# MURDER AT WHITEADDER HOUSE

JACKIE BALDWIN

Storm
PUBLISHING

To request permissions, contact the publisher at rights@stormpublishing.co

Ebook ISBN: 978-1-80508-291-0
Paperback ISBN: 978-1-80508-293-4

Cover design: Tim Barber
Cover images: Depositphotos

Published by Storm Publishing.
For further information, visit:
www.stormpublishing.co

## ALSO BY JACKIE BALDWIN

**A Grace McKenna Mystery**

*Murder by the Seaside*

*Murder at Castle Traprain*

*Dead Man's Prayer*

*Perfect Dead*

*Avenge the Dead*

*For Guy, my safe harbour in any storm.*

# ONE

Grace shivered as she left the warm cocoon of her car and tightened her woollen scarf around her neck. It was only mid-afternoon yet already the darkness was rolling in over the ragged waves at Portobello Beach. Twinkling Christmas lights punctuated the granite gloom. Festive good cheer spilled out of the pubs in a golden glow along with bouts of raucous laughter as she walked along the Esplanade towards the office, laden with parcels from her last-minute panic shopping. Her generous mouth curved in a grin as she thought of the Playmobile Hospital she had bagged from under another shopper's nose as his phone rang at an inopportune moment. Facing down his glare with a smile, she had turned smartly and marched to the checkout with it firmly tucked under her arm. It was Christmas Eve and she was looking forward to putting her feet up and having eggnog by the fire after her presents were all wrapped.

Arriving at the agency, her eyes widened. Talk about when the cat's away the mice will play, she thought, as she took in the fairy lights and fake snow. Good grief! It looked like Santa's grotto. She didn't know whether to laugh or cry. Since she had lost her son Connor three years ago, Christmas had been something to be endured rather than enjoyed. Maybe it was time to allow herself a few festive indulgences. Composing herself she pushed open the door to her office and stepped into the comforting warm fug. Christmas tunes were blasting out from a phone. Hannah and Jean were both applying the finishing touches to a real Christmas tree that to Grace's chagrin brought a lump to her throat in all its glory. Last Christmas she had wallowed in her misery, shutting out the world. What a difference a year could make.

'Do you like it?' asked Hannah, standing back to admire her handiwork with shining eyes.

Jean also turned to see her reaction.

Harvey, her Golden Retriever, came galloping out of her office festooned in tinsel and charged around her, barking and wagging his tail.

'I love it!' announced Grace, stooping to make a fuss of the dog and remove the tinsel before he caught it on something. 'You two have clearly been plotting again.' Despite Hannah being just nineteen and Jean in her early fifties, her two employees had formed an unbreakable bond and Grace considered herself lucky beyond measure to have found them.

'Mince pies all round,' said Jean, rushing off to get one of her signature tins filled with baked goodies.

'I'll grab the coffee,' said Hannah.

Grace flopped down on one of the easy chairs in reception and massaged her feet which were sore from her marathon shopping expedition.

'Did you get everything you needed?' asked Jean, nodding across to her discarded bags bursting with presents.

'I think so,' laughed Grace. 'There was one shop where I felt lucky to escape with my life! Christmas shopping is an extreme sport.'

'Well, it is if you insist on leaving it until Christmas Eve,' retorted Jean. 'I had mine all wrapped and under the tree on the first of December. I shop throughout the year.'

'Where's the fun in that?' asked Hannah, appalled. 'Mind you,' she said, giving side eye to her boss, 'even I don't leave things as late as Grace!'

'Okay, okay, don't mock the afflicted, especially when I come bearing gifts!' She fished around in her bags and pulled out a number of presents, which she added to the pile under the tree.

'I'm guessing that one's for Harvey,' grinned Hannah, pointing to the one shaped like a bone that was already being sniffed, as an object of interest, by one nosy Golden Retriever.

'How's the Christmas prep coming along, Hannah?' asked Jean.

Hannah groaned. 'It's such hard work. I had no idea.'

Grace and Jean looked at each other and burst out laughing. Hannah had decided to give her mum a break this year and cook Christmas dinner for the whole of her family, which consisted of her mum, three younger siblings and her own little boy, Jack.

'What time should I turn up tomorrow?' Jean asked Grace. As her son and daughter had opted to spend Christmas with her horrible ex-husband, Jean was joining Grace's family for Christmas at her mother's house.

'Come at twelve,' said Grace. 'Bring earplugs as I expect my sister's kids will be high on sugar by then.' She grinned.

'Looking forward to it.' Jean smiled.

Grace glanced at her watch. 'Right, you two, time to head home. I'll see you back here bright and early on the third of January.' As Jean and Hannah staggered out of the door laden with gifts, she poured herself another cup of coffee and switched off all the lights bar the ones on the Christmas tree. She really should have made the effort and got a tree for her flat upstairs, but she hadn't been feeling the festive cheer this year. Just a few weeks ago she had cherished hopes that she would be spending it with her ex-husband and love of her life, Brodie McKenna. Those hopes had been dashed for both of them when his pushy girlfriend Julie had triumphantly announced her pregnancy. Brodie was too honourable a man to walk away under those circumstances.

Her last big case had only finished a month ago and Grace had welcomed the break as it had been harrowing in the extreme. Now, though, she was starting to itch for something else she could sink her teeth into. If nothing else, it would take her mind off what had happened with Brodie.

# TWO

Grace glanced at her watch and sprang out of bed. It was Wednesday, 3rd January, and she was so over the whole festive period. Christmas day itself had gone really well, with even her mother in top form, particularly when jollied along by Jean who had way more patience with her than her daughters. It was more the period after Christmas that she had found hard to bear. A time for couples and families yet she was all alone in the flat with only Harvey for company. Aware that she was her own worst enemy at times, she'd refused the few invitations that had come her way and kept very much to herself, finding solace in long walks along the beach and nerve-tingling swims in the cold North Sea. There had been complete radio silence from Brodie which had hurt more than she cared to admit. However, she had made an exception for Hannah and Jack on Boxing Day, though she still squirmed with self-loathing remembering when he had bounced through the door of the flat and his face fell.

'It's not Christmas in here,' he said, his little face crumpling in disappointment. Grace had locked eyes with Hannah and they both looked equally horrified. Grace rushed to give him a cuddle.

'It was Christmas in here when I went to bed,' she said. 'But when I woke up Christmas had disappeared! There was a letter on the table from the Christmas tree.'

'What did it say?' he asked, wide-eyed.

'It said that it had gone off to have an adventure and the person who managed to find it would get an extra special present as a reward.'

'Mummy, can we go and look for Granny's tree?' he asked, tugging excitedly on Hannah's hand.

Grace pointed at the floor, but Hannah had already twigged.

'We could go and look in the office,' she said, injecting enthusiasm into her voice. They all disappeared down the stairs and Jack pressed his nose against the icy window of the agency.

'Mummy, I found it. The tree's hiding in there!' he shrieked.

Grace opened the door and switched on the lights.

'Hurrah, you found it!' She grinned. 'And look, there's your reward!'

Jack rushed to open the present under the tree and screamed in delight as he unwrapped it. 'Look, Mummy! It's a hopital.'

Hannah laughed. 'Thanks so much, Grace. He's going to love playing with that!'

'Crisis averted,' breathed Grace. 'Sorry, Hannah, I didn't think. His little face...'

Hannah rolled her eyes. 'Hey, nobody died.' The words floated in the air between them like a toxic cloud. *Except, someone had...*

Grace took charge. 'You're absolutely right. We can stay down here.'

'Mummy,' a small voice piped up. 'The hopital is broken.'

Hannah laughed. 'It's not broken, silly. It just needs to be built, and then it will look like the picture on the box.' She inspected the contents then put her hands up in horror. 'I think this might be a job for Grandpa,' she laughed.

Grace tried not to flinch. Hannah and Jack saw Brodie at least once a week now. She had never once pumped Hannah for information on how he was doing, though it had taken enormous self-restraint.

'I just wish these things would come ready assembled,' Grace had grumbled. 'I swear you'd need to be a time-served tradesman to handle it.'

Pulling herself back into the present, Grace pulled on her swimming suit and dry robe, pushing her feet into her battered sandals. She could hear Harvey padding about on the wooden floorboards in the kitchen.

'Boy, I'm coming,' she said, opening the door and putting Harvey on the lead. He tugged her down the stairs. When she opened the door, the wind almost wrenched it from her fingers. Harvey's hair stood on end as the wind whistled through his fur. Grace gulped, taking in the height of the foam-topped waves on Portobello Beach. This probably wasn't the best idea. Her mind drifted to the image of Brodie tucked up warm and cosy with Julie and her feet propelled her forwards onto the beach, anxious to shake the thought from her head.

Harvey pranced about waging war on some seaweed, shaking his head from side to side like it was some mythical creature to be slain. Her gaze softened as she watched him play. After a while her teeth were chattering so much they sounded like maracas. She called him to her and discarded her robe. Harvey lay down beside it, facing towards the sea, his eyes following her every move as she forced herself to dive headfirst into the waves. Gasping from the pain of the sudden chill, Grace struck out powerfully from the shore. At this time of the morning, it was impossible to detect where the blackness of the sea met the emptiness of the sky. As the chill burned its way through her body and gave way to numbness, she kicked powerfully, her head in the water, arms like pistons. Soon, her mind was empty of thought, and she existed only in the moment, her body just a bit player in the maelstrom around her.

She sent a few words out into the universe in the hope that they might somehow fall into the ear of her son, Connor, forever sixteen, who had died in this same water. Turning onto her back she glanced up at the stars, drinking in their beauty and feeling comforted by her own insignificance in the scale of things. Feeling rejuvenated and ready to take on the challenges of this new year, she flipped back over and swam for the shore where Harvey was waiting patiently for her.

# THREE

Grace entered the office with a freshly blow-dried Harvey in tow to find Hannah and Jean stashing all the Christmas decorations back in the cupboard.

'Happy New Year.' She smiled. 'Coffee, anyone? Hopefully, now that Christmas is out of the way, business should start to pick up again.'

'Please,' said Jean, settling herself at her computer. 'There's shortbread in the tin if anyone wants some.'

'Hot chocolate for me, please,' said Hannah, sliding behind her own desk and placing a shiny new notebook and expensive looking pen beside her own laptop.

'Christmas present?' asked Grace.

'Yes, from Brodie.'

'Was Jack looking forward to nursery this morning?' she asked.

'Yes, raring to go,' Hannah said with a gleam of pride. 'He missed all his little friends.'

Grace passed the tin around then helped herself and took her strong black coffee through to her own office. Harvey padded after her and settled down in his basket for a nap. The air felt a little stale as though it hadn't moved in a while. She opened the window but some papers immediately blew off her desk, so she closed it again. Firing up her computer, she got stuck in to some routine work including vetting some employees from a new care home that was due to open at the end of the month. After a bit of digging, she had vetoed two of the prospective employees on the basis that their social media posts had disclosed some rather unsavoury views in one case, and callous behaviour and a drunk driving charge for the other. The remainder seemed to check out, though.

Jean tapped on the door and entered.

'I've got a young woman outside asking to speak with you,' she said. 'She mentioned it was to do with her sister being missing. She's quite distressed.' Jean looked worried. 'Do you want me to make an appointment, or shall I send her straight in?'

Grace shut her laptop. 'I can see her now,' she said to the older woman. 'Could you ask Hannah to send in a tray of coffee when she's got a minute?'

Jean nodded and left. Seconds later she showed in a young woman who looked to be in her late twenties. She was thin to the point of gauntness and the dark shadows under her hazel eyes were suggestive of a number of sleepless nights. Her long chestnut hair was secured in a high ponytail.

'Hello, I'm Grace McKenna. Please, take a seat,' she said, walking over to the comfortable seating area around a coffee table with her notebook and pen in hand.

'I'm Eliza Anderson,' she said, a weak smile stretching her lips. 'Thank you for seeing me at such short notice. I've been going out of my mind with worry.'

There was a knock at the door and Hannah came in and deposited a tray with coffee and shortbread.

'Thanks, Hannah.' Grace smiled. She waited until Hannah had closed the door behind her before continuing. 'How can I help?' she asked, leaning forward, pen poised at the ready.

'It's about my sister, Beth – my twin. She's missing and I'm worried that something really bad has happened to her.'

'How long has she been missing?' asked Grace.

'Since the fourteenth of December. I haven't heard from her since. She just wouldn't do this. She knows how worried I would be. Something bad has happened to her, I just know it. I feel it in here,' she said, her eyes filling with tears as she placed her hand over her heart. Harvey stirred and cocked his head to one side, sensitive to the depth of emotion in her client's voice.

'Have you been to the police?' asked Grace.

'Of course, but they were worse than useless,' she said, scornfully. 'They more or less said that most likely she was loved up with some guy or lying in the gutter drunk out of her mind.'

'That's harsh,' said Grace. 'Any particular reason why they might have jumped to these conclusions?'

Eliza lowered her eyes and started fidgeting with her rings. She opened her mouth then closed it again. Her face grew red as if she was going to burst into tears. This would require careful handling.

'Look, it's okay,' Grace said, softening her voice and leaning forward. 'I'm not the police and my only wish is to help you find your sister.'

Eliza raised her eyes and looked at her once more as if to ascertain that she could trust her. She nodded.

'It's just hard, you know? Saying anything bad about her...'

'Then start with the good,' suggested Grace. 'What about your earlier life together? Twins, you say?'

'Yes, identical through and through. My mother loved the attention she got when we were out together and insisted on us dressing identically. She even gave us each two halves of one name. I'm Eliza, and my sister is Beth. She used to call us Eliza-beth collectively.'

'That's not weird at all,' thought Grace, keeping her expression neutral.

'When we were kids, it was fun to go along with it, I suppose. But she didn't let up on her controlling behaviour. She insisted we had the same friends, the same interests, and it was her way or the highway, I guess.'

'So you chose the highway?' guessed Grace.

'I was the older twin. Although we were identical, it was me who rebelled around age thirteen. I refused to wear the same clothes and scoured charity shops with my pocket money to try and forge my own identity. The more she pushed us together, the more determined I became to be my own person without dragging the spectre of my mother's dream child everywhere with me.'

'That must have been tough... on both of you,' said Grace. 'You said you were close?'

'We had been up until that point,' Eliza said, her bottom lip trembling. 'Beth wanted things to stay the same. She was still close to our mother and didn't want to upset her. I kept trying to push her away, but she clung to me like a limpet. I started to feel embarrassed when she sought me out at school. With my new clothes and bad attitude came a new group of edgy friends that I was desperate to fit in with. I ended up being really mean to her,' she almost whispered, guilt written all over her expressive face.

'Did that same dynamic continue?' asked Grace. 'You rebelling and her conforming to parental expectations?'

'No,' Eliza said, her eyes filling with tears. 'If I hadn't been such an idiot, none of it would've happened. Beth was so desperate to win back my affection that she started hanging out with the really bad kids at school, the ones that were on a mission to self- destruct rather than just trying to look cool. She started drinking. I was too wrapped up in myself to even notice. Until it was too late...'

'Go on,' prodded Grace gently, leaning forward to encourage her.

'A couple of years went by. At first Beth had been able to hide what she was doing from my mother. However, one day when we were about fifteen, she got blind drunk at school and assaulted a teacher. She insisted the teacher had groped her, but nobody believed her, least of all my mother. I tried to defend her, but no one would listen, and she was expelled. Things went from bad to worse after that. My mother ghosted her. We were living in the same house, but she looked right through her as if she wasn't there. It was as if somehow, she'd decided in her head that there was only one of us now with poor Beth reduced to an annoying phantom echo of me, like tinnitus or something.'

'That must have been hard for both of you,' said Grace.

'I felt really guilty. I still feel guilty. If it hadn't been for me, she would've been a goody two shoes all through school and had the life she deserved.'

'You don't know that,' said Grace, startled by the depth of emotion in Eliza's voice.

'I do,' she replied vehemently. 'Once I woke up to what was really going on with her, I tried to do better. I'd never been that into alcohol and I hated seeing what it was doing to her. Eventually, she more or less stopped eating. All she did was drink. It started at around five am when the shakes woke her up and continued until she passed out every night. She started wetting the bed, puking into a bucket. I was terrified as I realised she might not be able to come back from this.'

Grace had a feeling how this sad tale was going to end. Eliza seemed to be reliving it as much as telling it and, although time was marching on and she wanted her to get to the point, she recognised this was all coming from a place of trauma and let Eliza continue at her own pace.

'The day after we turned sixteen our mother packed her a bag and threw Beth out on the street. She was terrified and pleaded with her to change her mind. We both did. But she wouldn't budge. I threatened to go with her, but I didn't have the courage. I just stood and watched as she vanished from our lives.' Eliza leaned over and poured a glass of water with trembling hands.

'What about your father?' asked Grace. 'Couldn't he intervene?'

'I never knew him. He left when we were babies.' Eliza shrugged, her voice tinged with bitterness.

'So, what did you do after Beth left?'

'I stayed on at school, got serious about my grades and went to university. I've the barest minimal relationship with my mother. Beth was the only reason I didn't completely turn my back on her. She had no way of contacting me other than through her.'

'When did you last see your sister?' asked Grace.

'After she left home, I got some angry texts from her, always when she'd been drinking. She'd never tell me where she was. I didn't even know if she was still in Edinburgh. She blamed me. I blamed myself. She said I'd stolen her life. If it wasn't for me turning my back on her, she would never have got into drink and drugs. She'd send me pictures of squalid squats and drug paraphernalia.' Her voice broke and she covered her face with her hands, shaking.

'Go on,' said Grace gently, pouring her some more water from the jug.

'Once she even sent me a photo of some poor guy who'd obviously overdosed, still with the needle in his arm, and the caption, "Oops".'

Grace was shocked. There was a level of hatred there that seemed unwarranted but, she reminded herself, she was only hearing one side of the story.

'That must've been upsetting. Did she continue to maintain sporadic contact?'

'For the first couple of years and then nothing. My messages went unread. I began to worry that she might be dead.'

'When did she get back in touch?' asked Grace.

'It was the beginning of August. She sent me a letter to my mum's address. We arranged to meet for coffee. I was really nervous about what state she might be in, but she looked incredible, just bursting with health and vitality. In fact, if anyone looked a bit haggard it was me!'

'How had she turned things around?' asked Grace, curious now.

'She said that two years ago she was living on the streets. Her body was failing, and her mind had shut down apart from getting the next hit of alcohol. Day by day she let go a little more until she sensed she was near death.'

'So, what happened to change that?' prompted Grace, totally caught up in the story being revealed.

'Somebody offered her a place at a luxurious rehab clinic at Whiteadder.'

'Is that near the reservoir of the same name? Out in the middle of nowhere?'

'Yes. Not many people know about it being there. She didn't have to pay a penny. It's run by a charity apparently. Anyway, she was there for the best part of a year.'

'She didn't contact you in all that time?' asked Grace.

'Not once. She said that she wanted to once she started to feel better, but it was a condition of her ongoing treatment that she broke off all contact with the outside world.'

'That seems a bit extreme,' said Grace. 'I can understand it for the first few weeks but after that, contact with family and friends is usually encouraged.'

'That's what I thought, too,' said Eliza, 'but I didn't say anything. After all, there was no point.'

'How was she supporting herself? Did she have a job?'

'She seemed full of optimism for the future and was due to

start at Edinburgh College in September doing Highers. She was working at the Omni Centre in the cinema and living in a one-bedroom flat that the clinic had secured for her.'

'Do you have the address?' asked Grace.

'Yes, it was in Leith, but she wouldn't let me visit her there. She said it wasn't allowed.'

'How was she maintaining her sobriety?' asked Grace.

'The clinic was still supporting her. She had an appointment with them once a week at a local medical centre and they supplied her with medication.'

Grace was puzzled. The clinic sounded almost too good to be true. 'Did she keep in touch with you after that meeting?'

'Yes, though she claimed to be too busy to meet up. It wasn't long before I sensed something was wrong.'

'Did you think she had relapsed, that she might be drinking again?'

'I didn't know what to think. She would only text me, never phone. If I phoned her, she wouldn't pick up. She seemed edgy and paranoid. It was as if she felt someone was out to get her. She bought a new phone as she felt the clinic were monitoring her previous one.'

'The clinic?' said Grace, surprised. 'Why would she take against them? It sounded like they'd not only got her clean but offered ongoing support.'

'I don't know.' Eliza shrugged helplessly. 'The last text I got from her said she'd stopped taking the pills as they were poisoning her. By then she'd dropped out of college and was back to living on the streets. She said she was leaving the area and going to disappear so they could never find her again.

'I begged her to meet me one last time before she left for good, and she reluctantly agreed. She said she didn't want to put me in danger, but I insisted. She met me at the Natural History Museum in Chambers Street on fourteenth of December. We'd gone there a lot with our mother as children. When I first laid eyes on her...' She shook her head and teared up again. 'I was so shocked. I couldn't believe it was even Beth.'

'Drink can do that to a person,' said Grace.

'No, it wasn't that. I'm sure of it. She swore blind that she hadn't drunk at all. Before, when she'd been drinking, her breath would have that unmistakeable sour odour of booze. Her gait would be kind of exaggerated as if she was trying to concentrate on walking in a straight line. There was nothing like that.'

'I suppose it's unlikely that any deterioration, even if she had started drinking, would be that swift,' mused Grace. 'I don't suppose you took photos of her from each meeting so I can see the difference?'

'Yes, I did. The second time I figured by the state of her she was going to wind up dead and it might be the last time I'd see her.'

She scrolled down and handed over her phone. The two photos side by side were startlingly different.

'Can you send me these if we decide to open an investigation?' she asked, as she passed the phone back.

Eliza nodded. 'She was so fearful it hurt to see,' she continued. 'She kept on about how they were sending the snake to get her. "What snake?" I asked, thinking she meant a wee adder or something, but she shook her head. "I can't tell you," she said. "If I tell you they'll send it for you, too".'

'It sounds like she may have been having a psychotic break,' said Grace, sipping at her coffee.

'I don't know. I've been over and over it in my mind. She was terrified out of her wits for sure, but she really believed what she was saying. She said the drugs had poisoned her and that they were chasing her down so that no one would find out what they were really up to at the clinic. She said that she didn't have long. The pills had messed her up and if she didn't die from the pills, the clinic would finish her off.'

'This all sounds...'

'Crazy?' said Eliza, turning away from her. 'I know how it sounds, and at first I thought she was back on the booze or drugs. But it was more than that. Four months earlier she'd looked so well, but that day, the way she was holding herself, she looked proper sick. The weight had dropped off her. She looked emaciated. Even her voice had changed – it was hoarse and rasping when she talked. She was missing a couple of front teeth and had no energy. It felt off on so many levels.'

'And that was the last time you heard from her?'

'Something spooked her, and she ran off before we'd even finished eating. I tried to run after her but was stopped at the door by a security guard as we hadn't paid. By the time I got outside she was gone. Please, I need you to find her before it's too late.'

# FOUR

Grace sat back in her chair once she had finished bringing her team up to speed on their new case.

'Do you think Beth is still in Edinburgh?' asked Jean, her brow creased with worry.

'Impossible to say,' said Grace. 'She could've jumped on a train down to London and disappeared for good.'

'All that stuff about the snake gives me the shivers,' said Hannah. 'Their mother sounds a bit nuts, if you ask me. All that "Elizabeth" and acting like she only has one kid rather than two.'

'A few things Eliza said about the clinic did get me wondering,' said Grace. 'Something feels a bit off about them. For a start, private rehab facilities are notoriously expensive, yet Beth stayed there full-time for the best part of a year, free of charge.'

'Not to mention the follow-up care,' said Jean. 'I thought it was a bit suspicious, too, that they had to cut off all contact with family while they were in the clinic. It's normal to keep family away for two weeks and then have limited phone contact for several weeks before allowing weekend visits to help with motivation.'

Grace and Hannah stared at her.

'Not me!' she exclaimed. 'My dad's brother had a drinking problem. A bad one. His wife and kids stayed with us for a while. Most programmes are for twelve weeks or less.'

'Right, Jean, since you already know a bit about the system, can you do a bit of digging into the clinic and see how it differs from other programmes in Scotland? If they've a glossy brochure or website with testimonials, I want you to try and identify and track down anyone who has been to the facility. Scour the internet for people's experiences, good and bad. It would be good to canvass some local GPs as to whether they've heard of the clinic and whether it has a good reputation within the medical community.'

'Will do,' said Jean, scribbling in her notebook. She looked up, frowning slightly. 'Does this mean that we're buying into what Beth told her sister?'

'Not necessarily. I simply want to leave no stone unturned to give us the best chance of a successful outcome,' replied Grace. 'Hannah, I want you to create missing posters and show the two photographs we have of Beth side by side with a heading of "Has anyone seen this woman?" including our contact details. Also, can you email it to all the housing shelters in Edinburgh and any charities or agencies that work with the homeless? You'd better include all the drug and alcohol agencies, too. Explain to them that we've been instructed by her twin sister.'

'Won't that create a lot of false positives given that our client is her twin?' asked Jean.

'Yes, it may well do but those sightings should be easy enough to weed out from what we're looking for,' replied Grace.

'It must be so weird for Eliza,' said Hannah. 'Like having her very own Sliding Doors movie. If she'd got in with the bad crowd, maybe Beth would be our client and not the other way around.'

'We all have forks in the road,' replied Grace. 'Some of them may lead to a very different life. Others will double back and come full circle. It's impossible to know.'

'Like if you hadn't had Connor, then I wouldn't have Jack,' said Hannah, studiedly avoiding her gaze.

Grace went very still as a rush of emotion came over her. She and Hannah never talked about Connor. Not ever. It had become almost an unwritten rule between them and now she'd dropped him into the conversation like a small grenade. How was she supposed to react? What was expected of her?

'Yes,' she finally managed after a beat too long. The silence lengthened. She needed to fill it.

'Anything else you'd like us to do?' asked Jean, sensitive as ever and rushing in to fill the conversational void.

'No, not at the moment,' Grace replied. The moment had safely passed. 'I'm heading out to speak with Beth's mother to see if she can put me in touch with anyone who she might have trusted with her whereabouts.'

'What about Brodie?' asked Hannah. 'Can't he help?'

Grace flinched. *No, he bloody well can't,* she wanted to snap at her youngest employee. Since Julie's little bombshell at the end of their last case, she'd had to wave goodbye to her former easy relationship with her ex-husband, who had helped her out with her cases whenever he could in exchange for her reciprocal assistance with his own. None of this showed on her face as she smiled at Hannah.

'He works in major crimes, not missing persons, Hannah, so it wouldn't be appropriate. Our client reported it to the police and found them less than helpful, remember.'

'I suppose,' muttered Hannah.

'Anyway, the more information we gather the quicker we'll get to the truth,' said Grace. 'Our client needs us to give this case everything we've got.'

# FIVE

Grace had arranged to meet Eliza at her mother's terraced house in Musselburgh to get some more background information on the missing woman. Her client had thought that her mother might choose not to cooperate unless she was present. Fiona Anderson answered the door and her whole face lit up on seeing her daughter standing there.

'Eliza!' she gasped.

With a jolt, Grace realised it was the same look her mother would have on the rare occasions she dropped by unannounced. A pang of guilt stung her which she wrestled down.

'Mum, this is a friend of mine, Grace McKenna. Can we please come in?'

'Goodness! Where are my manners? Come in, both of you.' The diminutive scrawny woman in front of them sprang into action, ushering them through into an immaculate lounge.

'Please sit, won't you? I'll just put the kettle on.' The way she was swooping and fluttering made Grace think of a sparrow.

'I'll come and help you,' said Eliza, who hadn't smiled once since the door opened. Grace glanced around the chintzy room. There were no photos of the two girls together, which she thought was rather odd. Most families with twin daughters were happy to celebrate the fact. Of course, she had no idea of whether the single photos dotted around showing a child growing up into a young woman were all of Eliza, but given what her client had said she rather thought that they might be.

Suddenly, she could hear raised voices. Eliza must have explained why she was here then.

The door swung back on its hinges and Eliza walked in carrying a laden tray.

Her mother followed, her lips pressed into an angry straight line. She sat down and started to pour out the tea into dainty cups, her shaking hands causing the cups to rattle as she passed them round.

'Mrs Anderson,' Grace began. 'Your daughter, Eliza, has instructed me to look into the whereabouts of your missing daughter, Beth.'

'How dare you!' hissed the woman to her daughter, her face twisted in anger. 'I won't have our family name dragged down into the gutter with her. She made her bed, now leave her to lie in it, for all our sakes.'

For all she tried to hide it, Grace was shocked by her response. Being a mother wasn't something you could switch off like a tap, as she well knew. Why was the woman so vehement?

'Mum! Beth is in real danger. You can't just ignore this. I need you to tell Grace everything she wants to know.'

'Drama, drama, drama,' her mother muttered. 'I'm so sick of it all.'

'Mrs Anderson, could you tell me when you last heard from your daughter?' asked Grace.

The woman sighed but got her diary out of her handbag and flicked through the pages.

'She came to see me on the fourth of August. She tricked me. She pretended she was Eliza so I would let her in the door.'

'Beth shouldn't have had to do that,' snapped Eliza. 'You

saw her the day after I did. I've only seen her once since then on the fourteenth of December. No one has seen her alive since then.'

'What do you mean? Of course, she's alive,' said her mother. 'Why wouldn't she be? She looked healthy and well. Of course, I knew that it wouldn't last. I'm not stupid. She came in here bold as brass pretending to be you. She gave me the biggest hug which rather took me by surprise. We're not terribly touchy-feely in this family,' she added as an aside to Grace.

'Actually, that's just you,' muttered Eliza.

'Anyway, when she finally got round to admitting to her little deception, I wasn't best pleased and asked her to leave. I told her we had managed just fine without her and could continue to do so. I did wish her well for the future, but I knew it was only a matter of time until she found herself in the gutter again.'

'Mum, how can you be like this?' asked Eliza, her voice wobbling under the weight of unshed tears. 'Beth loves you. She always did. It was Beth who was the good one growing up, the one who only wanted to please you. How can you turn away from her? She still loves you despite everything. What kind of mother are you?' Her voice broke and she looked away, striving for control.

'The kind that did everything for that girl and had it thrown back in my face at every turn,' her mother snapped.

'Look,' said Grace. 'I completely understand how hard it is when your child acts in ways that you wouldn't wish for them, but the most important thing now, surely, is to make sure that Beth is safe.'

'I suppose,' she muttered.

'You don't want those harsh words to be the last thing you ever said to her, Mum,' pleaded Eliza. 'Help us, please!'

'Fine,' Fiona sighed, her face collapsing in on itself. 'What do you want from me?'

'When she was with you, did she mention a rehab clinic at all?' asked Grace.

'She went on and on about some place up in the wilds about half an hour from Edinburgh. It sounded more like a cult than a clinic to me.'

'Why do you say that?' asked Grace.

'Well, she sounded almost evangelical when she spoke about it. It all sounded a bit fishy. Apparently, she'd been up there living free of charge for almost a year. What are they getting out of it, that's what I want to know? If it's not money, then what?'

Grace thought she had a point. Such intensive support would not be sustainable even for a charity. Also, given that it was close to Edinburgh, she would have expected such a charity to be out banging the drum, raising money on a regular basis, not to mention carefully targeted ads and articles in the papers, yet she had never even heard of them before.

'Mum, look at this photo,' urged Eliza, scrolling through her phone until she found the last photo she had taken of Beth. She handed it over. Fiona swallowed hard when she saw it.

'You and I had both seen her four months before that was taken. Look at the change in her. I promise that she didn't smell of alcohol and wasn't slurring her words. Even a relapse couldn't account for it.'

Fiona looked up and frowned. 'But isn't that still the most likely explanation? Alternatively, could she simply have become ill? Maybe she picked up something when she was living on the streets?'

'It's impossible to say,' said Grace, trying to be diplomatic, though a relapse seemed the most plausible scenario. 'All we know for sure is that she was anxious and paranoid at that last meeting. She clearly felt, rightly or wrongly, that someone was coming after her from the clinic who wished her harm. Whether that harm was real or imaginary, it's impossible to tell.

Either way, it appears that she ran off in a distressed and vulnerable state and hasn't been heard from since.'

'What do you want from me?' asked Fiona.

'Do you have contact details for her friends from when she was last living with you?'

'She was quieter than Eliza at school. Apart from her sister she never really bothered with anyone until she started going off the rails. A right bunch of loudmouths she got in tow with then. I couldn't even tell you who they were after all this time.'

'Any other family members she was close to and might have told of her plans? A cousin, an aunt maybe?'

'We're a small family but I do have one sister. We're not in regular contact. I doubt very much Beth would get in touch with her, but I suppose I could give her a ring.'

'Do you still have any of Beth's things?' Grace asked.

'I've redecorated but both girls slept in what's now my spare room. They still have some stuff in there in the chest of drawers and the wardrobe. I couldn't quite bring myself to throw it out,' she muttered, averting her eyes.

Grace looked at her hunched-over body and sour face and couldn't help but feel pity for her. She'd let her happy family slip right out from under her. She knew a thing or two about that herself.

# SIX

Eliza pushed open the door to her old bedroom and motioned to Grace to follow her inside. This was no shrine to a departed child. The décor was cream and navy and there was little in the way of ornamentation. It could be a hotel room, the feeling of which was enhanced by white fluffy guest towels folded on the bed.

'It's like we were never here,' said Eliza, her voice thick with tears. 'I don't know how it's come to this. We were so happy growing up until I spoilt everything by shunning my sister. Even Mum, she was different, too.'

'Don't be so hard on yourself,' urged Grace. 'You were a teenager trying to carve out a separate identity. This isn't all on you. It doesn't need to be the end of the story either. You've time to fix things with your mother. Your sister, too, hopefully.'

Eliza nodded and wiped her eyes. She walked over to the wardrobe and pulled out four boxes stacked under empty coat hangers. Two were labelled Eliza and the other two Beth. She passed over the two belonging to her twin to Grace and rifled through the ones belonging to her.

'I can't believe she kept all this stuff,' Eliza muttered.

'There's a jotter in here from primary one! My diaries! I'd forgotten all about them. She'd better not have stuck her nose in these.' She flicked through one, cringing. 'I was such an idiot. These are coming away with me. I need to burn them.' Turning to look at Grace, she said, 'What is it? Have you found something?'

Grace held up a battered address book. 'Can you go through this and put a star beside any entries she was particularly close to or might have kept in touch with?'

'Sure, but like I say, when we were growing up, she didn't really have many friends.'

'What about teachers? Friends of the family?'

'There was one teacher she was close to. He tried to get her help when she was going off the rails. What was his name? Got it, his name was Seth Douglas, he taught English at Mussel-burgh Grammar School and was also her guidance teacher. He was fairly young so he might still be there. He was pretty cool for a teacher, really cared about the kids.'

Grace made a note on her phone. There was nothing else in Beth's box that she imagined could be helpful. It was expected but still disappointing.

'Wait a minute!' exclaimed Eliza, pulling out a glossy brochure from the bottom of the box. 'I didn't put this in here.' It was a glossy brochure advertising Whiteadder Clinic.

Grace dug deeper in her own box. 'There's one in here, too,' she said, surprised. Opening it up, a letter addressed to Eliza fell out. An identical one fluttered to the floor from Eliza's copy.

Eliza opened hers and motioned to Grace to do the same. One was a photocopy of the other.

*Dear Eliza,*

*If you're reading this then I fear that the clinic has found me. I might even be dead. I'm so terrified I can hardly breathe. It's too late for me. The drugs they have put me on have poisoned my body. I am rotting from the inside out. It's too late for me but there are others who might yet be saved – they have no one to fight for them. They choose their subjects carefully. People like me who no one will miss: addicts, the homeless, those on the fringes of society. Those who will not be believed. They'll tell you I'm mad, drunk, or using drugs. The one good thing they did for me was getting me clean. I got my life back but now they've destroyed it. I might have died as a lonely drunk in the gutter if they hadn't scooped me up but at least it would have been honest. They've messed with me in ways that I don't understand. Now they're sending the snake for me. The snake is real. Don't let it come for you. Take this letter to the police or someone who can help you. Send it to the papers but don't, whatever you do, go there in person. I wouldn't wish what happened to me on my worst enemy, let alone my twin sister.*

*It looks like Mum was right. You're going to have to live for both of us. I hope your life is amazing. I hope that you will always carry a little piece of me in your heart.*

*I love you.*

*Look after Mum for me and tell her I never stopped loving her, despite everything. Tell her to stop hiding the spare key under the flower pot. I sneaked in when she was out to put these letters in our boxes.*

*Beth*

Eliza broke down in tears and Grace pulled her in for a hug, her mind spinning. The letter was completely coherent apart from the mention of the serpent. What was all that about? Did it imply she was still delusional when she wrote it? Was it some kind of metaphor? There was no way of knowing.

# SEVEN

Grace put down her phone and sighed. A week had gone by and there had still been no positive sightings of the missing girl. Their poster campaign had resulted in no new leads as all sightings correlated with their own client's movements. The fact that they were identical twins was hampering their efforts. Annoyingly, the police were still not taking matters seriously enough. It looked like it would take a dead body to galvanise them into action and she fervently hoped that it wouldn't come to that.

She called Jean and Hannah through to her office. They looked as despondent as she felt as they settled on chairs in front of her desk.

'Jean, how's it going with the medical community? Have any of the doctors you canvassed made referrals there? Had they heard of the clinic? Do they think it's legitimate?'

Jean consulted her notebook. 'Well, I started with my own GP in Portobello. She hadn't even heard of it. I went round the practice managers of the other Portobello doctors, then extended the search to the whole of East Lothian and also three practices from each of Edinburgh's main areas. All but three of them drew a blank. A few of them said they were desperate for more rehab spaces for their patients as the waiting lists are crazy for the few that operate in the private sector. They were somewhat bemused at the idea of a clinic that didn't actively recruit patients as the unmet need is so great that they would have no problem filling every single space they had, even on a private basis. There are a number of high-functioning alcoholics working in the city right now who would be happy to throw money at a clinic to be pampered and weaned off alcohol. A lot of cocaine addicts, too.'

'What about the three who knew about it?' asked Hannah.

'They extolled the virtues of the place. They appeared to be of the view that it was so high-end that their referrals came by word of mouth at the top end of the business and media community. It might be insanely expensive, but their patients came back free from their addictions and have stayed that way ever since.'

'I suppose it's possible that they finance the charitable arm through the private clients, but I'm not entirely convinced,' said Grace. 'These doctors, I don't suppose they'd be willing to contact their patients and ask if they'd speak to us?'

'I can ask but even if they were willing, it's unlikely the patients would agree to speak with us. They may fear exposure to the press.'

'Give it a shot anyway. Say we would be happy to be bound by a confidentiality agreement,' said Grace.

'Can't you ask Brodie to lean on Missing Persons?' asked Hannah, her eyes beseeching. 'I mean, if it would help find Beth...?'

Jean glared at Hannah and shook her head slightly.

Grace sighed and ran her fingers through her short hair in frustration. He was literally the last person she felt like talking to. Yet just because their personal relationship had fallen off a cliff due to Julie's unexpected pregnancy, that didn't mean that they couldn't still have a professional one. She knew that Brodie had been keeping his distance deliberately until she got her head around the new situation. It was up to her to be the bigger person. Eliza had trusted her to find out what had happened to her sister. She owed it to her to put personal considerations to one side and not ignore a valuable resource.

'I'll call him,' she said, giving her youngest employee a quick smile. 'In the meantime, I need ideas for how we can get into that clinic and ask some questions.'

Hannah suddenly lit up with enthusiasm.

'How about I pose as a homeless alcoholic and try to get offered a place there?' she said, her voice rising in excitement.

'Absolutely not!' said Jean and Grace in unison.

Hannah's face fell. 'But... it's a good idea,' she said crossly.

'It's a dangerous one,' Grace said. 'We've no idea what they're doing up there. Also, it's not as easy as you think. You barely drink. Your bloods would be completely normal. You'd be found out in no time.'

'I suppose,' muttered Hannah, still looking somewhat offended.

Grace hid a smile and spotted a telltale twitch at the side of Jean's mouth, too. Hannah's impetuosity was something that needed to be kept in check sometimes. With age came experience. 'The same goes for drugs,' she added. 'If they took a sample of your hair, they'd know you were clean as a whistle.'

'Besides, even if our hypothesis that they're recruiting people from the streets is true, we can hardly have you sleeping rough for weeks or months just in case. Edinburgh is a large area. What are the odds they'd find you?'

They fell silent as they thought hard about a way forward.

'There's one surefire way to get their attention,' said Grace. 'Beth's twin could surface and either (a) pretend to be her, or (b) contact them looking for answers. They could hardly turn her away until they know what she knows.'

'We've never actively involved the client in an investigation before,' said Jean doubtfully. 'What if we put her in danger and something bad happened to her?'

'Yes, I know,' said Grace. 'Definitely only to be discussed as a last resort. In the meantime, I'll call Brodie and see if he thinks what our client told us is enough to warrant a visit from the police.'

'Of course,' said Jean thoughtfully, 'I suppose we don't necessarily have to go in all guns blazing. What if I went up there posing as Beth's mum? If I didn't accuse them of anything but was just looking for information to assist in tracking her down, then they could hardly either refuse to see me or object, could they? They'll want to pat me down and send me on my way. To do otherwise might invite undesirable negative publicity.'

'No, you're right,' said Grace. 'Don't say anything to alienate them, make sure you're admiring of the clinic and everything they've done for her. I imagine they know that she was estranged from her family. That might have been what made her such an attractive candidate.'

'What can I do?' asked Hannah, leaning forward in her chair.

'Go round some of the main housing charities in Edinburgh. There's Shelter, Bethany Trust... and I read recently about a great wee organisation called Streetwise. Tell them about Beth and send both photos through once you get a contact there. Check if they've heard any stories about people vanishing off the streets or suddenly being offered rehab places in a private clinic. Find out what areas are being mainly used for rough sleeping.'

'On it,' said Hannah, energised.

'In the meantime, I'll arrange to meet up with Brodie,' Grace said. 'He still owes us big time for the help we gave him in our last case. It's time for payback.'

# EIGHT

Grace fidgeted at the table in the café at Dobbies Garden Centre. She'd sweated over suggesting an appropriate place, somewhere that didn't scream date or intimate, or where either of them were likely to be recognised. This vast space filled with families and pensioners had seemed to hit the mark.

'Grace! Yoohoo!' yelled a voice across the crowded cafeteria. Grace gritted her teeth into a semblance of a smile and waved back. Dammit, one of her mother's old friends and her husband. Now, she'd get the first degree next time she visited her mother.

After a couple of minutes, the air shifted behind her and she realised he had arrived. Feeling a rush of heat to her face she strove for a normal greeting.

'Hi, Brodie,' she said, springing to her feet as though electrocuted, her voice coming out squeakier than she had intended.

'Grace, great to see you,' he said, an awkward smile hovering between them.

'How's Julie?' she asked, the words sticking in her throat.

'She's good,' he said, his expression giving nothing away.

'And the baby?'

'Julie had the twelve-week scan a couple of weeks ago and everything checked out.'

The baby that had come between them with the force of a juggernaut, she thought bitterly. Timing was everything. Only two months ago, Brodie had been on his way back to her when Julie had reeled him back in. She knew he wanted to be with her but having tragically lost their own son to suicide he wasn't about to walk out on another child. She pushed these thoughts to the back of her head. This was meant to be business not personal, she admonished herself.

'I hope all goes well,' she said, doubting very much that Julie would feel the same were the positions reversed. Underneath all that sweetness and light was a very bitter and twisted young woman, something Brodie was going to have to find out in his own time and not through her.

'The agency has a new case,' she said. 'I wanted to run it past you, see if you've heard any chatter on the grapevine.'

'Go on,' he said. 'It can't be any worse than your last one.'

'Don't be too sure. At first glance, it's a missing person case. A young woman aged twenty-eight with drug and alcohol problems.'

'So far, so not unusual,' said Brodie, scratching his head.

'Quite. This is where it gets a bit peculiar.'

'Go on,' said Brodie.

'She has a twin sister who she was estranged from until shortly before she went missing. Apparently, she'd been picked up off the streets by a weird rehab facility operating at Whiteadder. You know, the reservoir near the Borders?'

'That's certainly off the beaten track,' said Brodie.

'Anyway, apparently, she didn't pay a penny for her treatment and was there for nearly a year, after which they helped her find a flat and get a job while she was studying part time for her Highers. That's the point at which she contacted my client, her twin sister. She was clean, healthy and doing really well.' Grace showed him the first photograph and he studied it.

'So, what happened?' asked Brodie. 'I take it she fell off the wagon?'

'Eliza, our client, met with her four months after that pic was taken. She was anxious, paranoid and looked to have become severely unwell in that short period of time.' She passed across the second photo.

Brodie let out a low whistle. 'Quite the transformation.'

'Stranger still, she swore she was still clean, and our client backed her up on this saying there were none of the signs of alcohol use she had seen on her before. She was claiming that the pills the clinic had given her had ruined her health and she was terrified they were coming after her to bury the evidence.'

'Paranoid, looking wrecked physically. I don't know, Grace, it sounds as though the most likely explanation is that she fell hard, and her body is giving up the ghost. She could've been delusional.'

'Maybe you're right,' she said, deciding in that moment not to further increase his scepticism by sharing Beth's rambling about them sending the serpent for her. She needed him on board if she was going to obtain any help with her case. 'Can you lean on Missing Persons, Brodie? They've given my client the impression that they're barely going through the motions.'

'Not officially, but the husband of a member of my team works in that department. I'll see if she can bring her influence to bear. Do you have a sample of these alleged pills? Something tangible to account for her story?'

Grace passed across the brown bottle of pills she had found in Beth's box. It only had Beth's name and date of birth on it. There was no mention of the name or address of the prescriber. Brodie examined them and frowned.

'That's weird. You say she'd been living away from the clinic for months?'

Grace nodded. 'These apparently come from the clinic pharmacy at Whiteadder.'

'Could it be part of a clinical trial?' asked Brodie.

'None that I could find. According to her sister, Beth was adamant she hadn't signed up to any trials. On the face of it she appears to have deteriorated rapidly. Whether this has been caused by her lifestyle, or her medication, as she maintains, is impossible to determine without having this substance analysed.'

'Have you tried all the usual stuff?' asked Brodie, taking one out of the bottle and scrutinising it thoroughly. It was lilac and oval shaped with no markings on either side.

'Yes, of course. Unusually, it doesn't have any code imprinted on it, nor is the physical description recognised on any of the pharmaceutical databases.'

'That doesn't sound good,' said Brodie, looking worried. 'Of course, it could simply be a vitamin pill or something herbal. At the moment, you don't have enough to go on to launch any kind of police investigation. If you rock up at the clinic, they'll simply deny any wrongdoing and say they knew Beth was struggling and were trying to track her down to help her.'

'I know,' said Grace. 'That's why it's so important to establish what has happened to her.'

'Is it a British or American company?'

'It appears to be American, which rather begs the question of what they're doing over here in such an isolated location.'

'No other linked UK clinics?'

'No, it appears to be one of a kind,' said Grace.

They sipped their tea in silence for an uncomfortably long period.

Grace eyeballed Brodie. He looked away, unable to meet her eyes.

'What? Spit it out. You might as well tell me, or I'll imagine all sorts.'

'It might be best if you don't phone me for a bit. Julie has taken to checking my phone and goes ballistic if there's a call or text from you.'

'Are you kidding me?' said Grace, her voice rising in anger. 'Just what is her problem? It's not as though I'm on the phone to you all the time. These days it's usually about arrangements for Jack or Harvey. How can anyone feel threatened by that?'

'Look, I'm not disagreeing, Grace. However, you've got to consider the fact that she's pregnant and hormonal. I don't want to upset her. It's not good for the baby if she's riled up all the time.'

Grace knew that Julie didn't like her. During their last case her mask had slid off her face like melted wax and she'd spat bile at her in the street. She then wrongfooted Grace by lying to Brodie afterwards saying they'd had a cosy chat. Clearly, she was a manipulative liar and it pained Grace that Brodie had chosen her.

'I can see why you say that,' she said, removing the heat from her voice. 'But Brodie, she goes through your phone?'

Brodie reddened. 'Grace, she just needs a little extra reassurance right now. She'll relax once the baby comes – don't make this out to be a big deal.'

'Brodie, I'm sorry to have to say this but that's red flag behaviour and you know it!'

'Can you not see how inappropriate this is?' he snapped back, glaring at her now. 'I can't have my ex-wife sniping about my current partner. Don't force me to choose between you, Grace, because I'll choose the mother of my child every time.' With that, he pushed back his chair and stormed off.

Grace sat there in stunned silence, aware of a few covert glances in her direction including the friends of her mother. Drat. She drained her cup then scrolled through her phone for a few minutes to make sure he had already left the car park before she ventured out. She couldn't believe what had just happened.

What the hell was Julie playing at? There'd been no inappropriate contact between her and Brodie whatsoever. It was starting to dawn on her that Julie was determined to drive a wedge between them. It hurt. It hurt a lot, but maybe it was for the best, she thought wearily, as she deposited her tray and headed for the car park.

# NINE

Hannah shivered. The freezing cold penetrated her thick quilted coat effortlessly and she huddled further into her woolly scarf. It was below freezing already and Marek from Streetwise was taking her round the known sites where small pockets of rough sleepers existed on the margins of society.

It was a bit of an eye-opener for Hannah. Previously, she'd thought her family were hard up and barely eking out an existence. As she came face to face with real poverty for the first time, she felt ashamed and resolved to appreciate the roof over her head more. Without that, how did anyone manage to even function? Marek was young, cool without intending to be, and all fired up with a passion and altruism she had never come across before. It felt invigorating to be in his company. In exchange for his help, he'd got her to commit to a weekly shift at the soup kitchen and five patrols like this where they went around all the rough sleepers and checked on them, handing out hot drinks and sandwiches as well as blankets for those not adequately protected from the chill.

'Hey, Darren, how's it going?' he asked, squatting down to talk to a middle-aged man huddled in a sleeping bag whose face was grey with exhaustion. He was mumbling to himself, and his eyes were darting around like a fly not wanting to land. He flinched away from Marek but accepted the food and drink offered. Marek wrapped a foil blanket round his shoulders before moving on.

'Will he be alright?' asked Hannah, casting a backwards glance at him. He already resembled the dead more than the living as the snow started to fall.

'Probably not,' snapped Marek. 'Welcome to care in the community. He's a schizophrenic who's off his meds. His family had him committed years ago then buggered off.'

'Can't they section him or something?' asked Hannah. 'Get him the care he needs?'

'There are fewer and fewer secure residential hospitals. You can only compel treatment for so long then you have to let them go. Without support the world is a frightening place for the mentally ill. They can quickly become overwhelmed and turn to alcohol or drugs to help them cope. Then they decide those are preferable to their pills and the situation spirals out of control. It takes consistent follow-up and community support, but all the services are stretched to breaking point. He's one of the ones who fell through the cracks.'

'You know all their names,' said Hannah, impressed.

'Of course. They're people, and they deserve to be treated with dignity, irrespective of their situation.' Then he addressed the next person. 'Hey, Maria, going to be a cold one. No Duncan tonight?'

The young woman who looked only a little older than her answered them in a monotone, her face expressionless, eyes a blank slate, her body shivering uncontrollably with the cold. 'Dead,' she said, the words escaping in a bubble of spit, which lay there ready to freeze on her chin. She looked like she was so empty of emotion she would never feel again.

She was only in a long-sleeved t-shirt and tracksuit bottoms.

Hannah immediately peeled off her own coat and placed it around the girl, lifting her limp drug-tracked arms into one sleeve and then the other.

'I'm sorry,' said Marek. 'I know you'll miss him.'

'He was all I got,' she said suddenly, rousing herself. A tear glistened. She wiped it away. 'Thanks for the coat, love.'

They left their usual offerings and another foil blanket. Hannah pulled her hat off and ran back to give it to her as an afterthought, pulling it down low over the woman's purple ears.

'You didn't have to do that, Hannah,' said Marek. 'You need to put some boundaries in place if you're in this game for the long haul.'

'It's fine, I wasn't cold anyway,' said Hannah offhandedly.

Marek looked at her trying not to shiver and shook his head. He was smiling, though, and Hannah felt a strong tug of attraction. Hurriedly she pulled her mind back to the job in hand.

'I didn't show them the photos of the missing woman because they seemed so out of it,' she said. 'Should I have done?'

Marek shook his head. 'You wouldn't have got anywhere with those two. I've been on this beat since before you told me she went missing, and I've never seen her. I could show the photos to my boss, Jared, who's in tomorrow. You said she'd been on the streets rough sleeping years back. He might remember something from then as he's been in the job for way longer than me.'

'And as far as you're aware, nobody has been scooped up from the streets by some weird rehab clinic?'

'No, though I can't be completely sure. People go missing all the time. Sometimes they've died and been taken away in an ambulance. The lucky ones get taken into a shelter for a night or so and manage to get swept up by the system and supported. Even then some of them don't make it and end up back here on the streets.'

'It's so depressing,' she sighed.

'That there is part of the problem,' Marek said, giving her a cross look.

'How so?' she replied, stung.

'Compassion fatigue. Well-meaning people such as yourself come down here all fired up and do the odd shift. They come up against the system and just can't deal with it. They scuttle away back to their comfortable lives and do their best to forget about it.'

'You don't know anything about me,' she muttered, her cheeks fiery with shame. In her heart she acknowledged that apart from the commitment she'd already made, she didn't think she'd be able to keep doing this night after night with no real hope of making a difference. 'What about you?' she countered. 'You stayed.'

'Ah, that's a story for another night,' he said. 'Come on, we need to drive to the next place now.'

Hannah followed him to the car, her body numb with the cold. She had never been so intrigued by someone and very much wanted to get to know him better. That's if she could stop him thinking she was as shallow as a puddle. I've got hidden depths, she told herself, wondering if he felt as drawn to her as she was to him.

# TEN

The next morning Jean set off for the clinic and her appointment with the clinical lead, Dr Anna Campbell. She'd been surprised that her appointment had been made with someone so high up the food chain. Genuine concern at what had happened to one of their patients or damage limitation?

As she drove up the winding path through picturesque villages, she marvelled that all this was just a few minutes away from the A1, the main artery connecting Scotland with England. As the houses gave way to green fields and grazing sheep, she started to feel the isolation. There had been a hard frost followed by a smattering of snow. Her tyres slid on the ice as they climbed higher, but she managed to keep her nerve and carry on, the heater blasting to ward off the chill, her hands white as she gripped the wheel. The sky was a brilliant blue and the winter sun climbing in the sky. Normally she would have enjoyed the drive, but her mind was worrying away at the forthcoming interview. She'd never thought of herself as much of an actress so she hoped she could be convincing in her role as their client's mother. She'd memorised a few important facts just in case they delved deeper, but she was still a bag of nerves.

To calm herself she thought about her date for dinner the following evening with Patrick. He was taking her to a new Greek restaurant that had opened up in Stockbridge and she was really looking forward to seeing him again. It would be their third date and she felt as skittish as a schoolgirl. She liked him a lot and was trying to avoid getting her hopes up that it might develop into something special. She hadn't let on to Grace or Hannah as she didn't want to jinx it but maybe, if tomorrow went well...

She dragged her mind back to the task ahead. As she rounded a bend in the road, she could see the vivid blue of Whiteadder Reservoir stretching out below. She must be close to the clinic now. It wasn't on Google Maps, so she had memorised the directions from an atlas. It certainly wasn't visible from the road. After a few false starts she found herself bumping up a dirt track towards some woods hoping she wasn't going to wind up in another muddy farmyard. There were lots of Keep Out and Private signs along the way. Finally, she reached the end of the track, coming into an elegantly paved turning circle in front of a huge sandstone mansion. There was a high chain-link fence surrounding the property, which appeared to be extensive. Jean parked her car and approached the front door, her feet crunching on the gravel. Her arrival triggered ferocious barking from an unfriendly-looking Alsatian behind the fence. So far, she wasn't getting healing vibes.

She followed the sign for reception and was greeted by a friendly receptionist who looked to be in her early twenties. Her name badge said Lily.

'Mrs Anderson?'

'Yes,' Jean replied.

'Dr Campbell will be with you shortly. Can I get you something to drink?'

'No, thank you,' said Jean, remembering not to smile as she was supposed to be frantic about her missing daughter. The girl went back to her work and Jean glanced around. Everything looked very professional and was in a good state of repair. The décor was muted but elegant. Framed photographs of the clinical staff, fanned out around a larger portrait of the clinical director, Dr Anna Campbell, smiled down on her and she surreptitiously noted their names down on her phone so she could research them later.

Lily, the receptionist, suddenly appeared in front of her holding out her hand.

'I'm sorry, Mrs Anderson, but I'm going to have to ask you for your phone,' she said with a bright smile. 'It's company policy.' She lowered her voice discreetly. 'We have a number of celebrity patients who are very nervous about their treatment getting out into the public domain.'

'Oh,' said Jean, somewhat flustered and thankful Grace had insisted on a stiff password. 'I suppose that's alright.' She handed it over.

'Dr Campbell is ready for you now,' Lily said, and Jean followed her along a corridor where she was shown into a beautifully appointed office dominated by a large desk. Disappointingly there were no clues on the surface. That pesky privacy thing again.

The steel-haired woman who rose to greet her was tall and elegant with her hair swept up off her face in a chignon. It was hard to tell how old she was due to her fresh complexion and unlined face, but Jean guessed she was in her late fifties.

'Mrs Anderson, please do take a seat. I was very sorry to hear that Beth has disappeared off the radar. Such a lovely young woman. It was a privilege to get to know her. I considered her to be one of our success stories. It's very worrying. How can I help?'

Jean's voice broke as she imagined as a mother how she would feel if she were sitting here because of her own daughter. 'I don't know if you know this or not, but my daughter Beth and

I were estranged. She had pushed me over the edge until I just couldn't deal with the chaos anymore. It was eating me up.'

'I had heard that,' Dr Campbell said, her voice kind. 'Addiction is a terrible thing. It affects the whole family. It was so rewarding to help your daughter through that period in her life and reclaim all that wonderful potential.'

'You gave her a chance,' said Jean. 'And for that I'll always be grateful. I suppose one of the reasons I'm here today is to fill in the blanks. How did she wind up here, for example? Her GP hadn't heard of it. She hadn't consulted him about her drinking. This place must've cost a fortune. How did she manage to pay for it? It would've been way beyond my means. Not that I'm not hugely grateful to whoever made it possible.'

'We're a private institution with a top-end clientele but we also have a charitable arm which is equally important to us,' said Dr Campbell, her expression verging on pious. 'Our charitable work is funded by a number of wealthy donors to whom philanthropy is an important application of extreme wealth. We have an outreach programme with a mission to seek out those on the margins of society struggling with addiction, and endeavour to transform their lives so that they once again have meaning and purpose, with addiction no longer driving their personality.'

'Well, I'm incredibly grateful,' Jean said. 'Before she went missing for the second time, she came to visit me.' Was it her imagination or did the woman stiffen slightly in her seat?

'That must have been wonderful,' she said. 'After all those years to have her back in your home. I don't know much about her family circumstances. In fact, I'm sorry if this causes you pain... she told us she had no family.'

'There's only me, really,' said Jean. 'My husband left us when Beth was a baby. I haven't even been able to contact him to let him know she's missing, not that he cared. He had alcohol issues, too.' Grace had decided it was best that she didn't mention Eliza, just in case it put her in harm's way.

The woman nodded sympathetically, more relaxed now.

'She said that after she left here you helped her get a flat. She got a place at college to study for her Highers and got a wee job during the day. I really thought she was going to make it this time.' Again, the wobble in her voice. She was better at this acting lark than she'd given herself credit for. 'I've a photo of her I took the day she came round.' Fortunately, she had printed it off her phone already. She fished it out of her purse.

Dr Campbell took it and scrutinised it carefully. 'This is how I remember her. Such a delightful girl.'

'And this is one a friend took of her four months later,' she said, passing across the other photo.

Dr Campbell's eyes widened in shock. She opened her mouth to speak then closed it again. 'She must have relapsed. We need to readmit her right away,' she said. 'We don't turn our back on our patients when they leave here. We consider it to be a lifelong commitment. Tell me, when was this photo taken?'

Jean gave the date that Eliza had told them. 'I've had no contact with her since. We've put up missing posters all over the neighbourhood and down where the homeless congregate. No one has admitted seeing her. It's as if she's vanished into thin air. The police were no help either.'

'You went to the police?' the woman said, her face tightening.

'Well, yes, of course. She's a missing person. I thought they'd try to find her, but they seemed to give up before they even started. They assumed she was just back on the booze and sleeping it off in a squat somewhere.'

Was that relief she saw flicker in the woman's eyes? She was so inscrutable it was hard to read her. Time to get her on the back foot again.

'Of course, if she winds up dead in an alley somewhere, they'll have to look into it, but by then it will be too late. In my heart I feel she's already gone.'

Dr Campbell was by now striving to hide her irritation. 'It'll hopefully not come to that,' she soothed. 'We're going to start looking for her right away, I promise you. We need to get her back on the programme immediately, at no extra cost of course.'

'That's very generous but I feel she might be better off with me at home. I've learned from my mistakes. I intend to take very good care of her should I be lucky enough to be given a second chance.'

'I know that you mean well,' Dr Campbell said, 'but during her time with us we built up an in-depth profile on her mental and physical health, something that no other health provider or, indeed, caregiver could hope to replicate.'

'She did mention something about some pills,' said Jean.

Panic now unmistakably flared in the woman's eyes. She had clearly hit a nerve.

'We boost our patients' immunity with our own bespoke vitamin and herbal remedies,' she said.

'I don't know,' said Jean, looking doubtful. 'Maybe if you could show me around and let me get a feel for the place, that would help me to decide what I should do if she turns up. Would that be possible, today? I really can't face coming back. It took a lot for me to even come here but I just needed to see where she'd spent what might turn out to be the last year of her life. However, if you can't accommodate me to that extent, perhaps my next port of call should be the police? Maybe you'd rather show them around instead? I just need to check that everything here is as it should be. Then, if she turns up, I can guide her back here in good conscience.'

Jean could tell the woman didn't want to accede to her request but what choice did she have?

'If you could take a seat back in the waiting room. I'll see what I can do,' she said with a tight smile.

Jean thanked her and was escorted back by Lily. Dr Campbell could just be trying to get ahead of any blame attaching to the clinic and generating the wrong kind of publicity, but Jean sensed there was more to it than that.

'Did you know my daughter?' she asked Lily. 'This is her photo.'

Lily glanced at it. 'I did as it happens. I remember the day she left. She was so excited to be getting out and really looking forward to living her life now she was well again. I only really meet the clients when they come in and when they leave. It's a secure facility so I never see them the rest of the time.' Her face fell. 'I'm sorry. it must be so hard for you, not knowing what has happened to her.'

'Do you like working here?' asked Jean.

'Yes, I love it.'

'I've never noticed the clinic advertising for staff in the press. I expect they use one of those top-end recruitment companies.'

'The staff never changes much,' said Lily. 'They're all really dedicated. My dad is one of the doctors here, so I was lucky enough to be offered the job when the position came up, although I'd worked as a medical receptionist back in the States so was well qualified for the job.'

'Dr Walker?' asked Jean, reading the name plaque in front of her desk. 'Would he have been involved in treating my daughter then?'

'No, Dad works on the research and development side.' She reddened as though suddenly realising she might have said too much and, with a smile, busied herself in her work again.

Interesting, thought Jean. She picked up a magazine and flicked through the pages, not wanting to arouse suspicion by asking too many questions.

# ELEVEN

The door opened and in walked an attractive woman in a nurse's uniform who introduced herself as Head Nurse Frankie Garcia. She took Jean's hand between two of her own and squeezed gently.

'I remember your daughter, Beth. It was wonderful to see her blossom as she moved from the throes of addiction into a fresh-faced young woman ready to take on the world. I hope she returns to you safe and well. In the meantime, Dr Campbell has asked me to give you a tour of the clinic. Perhaps you'd like to hang up your coat before we start? We tend to keep things rather warm around here.'

Jean deposited her jacket on the elegant coat stand in the hallway then turned to face her guide.

'Follow me.'

For a moment Jean felt a pang of guilt at impersonating Beth's mother. Perhaps she, too, would have liked to see round the clinic and they were denying her that chance. Mind you, from what Grace had said, that was unlikely. She certainly wasn't blameless in the trouble her daughter had found herself in.

Nurse Garcia led her to a thick door with a reinforced glass window and keyed a number into the side panel. Jean had no chance of seeing it and probably wouldn't have remembered it if she did. As the door shut behind her with a soft whoosh, Jean immediately felt uneasy. From this point on she could only leave the clinic if someone chose to let her out. They walked up a flight of stairs with Jean struggling to keep up with the nurse's diminutive form.

'I can show you the room Beth stayed in during her visit,' she said. 'As luck would have it, we haven't filled it yet. Room thirteen. Just as well she wasn't superstitious.' She smiled, opening the door onto a light airy room with the kind of furnishings you would have in your own room at home.

'This is lovely,' Jean said, walking over to the window to look out. Although the view over the woods to the reservoir was stunning, she was a little unnerved to see not one but two Alsatians prowling around behind the high chain-link fence.

'They look a bit scary,' she said to Garcia with a smile. 'Do the patients ever get to go outside?'

Garcia's eyes hardened for an instant then she was all smiles again. 'It's another level of security. It stops people breaking in to cause trouble but also deters our patients from trying to escape before their treatment has been completed. However, I can assure you that with the right handling they're pussycats. The patients are encouraged to go outside for recreational purposes three times a day and the dogs are simply placed in secure kennels with a bone to occupy them during that time. We offer organised hikes, woodcraft, archery and all sorts of activities. In the summer we do kayaking and open water swimming on the reservoir.'

'I see,' said Jean, smiling, though it still seemed a bit off to her. Glancing around, she noticed the flat screen TV, music centre and well-stocked bookshelves. 'It all looks so comfortable. It really doesn't have a hospital vibe in here at all.'

'That's what we were going for,' said Garcia, her face dimpling. 'A home from home but with no stresses and strains to hamper recovery. The mind needs complete rest as it recovers.'

'What part of America are you from, if you don't mind me asking?' said Jean.

'Boston, Massachusetts,' she replied. 'I fancied something different, and I'd always wanted to visit Scotland. Though, I have to say, I'm not such a big fan of the weather.'

'What's next to see?' asked Jean.

'When people come to us, they're often dirty and unkempt. They've forgotten how to take care of themselves. Their self-esteem has completely collapsed and all that drives them is getting from one fix to the next. They've effectively lost their humanity. Once they've been detoxed and given clean clothes and a flattering haircut, we reward good healthy behaviours by visits to our indoor spa where they can have beauty treatments and start to take pride in their appearance again.'

'That sounds amazing,' said Jean. 'I'm so grateful my daughter got to come here. How did that happen, by the way? Her GP maintains he knew nothing about it.'

'Oh!' said Garcia, slightly flummoxed. 'I've no idea. I'm not involved with that side of things. We do have an outreach programme that goes out to actively find people we can help, so perhaps it was through that route.'

Their next port of call was the art therapy suite where Jean could see an impressive amount of framed art and all manner of equipment and resources.

'We even have a kiln,' said Garcia. 'If my memory serves me correctly, your daughter was a rather talented artist. Here's one of hers on the wall over here.'

Jean looked at it with interest. It was painted in oils and showed a coiled serpent ready to strike, its darting tongue sniffing for prey. The painting was stunning yet unsettling.

'Wow, I don't know what to say. She did make a few off-the-cuff remarks about the serpent coming to get her but I never took her seriously.'

Garcia stiffened and left quickly, forcing Jean to turn about and follow her.

'I'm afraid it was one of her delusions when detoxing,' she said, once they had left the room behind. 'Patients have all kinds of vivid hallucinations, bringing their own primal fears to the fore. Once we had a gentleman who kept seeing a mummy wrapped in bandages in his wardrobe mirror. He was Catholic and so sprayed shaving foam in the form of a cross over the mirror to keep the mummy from coming out. Of course, next he heard the sound of scraping, and the mummy was wiping away the shaving foam.'

'That sounds terrifying,' said Jean. 'So, you're saying that when Beth was detoxing, she conjured up this serpent and it was as real to her as you or me?'

'Exactly,' said Garcia. She opened the door into a games room with two badminton courts and lots of other equipment.

'Exercise is a healthier way to relieve stress than turning to drugs or alcohol. We encourage our patients to test that out for themselves. We also have a fully equipped gym and a swimming pool.'

It suddenly occurred to Jean that she hadn't seen a single patient yet. Glancing at her watch she said, 'Where is everyone?'

'They're all in various group therapy rooms at this time,' Garcia smoothly replied. 'That's why I was able to give you this tour. You'll appreciate that we owe our patients the strictest possible confidentiality in relation to their treatment here. If you saw someone that you knew, it could cause severe reputational damage.'

Jean thanked her for taking the time to show her around and left the way she had come after being buzzed out by young Lily. As soon as she walked out of the door the dogs started snarling at her, giving her a fright. Her mind was in turmoil after all she had seen and heard. However, she felt that she was no nearer the truth than she had been when she arrived. Although in many ways it looked like a wonderful place, she felt an under-current of something that had unsettled her though she couldn't put her finger on what had triggered it, no matter how hard she tried. She also thought that despite the explanation given it was odd that she hadn't come across a single person, staff or resident, during her tour.

Burying her hands in her pockets as she strode over to her car, she momentarily froze then continued walking. There was something inside her pocket that hadn't been there before. Mindful of the CCTV swivelling towards her she didn't take it out although by now it felt like it was burning a hole in her pocket. Instead, she calmly got in her car and drove off without a backward glance.

# TWELVE

Back at the agency they were all sitting in the comfy seats grouped around a large driftwood coffee table in Grace's office. She'd ordered in tasty bagels from the specialist shop in the high street and now, fed and caffeinated, they were all pondering recent events. Harvey had managed to score a bit of chicken that Hannah had accidentally-on-purpose let fall from her bagel. He was now slumped on her stockinged feet like a pair of comfortable slippers.

'You've made a really good contact there,' said Grace. 'It sounds like Marek is going to keep his ear to the ground for us.'

'He's such an amazing person,' Hannah said dreamily. 'He's really making a difference. He's even persuaded me to volunteer for some shifts.'

'I like his style.' Grace smiled, exchanging a knowing look with Jean. Hannah was clearly crushing on him. She moved across to her desk and picked up the letter that Jean had discovered in her pocket that morning. It was handwritten and unsigned. She read it out loud.

*I heard you say you're Beth's mother. Beth made such a lot of*

*progress here and was a lovely person. She doesn't deserve what*
*happened to her. Something here has gone very wrong. I wasn't*
*meant to find out but now I know some of what has been going*
*on. This isn't what I signed up for. Beth is going to die a terrible*
*death. It may already be too late to save her. Please meet me at*
*Wetherspoons, Musselburgh, tonight at 6pm. We need to talk.*
*I'll be wearing a brown and yellow scarf and have a copy of*
*National Geographic on the table. You can call me Gordon.*

'So, we have ourselves a potential whistleblower,' Grace
said thoughtfully.

'As long as the rest of them haven't twigged what he's up to,'
said Jean, sounding nervous.

'The serpent will be coming to get you, Jean,' said Hannah,
her hand imitating a snake's sinuous curves.

'About that,' said Grace. 'Having that painting of the
serpent on the wall was a bit weird.'

'I managed to get a picture of it,' said Jean. 'The receptionist
had taken my phone off me, but I asked if Garcia could send it
to me because art had been one of Beth's passions before she got
sick, and it would mean a lot to me to have a picture of her last
artwork. She wasn't keen but she could hardly say no without
arousing my suspicions, so here it is.' She opened an A4 folder
and handed round the copies she had made before lunch.

'That is SO good,' breathed Hannah. 'It almost leaps off the
page at you. It's super creepy though. There's something so
mean in the eyes.'

'For want of a better word, it looks evil,' said Grace. 'If that
was one of her hallucinations when detoxing, she must have
been terrified. Were there any other similar works on the wall?'

'What do you mean?' asked Jean.

'Well, you mentioned the delusion the man had about the
mummy coming through the mirror. Was there anything else
like that?'

'No, that was the only one,' said Jean. 'I did wonder at the time why she was even telling me that. It struck me as odd that she was giving such a frank account of another patient's psychosis. Even though she didn't identify them, shouldn't that sort of thing be kept private?'

'It sounds to me like they were aware Beth may have made comments about the serpent already and were trying to get ahead of it,' said Grace. 'It may not even have been painted by her at all.'

'You're not seriously trying to suggest that it's a real snake, are you?' asked Hannah.

'No,' said Grace. 'But I think that one way or another it was very real to Beth. It's possible they were using techniques like aversion therapy coupled with hallucinogenics and she was left with some residual effects.'

'You don't think they were brainwashing her, do you?' asked Jean, horrified.

'Without more inside information, it's hard to say,' said Grace. 'At least we've now got a bit of an in with this person inside reaching out.'

'You don't think it could be a trap, do you?' asked Hannah.

'A trap! Good heavens, I hope not!' exclaimed Jean. 'I must say that hadn't occurred to me.'

'Hannah's right,' said Grace. 'You need to exercise caution.'

'Maybe you'd better go,' said Jean, clearly doubting her ability to pull off the subterfuge again.

Grace thought about it for a minute. Of course, she was tempted. It was putting a lot on Jean to have her do it. However, it was Jean he had reached out to, and he was bound to feel skittish about the whole thing. Seeing someone different to who he expected might make him retreat. Also, as her employer she owed it to Jean to develop her skills and confidence. No, she was going to let her run with this.

'I think you need to do this one, Jean. Try to get his real name if you can.'

'Should I tell him who we really are?'

'I'm afraid you're going to have to play that one by ear. If things are going well, you can tell him. His main motivation in reaching out might be he's concerned about what happened to Beth. The fact he thinks he's talking to her mother might give us more leverage, initially.'

'I hate lying,' said Jean, shifting in her chair. 'Though I was shocked today to discover I was rather good at it.'

Both Grace and Hannah laughed. Jean was quietly religious and had a strict moral code for herself. Here she was discovering hidden vices she didn't know she had.

'Yes, but you're lying for a good reason and to help someone,' said Hannah. 'I'm sure that must be allowed somewhere in the God manual.'

'In the Bible, you mean?' said Jean, trying not to laugh.

'Exactly,' said Hannah.

'I'll be in the bar already, having something to eat from where I can see you both. So, you won't be in there alone,' said Grace. 'See if he could perhaps photograph or email some evidence to us of the things he's concerned about. The main thing is not to scare him off by coming on too strong in this initial meeting.'

'You can do it, Jean,' said Hannah stoutly.

'Go home and get some rest so you're fresh for later,' said Grace.

'Before I go, I'll email you the medical names I noted down on my phone before they confiscated it. There may be more people working there but this might be their entire medical team,' said Jean.

'Hannah, when that email arrives can you start researching those names? See when and where they graduated and what, if any, their specialties were? Look into postgraduate study and employments and what research studies they've been involved in. Check the electoral roll and get addresses for as many as you can. Some of them may be accommodated in the clinic, of course. See if there's a whiff of scandal attached to any of them. What are their reported interests, personal and professional? Have they ever been interviewed before or while they were at the clinic? Try to ascertain whether any of them have ever been connected with big pharmaceutical firms in the United States. Charge Nurse Frankie Garcia admitted to Jean that she was from Boston, Massachusetts, which is where a lot of these big pharmaceutical testing companies have their headquarters.'

'Is that all?' asked Hannah faintly.

'For now,' said Grace. 'I'm off to meet with our client and update her on how the case is going. I'll be back later, though, and I'll give you a hand then.'

# THIRTEEN

Grace headed further into Edinburgh, to the address she'd been given. Eliza lived in a stunning top-floor flat with fabulous views out to Carlton Hill at the back and down Leith Walk to the front. She suddenly realised that she didn't know all that much about her client. Hardly anything, in fact. When Eliza told her money was no object, she hadn't realised she actually meant it and had taken the case on intending to restrict her eventual fee as much as possible. Her mother certainly wasn't well off. Her small, terraced house was immaculate and well presented, but Grace suspected that she was struggling to keep it that way. Slightly out of breath from running up the stairs, she rang the doorbell on the smart blue door.

'Grace, come in,' said Eliza, throwing the door wide. 'Ben is working from home today, so I'll introduce you. Ben!' she yelled. A door opened and a tall gangly man who looked to be in his early thirties slid out into the hall. Dressed like an absent-minded professor in cords and a sweater, he looked unaccountably furtive as he shook Grace's hand. Maybe he was just shy, she thought.

'I'll make some coffee,' he said, still failing to meet her eye as he disappeared off in the direction of the kitchen, watched fondly by Eliza.

'Bless him,' she said as she led Grace through into a magnificent lounge with high ceilings and floor-to-ceiling views of Carlton Hill.

'It's beautiful,' said Grace. 'Looking at all that greenery you'd never think you were in the centre of Edinburgh.'

'I just love it,' Eliza enthused. 'Of course, working for the bank helped me get a decent mortgage rate which certainly helped.'

'What type of work do you do with the bank?' asked Grace, slightly curious.

'I'm an asset manager. I handle the portfolios of clients with a high net worth. It keeps the wolf from the door,' she said with a self-deprecating smile.

'Is Ben in banking, too?' asked Grace. 'Is that how you two met?'

'No, Ben works in software development. He thinks in code rather than English at times. We met at the gym. I came hurtling off a treadmill and crashed into him, even broke his glasses. Well, of course, I was mortified and immediately dragged him off to lunch and to go shopping for a new pair. He was unlike anyone I'd ever met before, really sweet. I guess it's a case of opposites attracting.'

After some more desultory small talk Ben came through with a laden tray and placed it on the coffee table.

'You're welcome to stay and hear what Grace has to say,' Eliza said, smiling up at him.

Did Grace imagine it or did an expression of fear flicker across his face? He turned away from her client to grab some coasters from a shelf.

'I would but I'm trying to meet a deadline,' he said with an apologetic smile. 'If I don't get this code through to the developer before the end of tonight the sky will fall down.'

'You work too hard,' Eliza protested, grabbing his hand but releasing it almost immediately.

'Before you go,' said Grace, operating on a hunch. 'Did you ever meet Beth?'

'No,' he said, his eyes widening in alarm. 'Beth was long gone by the time we met. When Beth finally got in contact, she would only agree to meet Eliza alone and in a public place.'

'I was so excited about introducing them,' said Eliza. 'Sadly, I never got the chance.'

Grace smiled and let it go but she was convinced he was lying. Once he was gone, she updated Eliza on the investigation thus far.

'I can't believe Jean impersonated my mother,' she said, looking bewildered.

'It might seem a bit extreme, but I didn't want to put your mother in any danger, and it was important to extract as much information as possible on that single visit. We might not have another chance to get inside.'

'No, I get that,' Eliza said, looking worried. 'There's no way she could have carried that off. These days she can hardly rouse herself off the sofa. I just want to be really clear that I don't want to put my mother at risk in any way. What if they have her address and go round to see her and it's a different person?'

'We've thought of that,' said Grace. 'Jean made sure to tell them that she'd moved since Beth had been away and she gave her own address, so they should've changed their records. The good news is that we've got details of their doctors and nurses from reception so we can start digging into them a bit more deeply. We've also been contacted by someone on the inside who might be considering dishing the dirt on what's really going on inside the clinic. He's meant to be meeting a member of the team tonight at six, if his nerve holds.'

'That would be amazing,' Eliza said fervently. 'But I'm also scared of what he might say. I'm terrified to think of what they might have done to her.'

'There's one more thing,' Grace said, opening the folder she had taken with her and pulling out one of the snake prints.

Eliza gasped and recoiled in horror.

'This was on the wall in the art therapy room and allegedly done by your sister. The nurse showing me round said it was a representation of a hallucination she suffered while detoxing. Does it hold any special significance for you?'

'Beth was terrified of snakes. We both were. This must be the serpent she was referring to. When we were really young, there was a weird man next door who had loads of snakes. He kept them in cages, but I remember a big one got out. Before he even realised it was missing, it had slithered across the lawn and into our house. It was massive. I think it was a boa constrictor. Anyway, Beth and I were playing on the kitchen floor with our guinea pigs, Bubble and Squeak. It was summer and the kitchen door was open. Before we knew what was happening it had taken Bubbles, Beth's guinea pig, and swallowed it whole. I got such a fright I dropped Squeak. She froze and it swallowed her, too. We were screaming and screaming. It looked like it wanted to eat us, too, but we were making so much noise it just slithered back outside. That was the last time we left the door open ever again. Probably explains why I chose a top-floor flat as well,' she said with a shudder.

# FOURTEEN

Grace's next port of call was Beth's old guidance teacher, Seth Douglas, who was still teaching at Musselburgh Grammar School. She'd arranged to go when he had a free period. The man who sat across from her in the battered and scuffed office was around forty and, although attractive, clearly had no sense of personal vanity. Despite the peeling paint and cheap furniture, he had clearly made an effort out of his own pocket to brighten the place up and added a range of fun quirky touches to appeal to a wide age range of kids. Instead of a chair opposite his desk there was a sofa with fun cushions so a distraught youngster could curl up there if they needed to. All of those things told her he was dedicated to his job.

After showing him her credentials, Grace leaned forward.

'I'm looking into the case of a missing person, Beth Anderson. I understand you were her guidance teacher and we're hoping she may have reached out to you?'

'She did,' he sighed, looking worried. He removed a slim diary from his desk and flicked through it for the exact date. 'Yes, she phoned me and pleaded to meet up, said she desperately needed help and she'd no one else to turn to.'

'Did you go?' asked Grace.

'Yes. I don't mind admitting I was a bit conflicted.'

'Why was that?' asked Grace.

He looked horribly uncomfortable and pulled at his tie like it was trying to choke him.

'I've known the twins since they were eleven,' he said. 'Eliza was always the stronger, more dominant twin. I felt when they were younger that Beth needed to step out from under Eliza's shadow more and forge her own separate identity. She seemed content to simply exist as an adjunct of her twin. They were both assigned to me throughout their time at school, both academically very able, but it was how they were developing socially that gave me cause for concern.'

'How so?' asked Grace.

'Eliza rebelled first when she went into secondary school. She became defiant and started giving cheek to her teachers – including me, I might add.' He smiled ruefully. 'She started hanging out with a different group of friends, the smart but edgy ones who were always looking to circumvent boundaries, you know the kind of thing.'

'Cider in the park?' asked Grace.

'Yes, some of that, too, although like I said, they might've been rebels, but they were smart cookies. They'd take it right up to the line but not beyond. I think all of them bar one ended up acing their exams and going on to university.'

'And Beth?'

He sighed. 'She was a poor wee soul back then. Her only friend was Eliza. Nobody else bothered with her. She was a pale imitation of her sister and why have the copy when you can have the real thing? That seemed to be the prevailing view amongst the kids.'

'The mother wouldn't have helped,' said Grace.

'No, she was a bit of a strange one. Instead of encouraging them to separate but still stay close she tried to force them together to the point where Eliza broke away from her twin altogether. It was hard to watch; the poor kid was utterly bereft. Without her protection she was bullied by the usual suspects. She spent a lot of time curled up on that couch sobbing her wee heart out. She honestly was such a sweet kid. Gave me a few sleepless nights, I can tell you.'

'What about later on?' said Grace.

'Well, she went completely off the rails. I had to advocate for her not being expelled two or three times. I think it came from a place of anger and hurt but nothing could seem to stop her falling. Once alcohol got a grip on her, it was game over. I realised pretty quickly that for her it wasn't just a bit of fun, a way to fit in, it was more than that. It consumed her. It ate her up, body and soul. Rather than want to help her and get her treatment of some kind, her mother turned her back on her completely. Her sister tried to distance herself as much as possible. By that time Eliza had grown out of it all and was focused on doing well in her exams. She'd no time for what she saw as her sister acting out. Beth had no one.'

'Apart from you?'

'Yes,' he said. 'Although even that wasn't completely straightforward. It was my first teaching post fresh out of college. I was a bit green. Anyway, one day, when she was fifteen, she asked to meet me here. She'd taken my refusal to give up on her as evidence that I'd feelings for her and made a messy attempt to kiss me. I was horrified and pushed her away reflexively. In retrospect, I didn't handle it very well, but she couldn't take what she saw as yet another rejection. Not long afterwards she was expelled for assaulting a teacher. I heard that she later left home and descended further into addiction. I kept tabs on her through her sister, but I always felt that I'd failed her. I don't mind admitting that it haunted me.'

'So, when she reached out?'

'I jumped at the chance to help her. I couldn't turn my back on her a second time.'

'I'm going to show you two photos,' Grace said. 'Can you tell me which one most resembled her the day you saw her?'

He studied them. 'The second one, sadly. I came out of school and found her lurking outside. She was in a terrible state, but adamant that she hadn't been drinking. I wanted to believe her, but suspected she'd fallen off the wagon and therefore was having a mental health crisis. It seemed the most likely explanation. She seemed terrified and paranoid and kept muttering about a serpent coming to get her. She said that she'd nowhere to go. Her mother had rejected her, and she'd been turned away by her sister's boyfriend.'

'What? Are you sure she said that?' asked Grace, startled.

'Absolutely. She'd no money and was desperate.' He shrugged helplessly. 'What else could I do but take her home with me?'

'How long did she stay with you?'

'A couple of nights. I took the next day off school and tried to work out how best to help her. She refused to go to a doctor. She said she'd no way of knowing which ones she could trust. I got her some bits and pieces: some new clothes, a rucksack, toiletries... then on the third morning when I woke up, she'd already gone. I'd hoped to persuade her to get help. I failed. I hate the thought of her out there wandering about in such a vulnerable state.'

'She's been missing now for nearly two months. It's not looking good,' said Grace. 'Did she tell you anything about the clinic where she was treated?'

'Yes, some charity operation up at Whiteadder. She said they'd got her clean. When she was admitted they made her sign an agreement to break off all contact with everyone she knew on the outside. Given she was there for the best part of a year, I thought that sounded draconian to say the least, but she said it worked because she'd never felt so good. She'd only been out a few weeks when she started to feel unwell. She still had no desire to drink but her joints ached, her hair started coming out in clumps and she was having problems with her memory. She started to wonder if it was the pills the clinic had her on, whether they were causing her symptoms.'

'Had she mentioned the problems she was having to the clinic?' asked Grace.

'She did but they said it was nothing to do with the pills and they asked her to go back in for monitoring to get to the bottom of it. She refused, saying they seemed more concerned about whether she'd told anyone about the pills than her welfare.'

'So she ran?'

'Not at first. She got home late from the library one night to find a black SUV with tinted windows outside her apartment. There were two security men dressed in black knocking at her door. She knew she couldn't go back there, or they'd force her return her to the clinic. That's all I know.'

Grace thanked him and left. If Beth was still out there alone and unsupported, she didn't much fancy her chances. It was even possible the clinic had already tracked her down and were holding her against her will.

# FIFTEEN

Hannah stood up from her desk wearily and stretched. She was stiff as a post from being hunched over the computer all morning researching everyone at the clinic. Harvey grumbled at being dislodged from her feet where he'd been sleeping. It was blowing a gale outside, and the windows were rattling in their frames as the rain lashed against them. Condensation had fogged up the windows, but she wiped a bit away to look out. The waves were pounding the sand with rhythmic intensity. She'd have to walk Harvey in the park after lunch as she wasn't going to risk him being carried off by a rogue wave.

The door opened, startling her, and Brodie walked in, soaked through.

'Hi, Hannah, is Grace in?' he asked.

'No, she's out interviewing someone,' Hannah said. She noticed that he looked relieved and felt sad. She hated the new awkwardness between them both. 'Is it something I can help with?'

'Another young woman and a male student have gone missing from Edinburgh in rather similar circumstances. I thought she should know. Both alcoholics who went to the clinic and were successfully rehabilitated. Again, they were put into accommodation owned by the clinic and went on to work and study opportunities. In each case friends came forward and reported them missing. They disappeared last night within hours of each other leaving no note or communication behind them.'

'What are the police doing about it?' asked Hannah, appalled.

'They're simply treating them both as missing persons, most likely due to relapsing back into their old patterns and lifestyle.'

'But you don't agree?' said Hannah, troubled by the plight of these additional missing young people who weren't all that much older than she was.

'No, I think it warrants looking into, but my hands are tied.'

'Coffee?' asked Hannah.

'Sure, thanks,' he said, folding himself into one of the comfy chairs. 'It might help me thaw out. That wind cut right through me.' Harvey drifted across, sending a guilty side eye over to Hannah.

'Relax, boy, I'm not offended.' She laughed, jumping up to pour a coffee from the pot and patting his big head on the way past. 'He misses you being around,' she said, handing over a full mug.

'I miss him, too,' he said. 'Unfortunately, Julie isn't terribly keen on having him around now that she's pregnant. She's worried he might go for the baby when it comes.'

'But that's ridiculous!' burst out Hannah. 'Harvey would NEVER do that. When have you ever heard of a Golden Retriever harming a baby? They don't have it in them.'

Harvey was looking from one to the other as though trying to figure out what they were talking about.

'It's not me you need to convince,' he said.

Hannah had to say she wasn't crazy about Julie. She'd liked her at first, but lately she'd begun to see a side of her that struck her as manipulative and controlling. Brodie clearly couldn't see it and Grace was adopting a hands-off approach. At first Julie had been super nice to Hannah and her son, but ever since she'd announced her pregnancy, they seemed to be seeing less and less of Brodie. With the benefit of hindsight, she now felt that Julie's interest in Jack had been fake all along and just her attempt to reel Brodie in by showing him what a good mother she'd make. Hannah now had her doubts about that one.

'Is there any chance you can give us their names?' asked Hannah, holding her breath. Brodie was normally a stickler for protocol, but they'd usually got round it by having something to trade that he needed for his own cases.

'I've thought about it... and yes, I will. You know how I feel about doing stuff like this, though. I'm giving you these names and addresses only because I'm worried about what is going to happen to these kids if I don't. It goes without saying – keep my name out of it. If this goes down the way I suspect it's going to, I'll be involved soon enough,' he said, handing over a piece of paper.

'Did their friends mention any pills they were on?' asked Hannah.

'No, they didn't. Missing persons' cases are incredibly frustrating. Most people have taken themselves off, but a tiny proportion will have been murdered or abducted and if it were up to me, we'd be far more proactive at the start in the hope of avoiding those bad outcomes. That window of time where we hang back and do next to nothing only gives any perpetrator time to cover their tracks.'

'Why don't the police do that then?' asked Hannah.

'It all comes down to resources,' said Brodie. 'Anyway, mind if I take Harvey for a walk? It's been a while.'

Harvey's ears pricked up at the mention of the magic word and he bounced to his feet, tail wagging.

'Sure,' said Hannah, laughing. 'I don't envy you going out in that,' she added, pointing to the driving rain.

'We'll be fine, won't we, boy?' Brodie grinned, turning up his collar and grabbing Harvey's lead from the hook. He opened the door and fought his way out against a sudden gust of wind that caused the papers on Hannah's desk to rise up and flutter off her desk. She shuddered against the sudden chill and turned on the electric heater. Her mum was picking up Jack from nursery today, so she had time to do some additional research on the two missing persons. She grabbed Jean's warm cardigan from the back of her chair and, huddling into it, she started to research the names that she'd been given, two lives that had gone horribly wrong.

# SIXTEEN

Jean spotted the man in Wetherspoons before he saw her. As agreed, he was wearing a brown and yellow striped scarf and had a copy of National Geographic magazine on the table in front of him. He was sipping from a pint of lager and his face radiated tension. She paused at his side and his startled brown eyes looked up into hers.

She sat down upon being invited with the drink she'd already ordered to avoid wasting time.

'I'm Fiona,' she said with a warm smile. 'What should I call you?' She asked even though she already knew who he was. Hannah had printed off sheets with photos, names and details of all the doctors and nursing staff at the clinic, pinning them to the board in Grace's room for them all to familiarise themselves with. Sitting before her was Dr Angus Macdonald, aged forty-two, a neurologist and geneticist who additionally specialised in substance abuse.

'Er, Gordon,' he muttered, looking away.

*Not a very good liar then*, thought Jean. *Perhaps he's on the level.* She didn't want to spook him by revealing she knew exactly who he was so simply nodded.

'Good to meet you, Gordon. I'm hoping you can shed some light on what may have happened to my daughter, Beth?'

He turned towards her, fully focused now. 'Honestly, I don't know what has happened to her.'

'Oh,' said Jean, disappointed.

'But what I do know about the clinic gives me cause for concern. My specialty is addiction medicine with a focus on neurology and genetics. I was headhunted by the clinic because of these specialisms and a series of studies I published whilst working towards a PhD at John Hopkins. It was an exciting opportunity. They promised money was no object in terms of research equipment and budget. I thought I'd landed my dream job,' he said, his mouth twisting bitterly.

'So, what went wrong?' asked Jean. She was worried that he was going to bolt at any minute. His muscles were twitching, and he looked pale and clammy, almost as if he might be sickening for something himself. His eyes darted about constantly, scanning for threats. Was this someone on the verge of a breakdown or someone they could take seriously? Either way she needed to tread carefully.

'I've been there five years,' he said. 'At first it was just a conventional rehab facility. We recruited patients who couldn't afford our services, which usually meant the homeless or those at rock bottom and willing to try to change for the better. In return, they had to agree to stay with us for a complete year and submit to a battery of tests using the most sophisticated imaging arrays. They also received the best of nutrition and healthcare, including psychological assessments. It didn't even end there. People can often change within the sheltered confines of a clinic but revert to type when they are discharged. We designed support packages including affordable housing with subsidised rent and regular monitoring. All they had to do was attend for monitoring one day a month. It was a pretty good thing we were doing, or so I thought at the time.'

'What happened to change that?' asked Jean, quietly sipping her drink.

'I don't know if I can do this,' he said, half rising out of his seat. 'They've eyes everywhere. Someone could have followed me here and be watching us right now. You don't understand how dangerous this is for me.'

Jean strove to keep her own voice slow and unhurried.

'My daughter is relying on you doing the right thing,' she said. 'You strike me as someone who got into this position to transform lives for the better. Clearly something has gone terribly wrong at that place.'

He sat back down with a thump. 'It's worse than you can possibly imagine,' he said. 'I could be struck off if anyone found out... the entire programme could be cancelled.'

'But don't you think you should try to bring it to an end if people are being harmed?'

'You don't understand. It's not so black and white as that. A few people may have been harmed, but the potential benefits are insane. If what's been happening here gets out, the whole programme will be shut down, which could have devastating consequences for future research that might benefit the whole of humanity.'

'What can you tell me about the lilac pills she was on?' she asked.

'You've seen those?' he asked. 'They're not meant to be giving them out yet. They're not ready. I... can't do this, I need to think. I'm sorry.'

With that, he swiftly got up and almost ran for the exit. Jean ground her teeth in frustration but knew it would be futile to go after him. A few minutes later she left, noticing Grace sitting two rows behind. As previously agreed, they didn't acknowledge each other and left separately, just in case Dr Macdonald had been tailed.

# SEVENTEEN

Grace stomped out onto Portobello Beach, her slender body bent against the wind and rain. She'd left Harvey behind in the flat, as even he would be miserable in this weather. Part of her wondered if she was bonkers for doing this, but the vulnerable part – which was larger than most realised – knew that this morning swim routine was what kept her alert, and helped her mind reset itself every morning. Shedding her dry robe, she plunged straight into the churning water, pulling strongly through until the waves were undulating in a more predictable way. She knew her limitations and wouldn't swim far today, striking out parallel to the Esplanade rather than swimming straight out towards the horizon as she usually did. The freezing cold water was always a shock to the system no matter how often she swam. This daily battle with the elements set her up to take on the challenges the day would bring. Or that's what she told herself, a rogue wave catching her by surprise and forcing salt water up her nose, causing her to splutter.

After a hot shower, a quick trot round Figgate Park with Harvey, and a bacon roll and coffee at The Espy, she felt ready to take on the world. It was still only eight thirty, but as she opened the door, Hannah and Jean were grabbing their first coffees of the day. Both of them were clearly bursting to speak to her.

'I think you'd better bring those through here,' said Grace with a smile, leading the way through to her large comfortable room at the back of the building.

After his usual meet and greet, Harvey retired to his basket in Grace's room for a snooze. He wasn't a fan of dark rainy mornings where the wind fluffed his hair up and blew sand in his eyes.

'Jean, you go first,' said Grace, forgoing her desk so they could all sit in the comfy seats beside the coffee table. As Jean put down her cup and smiled at them, Grace was struck by the change in her demeanour from a few short weeks ago. Even though she was predictably cagey about it, her new relationship must be blossoming. It was about time she met someone who was worthy of her.

'It was a man – dressed exactly as he said he would be. He said his name was Gordon, but I knew from the staff photos up in reception at the clinic that it was really Dr Angus Macdonald,' she said. 'Before I tell you what happened, it might help to know what Hannah found out about him yesterday?'

Hannah flicked through her new notebook. 'He's one of those genius types who went to university really young. He was fifteen, apparently. He got a scholarship to a posh private school down south and from there went to Oxford University. He's Scottish though, born in Edinburgh.'

'What did he study?' asked Grace.

'Not medicine at first. He got a double first in neuroscience and molecular biology. He then got accepted onto graduate programmes at John Hopkins in the US, where he did a PhD in Addiction and Genetics. After that he did an accelerated medical degree in Boston, then was hired by Magnum Pharmaceuticals, which is based there.'

'See if you can find any former associates or the current whereabouts of any parents or siblings,' said Grace.

'Will do,' said Hannah.

'The man was terrified out of his wits,' continued Jean. 'I get the impression that whatever he's got himself involved in, he started out with the best of intentions.'

'You didn't get any idea of what is going on at the clinic behind closed doors?' asked Grace, frustrated.

'No, but whatever it is I think it's pretty bad. He was shocked when I mentioned the lilac pills. He claimed they shouldn't be giving them out yet as they're not ready. On the plus side, they seem to have had great success with helping people get off drink and drugs in a sustainable programme with extended support once it finishes. He also said that the work they're doing could yield huge benefits for humanity so I think he's genuinely conflicted about what he should do.'

'What else have you found out about them, Hannah?'

'Well, the person in charge, Dr Anna Campbell, has given a handful of interviews in high-end magazines and although she's a doctor, she also has a degree in business which she got from Yale. She came across really well.'

'Any associations with US pharmaceuticals?' asked Grace.

'Yes, she was operations director for Magnum Pharmaceuticals before coming over here,' said Hannah, reading from her notes.

'Anyone else that might be of interest?' asked Grace.

'The person in charge of research and development is Dr Conrad Walker,' said Hannah.

'Yes, he's related to the young woman on reception, Lily Walker,' said Jean.

'Nepo baby?' said Hannah, pulling a face.

'To be fair she was very pleasant and seemed good at her job,' said Jean.

'I did find out one thing that was very interesting,' said

Hannah. 'All of them have a previous association with Magnum Pharmaceuticals. Even the nurse, Frankie Garcia. She was a practising nurse at John Hopkins, but ended up working as an administrator for several pharmaceutical trials.'

'I'm wondering if it might be a bit like money laundering...' mused Grace.

Hannah and Jean looked at each other with perplexed faces.

'I don't get it,' said Hannah. 'How so?'

'Well, I'm wondering if they're using a legitimate medical model for rehab as a cover up for unauthorised medical trials or experiments on human subjects,' said Grace.

'That would be insane,' said Jean faintly. 'If they got found out they'd be struck off and also face serious jail time.'

'They'd make a shedload of money if they didn't get found out though,' said Hannah. 'I don't get why they wouldn't do things the regular way though. Why try and short-circuit the process when the risks of being found out are so great?'

'You're right.' Grace smiled. 'It's probably a crazy idea.'

'Maybe they're just after proof of concept?' said Jean. 'Then they can dot the i's and cross the t's afterwards knowing it's all going to be worth the crazy expense of these things.'

'We may never know. Right now, all I'm concerned about is finding Eliza's missing twin,' said Grace with a sigh.

'Brodie was round here yesterday afternoon,' said Hannah.

'Oh?' said Grace, schooling her face in a neutral expression. 'What did he want?'

'Just to let us know that two other young people with a similar background to Beth went missing in similar circumstances. He gave us the names and addresses because they've only been flagged as missing persons, but he's worried about them. I said we wouldn't let on where we heard about it. They're called Lorraine Kerr and Tom White.'

'Did he say anything else?' asked Grace.

Hannah bit her lip and lowered her eyes.

'Come on, out with it,' said Grace.

'He said that Julie doesn't want Harvey around once the baby's born in case he harms it.'

Grace glared at her. 'He... what?'

'Hey, don't shoot the messenger!' said Hannah, holding her hands above her head in mock surrender. 'I did defend Harvey's honour. If it's any consolation, Brodie clearly didn't agree with it. I think he's also coming under pressure not to see Jack as much. I've been getting fobbed off recently with "Julie's tired" and other excuses.'

'I didn't know,' said Grace. 'I'm sorry, Hannah. I guess she's got Brodie exactly where she wants him at the moment. Anyway, our focus needs to be on our case. I don't like the sound of these other young people going missing. It's starting to feel like they're covering their tracks prior to shipping out.'

'I hope not,' said Jean. 'That would probably mean they'd never be held to account for what's gone on here.'

'The only way we would ever know what they'd been up to for sure would be a post-mortem,' said Grace grimly. 'And maybe not even then.'

# EIGHTEEN

Grace had arranged to meet the young woman who had phoned in one of the missing person complaints outside MacEwan Hall at Edinburgh University, the place where she herself had graduated. As she admired the stunning architecture and glanced around, she didn't envy the young students peopling the square. It seemed things were a lot harder for them these days than when she had been a student.

'Miss McKenna?' said a small voice from behind her.

'Olivia?' she answered with a smile to put the girl at ease, but with limited success.

'Yes, I thought we could go across to the library bar at Teviot,' she said. 'It'll be busy so no one will notice us.'

'Good idea,' said Grace, walking across with her. Once they were seated in the library bar with their drinks, Grace produced her credentials for inspection.

'Thank you for agreeing to meet with me. I've been instructed by my client to try and locate her missing sister. She went missing in what I believe are very similar circumstances to your friend. Can you tell me what you know?'

'Um... well, Lorraine and I became friends during Fresher's

Week,' said Olivia, her large owlish eyes peering earnestly at Grace from behind her glasses. 'Neither of us drink and we're also mature students, so I suppose initially we bonded over that. Instead of getting hammered in pubs we joined the hillwalking and kayaking clubs. As the term went on, Lorraine opened up to me about her life before coming here.' She paused.

'Go on,' encouraged Grace.

'It feels a bit disloyal telling all this personal stuff to a stranger. Are you sure she's in real danger?'

'It's a strong possibility,' said Grace. 'You won't only be helping Lorraine – there are others missing, too.'

'I suppose it's alright then,' Olivia said with a hesitant smile. 'She told me she was expelled from school at the age of fifteen after getting caught drunk in the science lab. She set it on fire with her Bunsen burner. Her parents were furious with her, but the more they tried to control her the more she rebelled. A year later, she ran off to live with some guy in a squat and her parents completely disowned her. Not long after that they split up and moved away. She was left living on the streets craving her next fix.'

'So how did she turn things around?' asked Grace.

'When she was eighteen, she told me she hit rock bottom. She stopped struggling and gave up. That's when a miracle happened. An American nurse and a doctor came by and offered her a free place at their rehab clinic. They said that once she was well, she would receive ongoing support. She would never have to spend another night sleeping on the streets. That was four years ago.' Olivia's eyes filled with tears, and she struggled to regain her composure.

'Take your time,' soothed Grace, trying to hide her impatience. She was also surprised. Lorraine seemed to have had an ongoing relationship with the clinic for a number of years – much longer than Beth had.

'She said it was some luxury clinic up in the hills. There

were others there like her. Over the year she was there some of them dropped out and disappeared, but most stayed like she did. It was like a fancy spa and there were all kinds of activities there she could do. The food was top notch. Even when she got out, they continued to help her, with accommodation, studying to get her Highers over two years and getting into university. All she had to do in return was go back there four times a year for tests. The data was used to improve care for those coming after her, so she didn't mind. She was doing so incredibly well and now this! It's so unfair!'

'When was the last time you saw her?'

'She hadn't been feeling well. Probably a bit run down from the end of term exams. She went to the clinic at the beginning of January, I remember that. Came back with some extra vitamins to try. Four days ago, Monday twelfth of February, I swung by her flat as usual on the way to the lecture theatre. She wasn't there. I haven't seen her since. Two days ago, I reported her missing to the police.'

'Had her bed been slept in?' asked Grace.

'I think so. The duvet was all rumpled... although she usually made her bed.'

'What about her keys or phone? Her passport?'

'I don't think she had a passport, as she'd never been abroad. Her keys were gone, but I have her phone.'

'You do?' said Grace, pleased at this unexpected stroke of luck.

'Yes.' Olivia looked a bit sheepish. 'Please don't tell the police. I was worried about her and thought they might just dump it in a box somewhere.'

'I'm going to have to take it from you – the police might be able to find something on it that could help her.' Grace held out her hand and the girl fished in her tote bag and handed it over with a sigh. 'Did she ever say anything negative to you about the clinic?'

'No, she used to love going there. She said it was like a pamper weekend at a spa. There was a nurse and a doctor there who treated her like the parents she wished she had. The nurse was American. I can't remember their names. I don't get it... why are you asking about the clinic? She would have told me if she was making a scheduled visit there. I saw her the night before. We were working together in the library, and I arranged to call on her in the morning, but she'd simply disappeared.'

'Did you speak to some of her other friends?'

'I was her only close friend here. I can show you her flat if you want?'

'You have the key?' said Grace, surprised.

Olivia reddened. 'We had copies of our keys made in case we got locked out or lost one. It's only a short walk away, in George Square. She lives alone in a garden flat there, so we don't need to get permission.'

In just a few minutes they were walking down the cobbled leafy square with the university library on their right softened by the central garden enclosed by railings. Olivia carried on down the right-hand side until she turned to open a gate and walk down a set of steps. Pausing at the bottom in front of the smart navy painted door with its shiny brass knocker, she glanced around furtively, then applied the key she was holding to the lock. The door swung open into a darkened hallway leading from the front to the back of the property. The flat was immaculate with quality furnishings far beyond the means of the average student, including a large flat-screen TV with surround sound. The kitchen appliances were modern. Grace opened the fridge. To her surprise it was completely empty and had been wiped clean. Olivia came up behind her.

'Where's all her food gone?' Olivia asked. 'She'd loads of stuff in there. I get chucking out your milk and veg if you're going away for a few days... but this makes it look as though she's not coming back.' Olivia rushed through to the bedroom.

'All her stuff is gone, too!' she yelled. 'Books, clothes, everything.'

Grace walked through and noticed also that the bed had been stripped with the duvet and pillows stacked neatly. They walked back through to the kitchen and sat at the table, lost for words. Grace turned her gaze upwards as she became aware of a small flashing red light. It didn't look like any smoke alarm she'd seen before. Jumping up she stood on her chair to inspect it. It wasn't a smoke alarm at all, but some fancy surveillance camera disguised to look like one.

'What is it?' asked Olivia, sounding alarmed.

There was no point in worrying her and Grace suspected it had been left there in error. She doubted anyone would be monitoring its feed now that Lorraine was no longer there.

'Nothing,' she said casually. 'Just being thorough.'

'I don't understand,' said Olivia, her eyes moist with tears. 'Has Lorraine just dropped out, left without saying goodbye?'

Grace shrugged helplessly. Either that, or that was what someone wanted them to think. She had a really bad feeling about what was going on here.

# NINETEEN

Back at the office, Grace paid a fee to do a search against the address that Lorraine had been staying at. As she suspected, it belonged to an American company she'd never heard of. She dug through the open file beside her for the last known address of her client's sister.

'Bingo!' she exclaimed as she discovered that the same company owned both properties. Now there was an unequivocal link between the two cases. Glancing at her watch, she saw that it was nearly time to meet Ryan Sinclair who had reported his friend Tom White as missing. They weren't students but worked as apprentices in a top Edinburgh hair salon called Xander's in the centre of Edinburgh.

She made a quick fuss of Harvey then left him in his basket with the door open as she updated Hannah and Jean on what she'd found out.

'Jean, can you try to find out who the office bearers are on that American company, please? If you succeed in doing that, cross-reference them against employees of Magnum Pharmaceuticals. I'm off to meet Ryan Sinclair.'

. . .

Walking into the small café in George Street with an enticing aroma of real coffee she hesitated. In the corner a young man who looked like a youthful John Travolta met her eyes with a guarded smile. She made her way over to him.

'Ryan?'

'Yes, please sit,' he said. 'I got you a water with ice and lemon to save you having to waste time in the queue.'

She smiled her thanks and took a sip. 'How well did you know Tom?' she asked.

'He was my partner,' he replied quietly.

'You used the past tense,' said Grace with a question in her voice.

'I have a bad feeling,' he said, placing his hand over his heart. 'I know Tom and he would never have just taken off like that. Not in a million years. He loved his job. We had so many plans together. We wanted to open our own salon one day.'

'Did you live together?'

'No, the terms of his lease didn't allow it. We were going to get our own place in a year's time.'

'When was the last time you saw him?' asked Grace.

'A week ago. We went out for dinner and drinks then he headed home as he wasn't feeling well, some kind of migraine,' he said.

'Had you noticed any change in him over the last few weeks?'

'Yes, he'd had some kind of bug he couldn't shake. I nagged him to go to the doctor, but he said he'd had enough of doctors, and it was just a case of waiting it out. He'd lost weight and his joints were hurting. Even his posture suffered as though it hurt him to stand up straight. The last time we slept together I noticed hairs on the pillow when he'd gone.'

Grace felt sick. Something awful was happening to these young people and she had to get to the bottom of it before it was too late.

'Do you have a key for Tom's place?' she asked, her heart heavy.

'Yes, of course, but I've already looked. He isn't there. You think he's sick, don't you? Really sick.'

'Honestly, I don't know,' Grace said. 'But I'm very concerned. Did you know about his past? Before he met you, I mean.'

'You mean about him living on the streets? Yeah, of course.'

'Did he ever mention anything about being treated for addiction at a clinic?'

'Yeah, some place up in the wilds near a reservoir. He shouldn't really have told me. They make everyone sign a confidentiality agreement.'

Was that why they'd been taken? Because they breached confidentiality? No, far more likely they'd got wind that they were sick. But how? Had the missing kids contacted them and told them? Or were they under some form of covert surveillance? She took Ryan's address and gave him her card in case Tom made contact, then took her leave.

A disturbing picture was starting to emerge, but she didn't have the resources to tackle it herself. She would need to involve the police. There was some kind of cover-up going on and she sensed things might be about to get even worse. What on earth were they getting up to at Whiteadder?

# TWENTY

Grace headed straight for St Leonard's police station where Brodie and his team were based. She'd phoned ahead and made an appointment, not wanting the humiliation of being turned away at the desk in a building she used to work in.

She was buzzed through on arrival and met on the other side of the door by Brodie. They made awkward small talk until she was seated across from him in his small, cold office.

'Cold?' he asked as she suddenly shivered.

'A bit,' she said and watched as he switched on the electric heater for her benefit. He looked thinner. It must be all that vegan stuff Julie was feeding him. He'd lost the twinkle in his eyes. Mind you, that could be down to his changed feelings towards her. Concentrate on the job in hand, she scolded herself.

'I spoke to the two missing kids' friends,' she said urgently. 'Basically, that's three young people missing now, in similar circumstances, with a common denominator of having been homeless, addicted and invited to take up a lengthy residential place at Whiteadder Clinic.'

'I hear you, Grace, but my bosses are reluctant to go in hard here. It's perfectly possible, likely even, that each of them has simply fallen off the wagon and gone back to their old ways. It's easier than people think to simply walk away from your life and disappear.'

'But what if it's something to do with their previous treatment at the clinic? Isn't it possible that with so much at stake, the clinic is tidying up their mess with a view to pulling out of Scotland? It's an American company.'

'That's partly what makes it so difficult,' said Brodie. 'We have to bear in mind that we're dealing with foreign nationals and a company with links to big pharma in the US. If we go in mob-handed without clear evidence they'll bury us in litigation for years.'

'I've now had access to each of the two flats where the missing kids lived. I carried out a Sasine Search and they're all owned by a letting agency that links back to Whiteadder.'

'So? You've already established that they provide ongoing support to their patients.'

'The ones we know about only go missing when they're sick. How does the clinic even know that? I'm wondering if the reason they're so helpful with accommodation is that they're continuing to monitor them without their knowledge or consent?'

'Did you find any evidence of that?' asked Brodie wearily.

'I did find something in Lorraine's flat. It looked like a surveillance device concealed within a smoke alarm. It may well be that there is something similar in the boy's flat. I didn't feel like I could start to pull things apart. If the police officially searched the properties, I'm sure they could stumble upon it, if it's still there.'

'Grace, are you alright?' Brodie said, shifting in his seat with a squeak. 'You're sounding a bit... well, paranoid?'

Grace stiffened in anger. 'Call it a hunch. Remember those?' she said, her voice laced with sarcasm.

They stared at each other over his untidy desk, eyes narrowed in hostility. She'd known they were in for a bumpy ride after he decided to stay with Julie, but she hadn't expected him to start doubting her professional judgement.

'Brodie, what's going on?' she said quietly. 'Is there something you're not telling me?'

He ran a hand through his thick dark hair making it stand on end like a punk rocker. Normally, she'd have stifled a smile, but she'd never felt less like laughing. She let the silence congeal between them until he brought it to an end.

'Look, Grace, I don't know what's going on but the word from on high is to leave this well alone. The Super got wind I'd been asking questions about the missing kids and tore me off a strip. Word is, he got a strip torn off from his boss and so on, all the way up to the top.'

'Since when have you let office politics stop you?' scoffed Grace. Suddenly, she slapped her head.

'Oh, I get it, now you're having a baby with Julie, the Super has you like a nodding dog in his pocket. How can you be so spineless?' she raged. Now that she could feel the anger ignited within her it started to blaze out of control. He'd hurt her more than she'd acknowledged to herself by running back to Julie, just as he was on the verge of committing to her again.

'Oh, grow up, Grace,' he snapped. 'How about living in the real world for a change? I'm sick of your holier-than-thou attitude. Maybe if you hadn't shut me out when Connor died, we wouldn't be in this mess.'

They both stared at each other, shocked. For so long they had skated round all this without clearing the air between them. Grace felt a tsunami of emotion rise up, threatening to engulf her. Not here. Not now. Abruptly she sprang to her feet and walked out of the room. There was no way she was going to break down in front of him. She didn't even know who he was anymore.

'Grace! Wait!' he yelled after her. She carried on walking, her head held high. She was halfway down the long corridor when the Super, Julie's father and her former boss, stuck his head out of his office, wondering what all the commotion was. He opened his flaccid mouth to emit his usual sarcastic comments. Furious, she turned on him and held her hand up to silence him. What she really wanted to do was make a rude gesture, but she refrained. In silence she continued her march out of the police station, determined never to return. She would have to figure this out on her own.

She burst out of the station then hurried down the road to where her car was parked, her tears mingling with the lashing rain until she couldn't tell which was which.

# TWENTY-ONE

'So, what's he like then?' asked Hannah, leaning her chin on her hand and fixing her unblinking stare on Jean. They were having a working lunch. Jean had brought in sandwiches for them all so they wouldn't have to brave the wind and rain. The dark slate-grey of the sea made it difficult to know where the sky ended, and the sea began. The wind hurled sand viciously into anyone who was foolish enough to walk along the Esplanade today.

'Who?' asked Jean, playing for time, hurriedly stuffing a brie and cranberry sandwich into her mouth.

'You know who I mean. You've been out with him three times now. Is he going to be a keeper, do you think?'

Jean rolled her eyes. There was no way that Hannah was going to let her off the hook. Grace raised her eyebrows, and folded her arms, sitting back in her seat.

'Fine,' groaned Jean. 'I'll tell you. His name's Patrick Vaughan. I met him through the church. He's a widower with two teenagers, a boy and a girl.'

'Have you met them yet?' asked Hannah, cutting straight to the chase as always.

'Not yet. It's too soon.'

'Does he have a GSOH?' demands Hannah, eyes narrowed.

'A what?' asked Jean, bewildered.

'A good sense of humour,' supplied Grace with a smile. It warmed her heart to see Jean blushing like a schoolgirl.

'Well, we certainly have a lot of laughs together,' said Jean. 'Tonight he's taking me to the Traverse Theatre to see a play. We're having dinner first,' she supplied, her eyes sparkling.

'Now we just have to get Grace sorted out,' said the irrepressible Hannah.

'Not so fast, missy,' said Grace. 'I think you should be dipping your toe in the dating waters next.'

There was an awkward pause. Everyone knew that the last time Hannah had dated was three years previously, when she'd been involved with Grace's dead son, Connor. The relationship had given her an adorable son but also trauma from his subsequent suicide. Grace wanted her to move on with her life but was starting to wish she'd never opened her mouth.

Hannah looked bashful. 'Actually, there is somebody I might have my eye on,' she admitted. 'It's the guy I've been seeing in connection with our case, Marek. He asked for my number. If he was to ask me out, would that be okay, as he's not directly involved?'

'Of course.' Grace smiled. 'If he works with the homeless his heart must be in the right place.'

'Watch this space,' said Hannah, tapping the side of her nose.

'Right,' said Grace, glancing at the clock on the wall. 'Time I wasn't here. I have to go and see our client. Jean, I take it you've heard nothing further from Dr Macdonald?'

'No, should I push for another meeting?'

'Yes, things seem to be accelerating now. The clinic may well be looking to shut down and erase all incriminating evidence of what they've really been getting up to.'

'Including people?' asked Hannah, looking worried.

'Perhaps,' said Grace. 'Keep your ear to the ground in relation to your volunteer work, see if you can bump up your shifts. I think the time may have come where we need to be more open with people so that they understand the urgency. Have there been any more leads in relation to your poster campaign?'

'No, there's been nothing for days now, not even the crazies,' sighed Hannah. 'How did it go with Brodie? Isn't there anything he can do to help us?'

'No, I'm afraid we're on our own for this one,' said Grace. 'I'll be back before closing time. Do you mind if I leave Harvey here, or would you rather I popped him back to the flat?'

'Are you kidding me?' said Hannah, eyes wide in horror. 'He's like a furry hot water bottle on my feet. Leave him where he is!' Harvey looked smug.

Grace laughed and left them to it, her smile melting off her face the minute she was outside. It was exhausting pretending everything was all right when she was still pretty shaken up by her row with Brodie earlier. Maybe she had been viewing the past through rose-tinted spectacles. Today had reminded her that the death throes of her marriage hadn't been pretty. Maybe it was just as well that he had thrown her over for Julie. After all, if he had loved her as much as he led her to believe, he should have fought harder for her. It was a painful lesson to learn.

Jean and Hannah were right. It was time to stop being a doormat and get herself back out into the fray. Surely there had to be at least one nice guy left in the city of Edinburgh?

## TWENTY-TWO

Grace jogged up three floors to her client's flat and paused to catch her breath before ringing the doorbell. She was still a little early. Suddenly, she was startled by the sound of smashing glass and raised, angry voices. Were Eliza and Ben having a fight about something? Grace felt awkward listening in, but she really had no option. What if it was relevant to the case? Moving closer, she put her ear to the door.

'How could you do that?'

'What? What did I do?' he shouted. 'You're only pissed with me 'cos she went missing. How was I meant to know that would happen? She's trouble, Eliza. I couldn't have her derailing everything we've fought so hard to achieve. She's a burnt-out alchy or worse. Open your eyes! She'd have bled you dry either emotionally or financially.'

'I told you she was clean! Why won't you believe me? And even if she wasn't, she's my twin sister. Saying you hate her is like saying you hate me. Don't make me choose—'

'Because you'd choose her,' he finished for her. 'I'll be back for my things.'

Grace jumped and flattened herself against the wall as the

door swung open and Ben rushed past her, his face contorted in an ugly scowl. She watched him run down the stairs and turned to the open door. She could hear the sound of sobbing from within. She felt a bit awkward after hearing them row, but decided to press on. Tentatively, she knocked on the door. 'Eliza, it's Grace. Okay if I come in?'

Eliza poked a tearstained face round the door and motioned to her to enter.

'Why don't you sit down, and I'll make us both some tea?' Grace said.

Eliza nodded, not yet able to speak, and led the way into the lounge where she threw herself down on the couch. Grace walked past her into the kitchen where she made a pot of tea and scrounged up some biscuits. When she was opening the fridge to get milk, her eyes were drawn to a photo of the twins which had been made into a fridge magnet. They were indeed indistinguishable from each other.

She carried the tea tray through and poured a cup for them both. Eliza had wiped away her smudged mascara and now looked more composed, although her eyes were still moist with tears.

'I couldn't help overhearing...' began Grace.

'She came round to the door pleading for help, saying she was in real danger, and he sent her packing. Who does that? I don't know how I can ever forgive him. How could he keep something so important from me? He knew I was worried sick about her.'

'When was this?' asked Grace.

'It was exactly two weeks after I came to see you, can you imagine? If he'd only let her in, all this could have been avoided. She could be safe. God knows what's happened to her since then.'

'At least we know that she was alive two weeks after she disappeared off the radar. That's got to be a good thing. As for

Ben... I know how angry you must be, but you can hardly blame him for jumping to conclusions in the circumstances. I guess he was probably trying to protect you in his own way.'

Eliza took a sip of tea and then another. She was slowly calming down. Grace sipped her own tea and waited until she judged it safe to continue.

'Do you think that your sister would have mentioned to the clinic that she had an identical twin?'

'No, I know she didn't. At the time she started treatment there, she'd cut us out of her life so irrevocably that I doubt it would have even occurred to her. Later, when I met her, she mentioned she was glad they didn't know I existed, and it comforted her to know that at least I was safe. She said she'd thought about telling them while she was there, but was too ashamed and felt that part of her life should remain buried for good. It was best to start over with a clean slate. She thought I'd only look down my nose and judge her.' Fresh tears spilled from her eyes.

'The reason I came to see you today was that two other young people have gone missing in similar circumstances. Both were addicted to alcohol and living on the streets when the clinic offered them a place and helped them turn their lives around.'

'You don't think the clinic has murdered them all, do you?' asked Eliza, her voice rising in fear.

'There's no evidence to point to that at the moment. We're in touch with a whistleblower from the clinic, but he's clearly terrified and hasn't given us much to work with yet. We need to get inside,' said Grace, frustrated. 'From a conversation I had with someone in the police, it sounds as though they're being protected by a wall of silence flowing down from the top. Someone must have brought some serious influence to bear on the situation.'

'What chance do we have, if they've managed to nobble the police?' asked Eliza, wringing her hands in despair.

'One way or another, we're going to do our best to expose them if they're carrying out unauthorised procedures under the guise of helping people,' said Grace with renewed determination. 'We're going to get to the bottom of this.'

'Or die trying?' said her client with a watery smile.

'Let's hope it doesn't come to that,' said Grace grimly.

# TWENTY-THREE

Hannah had already had her tea and Jack was tucked up in bed. She'd thought he'd never go to sleep, but the final story had done the trick. Hannah's mum was staying in tonight, so she was free to work the case. The frost was crisping on the ground and the moon had risen in the starlit sky as she wrapped up warmly and headed out carrying a large bag of blankets, gloves, hats and scarves she had scrounged off everyone she knew, together with some good charity shop finds. Grace's sister, Cally, had been particularly generous, and her son, Hamish, had promised to come out some nights as well. She thought he'd drop her as a friend once he started uni, but they were as tight as ever. Despite his unsettling resemblance to his cousin Connor, Jack's deceased father, he was much easier to be around and a whole lot less intense than Connor had been.

She got the bus into town. Her first stop was at the soup kitchen in the bowels of the Grassmarket. As she hurried down the steep steps, she felt a bit vulnerable in the dark and couldn't resist glancing behind her a few times. She knew Grace would have wanted her to go the long way round, but she was already running a little late and this would catch her up a bit.

She arrived at the church hall that served as their base and although her heart leapt at the sight of Marek, she didn't greet him but just quietly mucked in doing what needed to be done. There were a lot of people queuing to get in tonight because of the extreme cold, and Hannah couldn't help worrying that some of the older and frailer might not make it through the night. She passed out her supplies to those who looked the most in need, but it didn't take long before her stores were exhausted. She'd been allowed to put posters of Beth, Lorraine and Tom up on the noticeboard with a note asking anyone who might have seen them to tell someone on duty. They had the heaters blasting in the church to give the visitors some respite while they had their soup and sandwiches. To Hannah's disappointment, no one came forward. The evening flew by, and Hannah could feel her eyes blurring with tiredness. As the last of the stragglers shuffled out, she turned to grab her coat off the hook.

'Hannah, wait up!'

Marek had materialised by her side. She'd barely exchanged two words with him all night. 'I'm just heading off,' she said. 'I feel bad for them all out there. It's well below freezing tonight, for sure.'

'I know, it's grim. Part of doing this is accepting you can only do so much, even if it's not enough.'

Hannah sighed and shrugged on her old coat. 'I suppose. I don't know how you do it. Nobody should have to sleep out on the streets on nights like this.'

'I can't argue with you there,' he said. Hannah prepared to move past him. It'd been a long day, and she was beyond exhausted.

'Why don't we have a quick drink before heading home?' he said, his chocolate brown eyes locking on to hers. 'It's good to decompress sometimes.'

'Oh... who else is going?' she asked casually.

'Just us, I think,' he said, glancing round at the remaining two workers who were in their seventies at least.

'Sure, why not?' she said, playing it cool, though her heart rate shot up like a racehorse out the gate.

They ended up at Greyfriar's Bobby, from where they could both jump on a bus home. There was a welcome blast of heat as they headed in the door, and they managed to find seats together as they squeezed in behind a table. The fug of the pub and the warm rumble of the regulars' banter relaxed her. Marek went to the bar and came back with a pint of lager for himself and a glass of white wine for Hannah. He looked really embarrassed and, suddenly, could barely look at her.

'What is it?' she asked, alarmed.

'Er, the bar man wants to see some ID,' he muttered. She looked across and saw a burly man standing staring at her, his arms folded, a scowl on his face.

Feeling humiliated, she slid out from behind the table and thumped her driving license down on the bar.

'Sorry, love. You'll be glad of it when you're older. Can't take any chance with my licence.'

'Let's never speak of this again,' she huffed to Marek, as she joined him behind the table.

'You're so cute when you blush.' He grinned, only to receive an unfriendly poke in the ribs from Hannah.

'Ouch, message received,' he said, rubbing at his side.

'You're hardly ancient yourself,' she said. 'How old are you, anyway?'

'Twenty-seven.' He smiled.

*Probably thinks I'm a stupid kid then*, thought Hannah gloomily. They sipped their drinks for a couple of minutes in silence.

'I was surprised when you came back,' Marek said. 'We get a lot of people come down on a whim. Well-intentioned but with no staying power.'

'Well, I like to see my commitments through,' said Hannah. 'Or in other words, I'm stubborn.' She grinned.

'What did you say your day job was?' he asked.

'I didn't,' she said, giving him a considering look. She wanted to tell him about the agency. After all, it was a cool job and she'd lost major street cred with being ID'd by the barman but, still, something held her back. She'd wait until she knew him a bit better.

'I work in a legal office,' she said instead. After all, it wasn't that far from the truth. 'How about you?'

'Well, I'm involved in the church, obviously, but aside from that, I work as a nurse at the Royal Infirmary.'

'Cool,' said Hannah, wishing she had told him the truth now. After that the conversation flowed until the barman rang the bell for last orders. As they walked to the bus stop, he paused as his bus was on the opposite side of the road from hers. He leaned across slowly and kissed her on the cheek, but the slow lingering look he gave her afterwards made her shiver with delight.

'See you soon,' was his parting shot as he dived across the road just in time to catch his bus.

Hannah watched his bus until it rounded the corner and was hidden from view. She hadn't mentioned that she had a son, and he hadn't asked whether she had children. Why would he? She was only nineteen. She could have mentioned it, but something had held her back. Since their last case, when Jack's safety had been threatened, she had vowed to keep him safe. Before, she would bring him to the agency after nursery and have him collected by one of his grandparents or wait there until she was finished, but that rarely happened these days and she tended not to let on to people that he even existed. It was safer that way. It was early days with Marek, and she saw no reason to deviate from her usual policy. Her bus arrived and she quickly jumped on. It had been an interesting night.

## TWENTY-FOUR

Grace walked briskly along the beach at Portobello, bending her body into the wind and rain. It was only just gone seven and still dark. Harvey trotted at her side, undeterred by the weather, his snout up tasting the air. Suddenly, he let out a growl deep in his throat and took off in a straight line to the water's edge, his head down.

Grace groaned. What old mouldy jellyfish was he going to present to her now? She chased after him, calling his name, but he ignored her.

As she drew closer, he started barking and tugging on something. A shiver went down her back. The moon slid from behind the clouds, and she gasped in horror as she saw the body half in, half out of the water. Her heart gave a massive thump and then resumed its normal rhythm.

'Harvey, come to heel!' she commanded, standing still and holding out a treat. Reluctantly, he released the body and trotted to her side. Hurriedly, she snapped on his lead and gave him the titbit. The body had clearly been in the water for some time and was floating face down. Her heart pounding in her chest, she forced herself to study it. Long chestnut hair mixed with seaweed. The build and height looked similar. From the back it could be Beth. With shaking fingers, she hurriedly called up Brodie's number. Thankfully, he picked up straight away.

'Brodie, there's a body on Portobello Beach, a female. It's been in the water some time. I need you to get someone down here. I haven't disturbed it. I think it might be Beth...' she said with a catch in her voice.

'I'll be down with a team as quick as I can, Grace. Hold tight.' Just as well she hadn't gone for a swim this morning. The thought of bumping into the trailing corpse gave her goosebumps. She retreated to the wall dividing the sand from the Esplanade and sat there with her legs dangling over the edge facing the sea, never taking her eyes from where she knew the body lay. The tide was still coming in, so it wasn't going anywhere for now. Harvey flopped down in a huff on the Esplanade side of the wall. He couldn't understand why his human wasn't in a rush to deliver his breakfast.

For the last three years she'd dreaded a body being washed up on the beach in case it was her son, Connor. It had never happened, but it had also been harder to move on without a body to lay to rest. Harder to accept that he had really gone.

By the time Brodie and his team arrived it was still mercifully quiet on the beach and light was sliding over the horizon. The wind and rain had abated slightly but Grace was still chilled to the bone and in desperate need of coffee.

Seeing his familiar figure stride over towards her she felt numb but relieved to know she wouldn't have to guard the body any longer. Harvey jumped to his feet, tail wagging like a metronome.

Brodie ruffled his fur then turned towards her. 'Grace, thanks for staying put. Sorry we couldn't get here any quicker, but I needed to bring a whole forensics team with me to recover the body.'

'No problem,' she replied with a faint smile. 'I couldn't risk anything happening to it. I'd like to think if it had been Connor someone would have done the same.'

She peeled her frozen legs off the wall, stumbling a little. Brodie reflexively grabbed her then let her go abruptly like she'd given him an electric shock.

'Relax, Brodie. I just tripped, for goodness' sake,' she snapped, annoyed with him for all sorts of reasons. She tugged on the lead and Harvey trotted beside her after a last sad look at Brodie. It was a shame for the dog. She wished Brodie had the gumption to stand up to Julie but hey-ho, she acknowledged bitterly, it was none of her business.

She let herself into the flat and fed Harvey before making breakfast for herself. She took it over to the large bay window and sat down at the table to watch what was going on. Now that it was almost fully light, a motley crew of avid onlookers were hanging over the wall, camera phones at the ready. It made her feel queasy. Turning away from the scene below, she got changed into her office garb and was putting folders in her briefcase when the buzzer rang.

'Grace? It's me,' Brodie announced. 'I think you're going to want to hear this.'

'Come on up,' she said and opened the front door, hearing his footsteps moving towards her. She poured him what was left of the coffee and sat down opposite.

'Thanks,' he said gratefully, taking a sip. 'That's the body on the way to the morgue. I don't actually think she's been in the water all that long, but we'll see what the pathologist says. From the look of her when they turned her over there's a distinct possibility it could be one of the missing girls.'

Grace got her phone out and showed him the two pictures of her client's sister.

'They're not dissimilar. Is it Beth? This is her in the photo. Or the other missing girl, Lorraine Kerr?'

Grace scrolled through until she came to the pictures she'd been sent by Olivia, Lorraine's friend.

'Honestly, it could be either or neither of them, said Brodie, looking at the images intently. 'The corpse is bloated, and the face took a beating on the rocks so it's hard to identify, but dental records and DNA tests will hopefully reveal the truth of the matter. Their age, build and hair colour are fairly similar from the photos.'

'If the body is Beth or Lorraine Kerr then that might mean that the clinic has killed before or might kill again,' said Grace, jumping to her feet and pacing up and down. 'Don't you see?'

'I'm not saying you're wrong, Grace, but it's too early to jump to conclusions.'

'How can you say that? It's obvious that the clinic is involved. You need to take action on this, Brodie. How many more young people need to die before the police wake up to what is going on here?'

'My hands are tied, Grace. The Super has made his position clear.'

'Then take it to someone else!' she said, not even trying to keep the disgust from her voice. 'The Super is an idiot, but even I didn't have him pegged as being corrupt.'

Brodie jumped to his feet, his expression furious. 'Will you just back off, Grace! Stop poking your nose into things that don't concern you. You're too much sometimes, you really are. These guys could bury us in costly litigation for years. We can't just go barging in mob-handed on a hunch.'

Grace stared at him in stunned silence. It wasn't like him to lose his rag like this. Usually, she was the one to get all fired up. After an awkward pause, Brodie sat back down.

'The clinic is near Whiteadder Reservoir. It's very deep. Wouldn't it be easier to dump the body there, if it's involved?'

'Yes and no,' said Grace. 'I think it would be far too risky for them. A reservoir has no outlet so if the body got disturbed or tangled in weeds it could come back to bite them. Plus, if it's discovered on their doorstep in such an isolated location it would lead the police right to their door. Plausible deniability would go right out the window.'

'True,' sighed Brodie. 'It's unlikely the body went in at Portobello. There's any number of locations down the east coast that are more likely to be the source of the body drop. I'm going to need to consult with an oceanographer on that.'

'They clearly intended for the body never to be found,' said Grace. 'This will put a real spanner in the works if the body traces back to the clinic. It could be the break we need... but at a terrible cost.'

# TWENTY-FIVE

Grace followed Brodie out as it was time to head into the office. Jean and Hannah were already assembled, looking downcast and talking quietly as they sipped their coffee. Entering with Harvey, she sat down in the front office and apprised them of what she had learnt so far.

'That poor girl,' said Jean with a shudder. 'When will we know for sure if it's Beth or Lorraine?'

'Hopefully, later today,' said Grace. Her stomach churned at the possibility of having to tell Eliza that her twin was dead. 'If it is either of them, then we must leave no stone unturned to expose what's happening at the clinic. Brodie seems to think they're so well connected that the police have been persuaded to look the other way. They've been running scared of what the big pharma legal team will do to them if they knock on the clinic door. These guys fight dirty.'

'But that's insane,' snapped Hannah, her eyes flashing with anger. 'What's the police for if it's not to protect ordinary people from being preyed upon? Didn't Brodie stand up to his bosses?'

'Not so far, but hopefully that will change,' said Grace.

'I thought he was better than that,' muttered Hannah.

'So did I,' said Grace with a sigh.

'Julie's dad thinks he owns Brodie body and soul now that they're together,' raged Hannah.

Grace and Jean looked at each other. They had rarely seen Hannah so riled up. Grace suspected she was feeling stung at what she perceived as Julie's rejection of her and Jack, not to mention Harvey.

'Anyway,' said Jean, diplomatically changing the subject. 'I haven't heard anything further from Dr Macdonald. I think we need to force the issue. If he realises the police might be closing in, he'll surely want to position himself as being on the side of the angels.'

'Agreed,' said Grace. 'We know where he lives. I think we need to pay him a visit. Time is no longer on our side. I'll come with you and if he doesn't play ball, we can threaten to involve the police.'

Hannah picked up her voluminous notebook and flicked through the pages.

'He lives at Lammermuir Cottage, out past Nunraw Abbey. He's married to a woman called Carina, who's American and a molecular biologist at the clinic. They have no children.'

'I don't like it that he has a wife associated with the clinic,' said Grace. 'She could be even more heavily involved than he is.'

'There may be people who are only involved in the rehab side,' said Jean. 'If we can locate some of them, they're likely to be horrified when they discover what the clinic is really getting up to.'

'We need to lean on Dr Macdonald to get us inside the clinic in some capacity. It's impregnable from the outside,' said Grace.

'Can't you pay someone to hack into their systems?' asked

Hannah. 'If we could only have a peek in their files that might tell us everything we need to know.'

'Anyone who might be capable of such a thing would charge way more than we could ever afford to pay,' mused Grace. 'Wait... there is one possibility. It's a long shot, but it might just be the answer to our prayers. Eliza's partner Ben is some sort of computer genius. With her blessing, maybe I could persuade him to help us? I overheard a ferocious row between them recently. It would give him a way to get back in her good books.' She stood, glancing at her watch. 'I'll head out now to try and track Ben down.'

'When do you want to confront Angus Macdonald?' asked Jean.

'I'll swing by and pick you up at six,' said Grace. 'Hopefully, he'll be home by then. We need to switch into top gear with this case now. I have a horrible feeling that the clinic is now tying up loose ends and preparing to ship out.'

# TWENTY-SIX

It took Grace the best part of an hour to battle through the Edinburgh traffic and park her car at Greenside due to extensive roadworks. She knew that her client had been mainly working from home, as had Ben, so thought she had a fairly good chance of catching them in, even though her client hadn't picked up when she tried to call. Her phone was probably on silent so she could work in peace. She'd wrestled with herself about whether to tell her client about the body washed up on the beach, but had decided against it for now. It might not be Beth. Better to say nothing until she knew for sure.

Ringing the doorbell, she was initially pleased when Ben answered the door. They must still be together, which boded well for her request. However, she quickly realised something was seriously amiss.

'Eliza's missing!' he said, his voice tinged with panic as he almost pulled her inside the door.

'Missing? How long for?' asked Grace, following him into the lounge where he continued to pace up and down, clearly distraught.

'Since yesterday morning. I woke up and she was gone. She

hasn't been into work, and I've contacted all her family and friends. No one's seen her.'

'You didn't have another row?' she asked, her tone neutral.

'No, I apologised after the last time. I realised I'd been in the wrong and it was all sorted out.'

'Have you called the police?'

'Not yet. It seemed so final,' he said, his voice catching in his throat. 'And after what happened with her sister, I thought they'd do a big fat zero anyway.'

'Have you any ideas where she might have gone?'

His expression stricken, he turned to her. 'It sounds crazy but… she was banging on about the clinic that last night, all hyped up. She'd some insane idea of turning up at their door pretending to be her sister. She said if they hadn't already killed her twin, they would have no reason not to take her inside. That way she could finally find out what they've been up to. She can't have actually gone there, though… right?'

Grace sucked in a breath and put her head in her hands. This was bad. This was very bad. She had one dead girl on her hands and now her client may have gone rogue and was in very real danger.

'Okay, Ben, listen to me now. You need to report Eliza missing to the police and tell them what you told me. I need to also tell you… a body of a young woman came in on the tide at Portobello this morning.'

Ben turned white.

'We don't have an identity yet, and it could be completely unconnected.'

'Was she murdered?'

'We don't know,' she said. 'The reason I came here today was actually to see you. I wanted to see if you would be able and willing to attempt to hack into the clinic's server to see if we can get an inkling of what they're actually up to in there. My guess is they're using the homeless population to conduct experiments on, under the guise of treating their addictions. The unusual degree of support afterwards could be all about monitoring them for side effects.'

'When I think about how I turned Beth away... how I didn't believe Eliza... I've been a complete jerk, haven't I?'

'This is your chance to make up for it,' she urged. 'Do you think you can do it?'

'It won't be easy, but I'll throw everything I've got at it.'

'Be careful – you'll need to cover your tracks as best as you can. These people are very dangerous. I've a feeling they're willing to kill anyone who gets in their way. My gut tells me they've learned what they can and they're getting ready to bury the evidence and pull the plug on the whole operation before running off back to the States.'

'What do I have to go on?' he asked.

'Here's the clinic website and a list of all the main players,' she said. 'I want everything you can dig up on them but the main focus is trying to breach their firewalls without alerting them to your presence so we can see exactly what kind of experiments they've been running, and the names and addresses of patients where possible.'

'The thought of them experimenting on Beth makes me feel sick to my stomach. I'm going to nail these guys to the wall. If it helps Eliza, then I'm all in,' he said, taking it from her.

She left him her phone number and the address of the agency, telling him to call her day or night and she'd pick up. They were up against the clock now, and with every second that passed the danger could only increase.

# TWENTY-SEVEN

Grace was heading back out from Edinburgh when Brodie called. Continuing to drive she accepted the call.

'Hey, Brodie, has the post-mortem been done?'

'That's the reason I'm calling. Can you swing by the office?'

'Yes,' she said, switching lanes. 'I'm in Edinburgh now. I'll be with you shortly.' Her stomach churned as she worried that he might be going to tell her that the dead body was Eliza or Beth. Grinding her teeth at the slowness of the city traffic she nonetheless managed to make good time and pulled into St Leonard's police station just twenty minutes later.

She was buzzed through as soon as she announced herself and met by Brodie at the top of the stairs.

'Thanks for coming,' he said, his expression deadly serious. He led the way along the corridor to his office and closed the door behind her. Grace sat in front of the desk and waited as he called up the photographs of the body they had recovered from the sea earlier that day.

'The pathologist got the shock of his life when he opened up the bag to start preparing the body for the post-mortem. He said he'd never come across this before. It turns out someone had got there before him.'

'What do you mean?' Grace asked.

Brodie turned the computer towards her. Grace gasped as she saw a close-up photo of a woman's abdomen, with an unmistakable post-mortem scar.

'She had this on her before he started?'

'Yes, when he opened her up, she was hollow inside. All her organs had been removed. Even her brain. Someone had already conducted a post-mortem.'

'It was the clinic,' said Grace in horror. 'I'm certain of it. They carved her up, took what they wanted then just chucked her away like she was garbage. It's monstrous. Have you been able to identify her?'

'It isn't Eliza, Beth, Lorraine, or anyone else you've brought to my attention so far,' he replied, and Grace let out a shaky breath. 'We're still searching through our missing persons database and cross referencing any mention of having been homeless. It's going to take a bit longer to find out who she was. I'm afraid we still don't have any grounds to get into the clinic. There's no apparent link.'

Grace wanted to tell him about her client's plan to infiltrate the clinic masquerading as her twin, but decided to keep it to herself for now. She didn't want to encourage the clinic into the further killing off of their scientific subjects until she'd managed to haul her out of there, hopefully still in one piece.

'Is there any way you could manage to keep this out of the press?' she pleaded. 'If the clinic get wind of it, they might panic. To the best of my knowledge there are still vulnerable people up there under their complete control.'

'Sorry, Grace. That ship's already sailed. The press know that the body of an unidentified woman washed up at Portobello. Nothing was leaked about the fact she was missing her internal organs though. That information is strictly need to know. We couldn't post a picture of her either. Her face... well, let's just say it wasn't pretty.'

'That gives us a little bit of time then,' she said.

'Grace? What aren't you telling me?' he said suddenly.

'Nothing!' she said. 'Is the official line still that the clinic is out of bounds for investigation?'

'I didn't exactly say that, Grace,' he said, looking exasperated.

She gave him a long hard look. There was a time once when she would have bet her life on his integrity. Right now, she wasn't so sure. Was Superintendent Blair grooming him to be his successor now Brodie had settled down with his daughter and a baby was on the way?

Brodie slid his eyes from hers and stood up.

'Thanks for coming by, Grace. I appreciate it. Keep me posted in case our cases do intersect.'

*What? So you can run off to your boss and give him a heads up?* She gave him a polite smile and left. This whole thing stank of a cover-up. But how had the clinic nobbled the police? Was it money or blackmail? She hoped to God that Brodie wasn't involved, but if he was agreeing to look the other way then he really wasn't any better than the others.

She was about to press the button to go through to reception when she realised that she'd left her phone on the desk. Wearily, she trudged back up the stairs but as she mounted the last few steps, she became aware of raised voices coming from the direction of the Super's room. She slipped into Brodie's room, grabbed her phone then, hugging the wall, she crept closer to listen.

'You've got no business allowing that woman to run amok in the police station!' Blair shouted. 'I wouldn't trust her to take out the trash.'

Right back atcha, thought Grace, insulted. She was surprised to hear Brodie shouting back at him.

'That's ridiculous. You're talking about a decorated police officer who brought more than her fair share of glory to this department whilst under your command.'

'Until she flaked out and had a breakdown,' Blair spat. 'Fat lot of good she was to us then. She could hardly find her way to her own car, never mind track down criminals.'

'She was ill, not incompetent,' Brodie said, his voice like gravel. 'We'd just lost our child.'

'Yes, well, er—' spluttered Blair, at last joining the dots and realising he had been indiscreet. He changed tack. 'How do you think Julie will feel when I tell her that you're still having cosy chats in your office with her? She can't stand Grace. Can't say as I blame her,' he muttered.

'I thought they got on all right,' Brodie said, perplexed. 'Julie's never said anything to me.'

Grace had an insane urge to laugh. At least Brodie had stood up for her. That meant a lot. She turned to leave again, but Brodie's next words had her creeping even closer.

'You've told me to back off the clinic at Whiteadder. I want to know why,' he said, his voice strong and determined. 'The body we recovered from the sea had already had a post-mortem performed on her – that points to something medical. I mean, she was completely empty inside. Are you not alarmed by that? About what we might be dealing with here?'

'Of course, I'm alarmed,' Blair blustered. 'But what on earth makes you think the clinic was involved? Has that woman been dropping poison in your ear?'

'If this all implodes and it transpires the police were busy looking the other way, how do you think it's going to look?' demanded Brodie.

The Super was nothing if not motivated by self-interest, thought Grace, holding her breath.

'Look, my hands are tied,' he exploded. 'For now, that is.'

'What does that mean?' asked Brodie.

The Super walked over and closed the door. Grace flattened herself against the wall. She was unable to distinguish anything further from the low rumble of voices and crept back down the stairs. As she left the police station and took a deep lungful of the crisp winter air, she pondered on what she had heard, glad that Brodie was questioning his boss on the apparent moratorium in relation to the clinic. Whether she got to hear about it from him, time would tell.

# TWENTY-EIGHT

Grace and Jean had been sitting in her car for a couple of hours already. It was nearly eight pm.

'I do hope that our client's alright,' worried Jean. 'Do you think the clinic fell for it?'

'I suspect so, or she'd have been back home by now. Ben promised to message me the minute he heard anything from her.'

'If our meeting with Angus Macdonald goes well, he might be able to tell us what's happened to her,' said Jean.

'We have to tread with caution,' said Grace. 'Everything he says must be treated with extreme scepticism until proven to the contrary. Also, his wife is still an unknown quantity.'

'Do you think Ben is going to be able to hack into the clinic's records?'

'I hope so, but I don't have high hopes... I imagine they'll have top-notch security features.' Grace had decided to keep the details about her meeting with Brodie to herself meantime. Things were awkward enough.

'Another sandwich?' asked Jean, pouring them each some coffee from a large flask. She'd really gone to town for her first ever stake-out. Grace accepted gratefully, keeping her eyes trained on the entrance to the remote sandstone house across the single-track road. They'd managed to find concealment up a wooded farm track that hid them from sight, but still enabled them to watch the comings and goings of the house opposite. Despite the chill of the night, Grace wound the windows down after checking that Jean had no objection. It was pitch black and the stars glittered all over the sky. Bats flitted through the trees, moving so quickly it was hard for the human eye to track them. Up here in the Lammermuir hills and away from the light pollution of the city, it felt as if they were at one with the vastness above them. Suddenly an owl hooted loudly, startling Grace from her reverie.

'That nearly gave me a heart attack!' exclaimed Jean, clutching her chest.

Grace shushed her, pointing to car lights shining through the trees. Was this him?

After a few seconds they had their answer as the car slowed. It turned into the driveway. Grace and Jean hurriedly exited the car and ran forward, keeping their bodies low so they were out of sight to the occupant of the car. Only one person got out and he was clearly male. Grace walked forward, clearing her throat gently.

Dr Macdonald swung round, his eyes wide with fear. The fear only dissipated a notch when he recognized Jean. 'How did you find me? And who's she?' he asked, nodding towards Grace.

'We'll tell you everything in a moment,' said Grace, trying to sound firm but unthreatening. 'Is your wife home?'

'Leave her out of it,' he snapped. 'She's working late tonight.'

'In that case, may we come in?' asked Jean. 'It's freezing out here and we're much more visible to anyone driving by.'

He looked torn as though he couldn't decide what to do for

the best before muttering, 'Fine', and turning his back on them to open the door.

Inside, no expense had been spared. The interior was painted in period style and the house was filled with expensive looking antiques with a few eclectic modern pieces seamlessly blended in. Even the rugs on the sanded wooden floors looked expensive. This apparent luxury suggested that the doctor and his wife might sit near the top of the clinic medical staff.

'You'd better sit,' he said, gesturing to the sumptuous sofa and positioning himself on an upright occasional chair to one side of them.

Grace nodded at Jean to kick things off.

'I lied to you,' Jean said to him straight off. 'I'm not Beth's mother.'

'Then who the hell are you?' he asked, springing to his feet and looking wildly about him, his face twitching with stress. 'Reporters?'

'We're private investigators,' she replied, 'instructed by the family.' She passed up one of her business cards to him. He studied it, his hand shaking, before sitting back down abruptly, like his legs wouldn't hold him up.

'How much do you already know?' he whispered, sweat beading his forehead.

'We know enough,' said Grace. 'Are you aware that there was a body found at Portobello Beach today? Likely one of your patients, as a post-mortem had been performed on her already. Can you tell us who she was? Her family have a right to know what happened to her.'

Dr Macdonald put his head in his hands and groaned. 'I honestly don't know, though I'm sure I could find out with a bit of digging. People have died at the clinic before, but usually due to some pre-existing damage to their organs that we were unable to heal. I swear to you, I'd no idea what they were up to when I started there. I'd pioneered an incredibly effective approach to addiction. It was the culmination of my life's work. We were taking people off the streets, the most desperate people, bereft of all human dignity, and pressing the reset button to give them their lives back.'

'Were you aware that the clinic was monitoring participants by spying on them with hidden cameras?' asked Grace, trying to keep the note of censure from her voice. She wanted him onside.

'Yes,' he admitted. 'But only so we could monitor their progress and catch them before they fell.'

'But perhaps that's not the real reason they were doing it?' said Grace. 'Perhaps they were monitoring them from side effects for the experimental drugs they were pumping them full of.'

'I've not known about that for long. I was horrified when I found out the real purpose of the clinic.'

'And yet you did nothing?' Grace said.

'I made contact with you,' he said, nodding over at Jean.

'But after we met in Wetherspoons there's been nothing but a wall of silence,' said Jean.

'That makes you complicit, as far as we're concerned,' said Grace.

'You don't understand!' he exclaimed. 'I wanted to help Beth's mother, I really did, but then I found out something that... complicated things.'

'Go on,' said Grace, determined not to let him off the hook until he'd agreed to help them.

'My wife is involved,' he whispered, as though she could hear him. 'She's a top-notch research scientist. I overheard a conversation between her and Dr Walker at the clinic. They didn't know I was there.' He swallowed hard. 'They were talking about a patient who'd died after being released from the clinic. Something to do with the degradation of cell tissue. My wife was arguing with him that the drugs protocol should be scrapped. She said there have been too many deaths. The experiment should be considered a failure as the collateral tissue damage was too high. How can I turn my own wife in?' he asked, his face anguished.

'They're experimenting on people without their consent. We're not talking about a new moisturiser here. We're talking about a complete bodily disintegration. How many people have already died at the clinic? Tell us!'

'I can't. I honestly don't know,' he protested. 'Can you even say with certainty that the body that was found is one of ours? It might not be anything to do with us even if there is an association with the clinic.'

'And if there is?' said Grace, her voice hard. 'Then you and your wife are complicit in murder.'

'My wife and I have killed no one!' he shouted.

'Maybe not, but you are clearly complicit in covering up the crimes,' said Grace. 'That will hardly be looked on favourably by a jury if it goes to trial.'

He slumped back in his seat like a burst balloon. 'What exactly do you want from me?'

'You need to get me and another member of my team into the clinic. Hannah is nineteen. Neither of us has any medical training, so we'd need to blend in to the support side. I can't use Jean as they'd recognise her from her previous visit. I need a detailed map of the whole facility from you, with appropriate passcodes to move between different areas, and a set of scrubs for each of us, complete with stethoscopes.'

'You're not planning on treating any patients whilst there, are you?' he asked in alarm.

'Hardly,' said Grace. 'But we need to get around to see what's actually going on. Your bosses are bringing pressure to bear on the police. They seem inexplicably reluctant to get involved. I plan to bring them evidence that they can't sweep under the carpet.'

'It might also be useful to have the shift change rotas,' said Jean.

'I have access to those,' he said, making a further note on his phone. 'You know, when I came to work here, I thought I was doing a good thing. We were transforming people's lives for the better. The addiction profile I developed has an incredibly high success rate in a very hard-to-treat population. They told me they were planning to open more clinics depending on the success of this one. It could've been rolled out nationally. We could've been the envy of the world.' His eyes shone as he contemplated his golden future, then clouded as he fell back down to earth with a thump.

'We need a list of all the patients you treated on the addiction side, together with their addresses on release. We need to check on how many are still well.'

'Not everybody would've been given the experimental drug protocol, if that's what's happening,' he said. 'It's just not how experiments are done: there must have been criteria of selection as well as a control group who didn't receive it. And I really do know nothing about any extra medication they were given.'

'So, you really didn't have anything to do with the development of the lilac pills?' asked Grace.

'No,' he said, looking bewildered.

'Could it be that the experimental pills were issued once rehabilitation was complete?' asked Grace. 'Perhaps the whole rehab plan was really to optimise the health of test subjects so that they were fit and healthy enough not to give skewed results? They wanted an anonymous population to experiment on who no one would miss and whose possible deaths would be unquestioned. Really, if you think about it, without you and your rehab team this whole experiment could not have taken place.'

Angus looked horrified. 'My wife was hired first... not long after we were married. She worked with Magnum Pharmaceuticals initially, then they invited me to apply and for us both to relocate over to Scotland. She can't have been aware of what their intentions were... could she?'

Grace felt some sympathy for him. He'd been naïve and too trusting, but now was stuck between a rock and a hard place. 'Or, she may have known all along. I know this is hard, but remember the first tenet of practising medicine: do no harm.'

'My wife believes passionately in the power of medicine. If she's truly involved in this up to the hilt, she'll be doing it for what she considers to be the greater good. Although she's a doctor, she's never treated patients. She was always drawn to pure research. She must believe these experiments have the potential to assist humanity in some major way.'

'You don't really believe that though, do you?' asked Grace, her tone scathing. 'That the needs of the many always outweigh the needs of the few?'

'No. As a doctor, how could I? But you're asking me to betray my own wife. From what I overheard, she wanted the clinic to stop what it's doing. Maybe she could help you as well?'

Grace shook her head. 'She's clearly been heavily involved in the experimental side. I'm in no position to say or do anything that might compromise the judicial investigation that'll be coming. Plus, she might warn Dr Walker. What if some of these trial subjects are still alive? Telling your wife could be signing their death warrants.'

'She wouldn't...' he began, tailing off into silence.

'You don't know that,' Grace admonished. 'Maybe you don't know her at all.'

# TWENTY-NINE

Hannah was shattered. It had been a long day at the agency. Jack had been at his grumpiest after managing to flush his current favourite toy down the toilet so it could have a big adventure, then discovering it couldn't come back. She'd longed to settle down on the couch in front of the fire and watch something mindless with a cup of hot chocolate, but instead she'd forced herself out into the freezing cold night once her mum returned to watch Jack and her younger siblings. It wasn't just about the case. She'd made a commitment and intended to honour it. As she stood, stamping her feet to keep warm at the bus stop, she also felt a warm glow inside at the thought of seeing Marek again. She wondered if he would suggest a drink after work again? Just in case, she'd slapped on some makeup and left her hair down to try and avoid the whole ID debacle that happened last time. Her bus arrived and she jumped on. The bus was fairly packed, and the windows were fogged up. It didn't take long to arrive at her destination.

Walking into the community hall, she threw off her coat and got stuck in serving soup and sandwiches. Already she was starting to recognise some of the regulars, and she enjoyed a bit of banter with them. It did her heart good to see them huddled by a heater getting a bit of warmth and food in their bellies to ward off the chill. She berated herself for her reluctance to come out tonight. As there was a momentary lull, she glanced at those sprinkled around the hall, some conversing with others, most choosing to isolate themselves in their own solitary bubble.

'Hey, kid,' said Marek at her shoulder, dodging back as she swiped him with her dish towel.

'Enough of that,' she scolded. 'At least I'm not on the fast track to middle age, like some.'

His face fell comically.

'See? You can dish it out, but you can't take it,' she teased.

Marek held his hands up in surrender. 'Truce! I come in peace. Once the last of the stragglers are away, I'm heading out with flasks of soup and leftover sandwiches. Are you coming? Thought we could grab a drink afterwards like before, if you're up for it?'

'Sure,' said Hannah. 'It's going to be a cold one tonight. Do we have any extra blankets?'

'One or two. Not enough to go round, unfortunately,' he said, sounding worried.

'I've a few warm hats,' said Hannah. 'A lot of body heat is lost from the head. My colleague Jean has been busy knitting.' She grinned.

'And do you knit?'

'Hahaha, you're funny,' snorted Hannah. She finished the last bit of clearing away.

Hurriedly she locked up and left to join Marek in the car.

Their progress across those areas in the city where the homeless gathered was slow. The cold pierced them like daggers. Most had gone to sleep huddled for warmth as best they could. There were several heart-stopping moments where Hannah thought that a rough sleeper might be dead, but they didn't have to call an ambulance and most stirred to partake of hot food and drinks. Some were already wearing hats or had hoods pulled over their heads but those who hadn't eagerly took the warm hats Jean had knitted. With a renewed sense of urgency, Hannah asked everyone they encountered if they had seen Beth. Although he didn't try to stop her, Marek looked increasingly disapproving as she questioned them. She also asked if they could remember young people being taken from the streets. Everyone shook their heads and turned away, unwilling to engage with her. A few of them even looked fearful, like they thought she was there to hurt them or something.

'I don't get it,' sighed Hannah, as they walked to the pub after doing welfare checks and handing out the last of their supplies. 'This is a crime against their community. Why are they closing ranks?'

'Because they're scared. Because they don't know or trust you yet? So many people have let them down in the past. It's hardly surprising. I can't say that I'm all that comfortable with it either, Hannah. From now on if you want to play detective you can leave me out of it. You're starting to undermine the good work that we're doing here.'

Hannah squirmed. She hated to say it, but she could see his point. Why did life have to be so complicated?

'That office job,' he continued, his teeth clenched in anger. 'Where do you work exactly? The police?'

'No!' said Hannah. She weighed up her options and decided to come clean. What choice did she have? One way or another, he was on to her. She wouldn't say anything about the clinic at least.

'I do have an office job... but it's in a private detective agency.'

'Okay... so, what's with all the questions then?' he asked. 'I need to know you're not putting the people we're trying to help at risk.'

'We're trying to trace a young woman who went missing,'

she said. 'She used to be part of the homeless population in Edinburgh, an addict. I was just trying to find out if any of them had seen her recently, that's all.' She felt guilty for not saying more, but she could hardly share the whole truth.

'Might have known you'd have an ulterior motive for traipsing about here in the cold. I take it that's why you pretended to give a damn, so I would give you access to them all?' he said, his voice bitter.

'No!' she exclaimed. 'That's not it at all. I thought we were friends?'

'Friends don't lie to each other,' he said dismissively. 'I'll drop you at home.'

'No, it's fine,' she muttered. 'I'll get the bus.'

'I get it, you don't even trust me with your address, that's what great friends we are,' he scoffed.

Hannah's eyes filled with tears, but she turned away so he wouldn't see. This whole evening had been a bust. No wonder Marek was sore at her, but what else could she have done? It was her own stupid fault for allowing herself to get attached to him.

'I'm sorry you feel that way,' she said. Hunching her shoulders against the bitter cold she left him standing there and walked away. When was she going to learn that sooner or later everyone let her down? It was best not to get involved.

# THIRTY

Grace plunged into the icy waters at Portobello Beach with a convulsive shiver. Although it was still pitch black, she could see a slight lightening at the horizon. It never bothered her swimming in the dark; in fact, she welcomed it. It had a way of getting her puny earth-borne worries into perspective, swimming beneath such a dazzling display. The pinprick points of lights she was seeing had taken millions of years to reach her, their stars perhaps no longer in existence, their light a last signal from a dying civilisation.

After a protracted discussion with Angus, which had seen them being rushed out of the back door when he heard his wife's car pull into the driveway, he'd agreed to help them, his repugnance over what might be happening at the clinic winning out over his fear and loyalty to the company. He'd also said he would sound out his wife to see if he could bring her round to his way of thinking without alerting her suspicion. He was clearly terrified that she was involved up to the hilt and what that would mean for their marriage. She didn't envy him.

Her shoulders tiring, she lay on her back for a few moments. The sea was calm this morning and she felt at peace as she floated on the incoming tide, ready now to face the challenges ahead. Flipping back over, she struck out strongly for the shore where Harvey lay waiting patiently. A single woof acknowledged he'd noticed she was on her way back and was impatient now for his breakfast.

Grace sat having coffee with her team, Harvey sitting to attention as if he considered himself to be part of the briefing, too. 'So, we're clear on the plan then,' she stated. 'Hannah's going to be presented by Dr Angus Macdonald as another candidate for rehabilitation. He's going to say he was at the university medical library in Edinburgh when he saw her puking her guts up on the street. He stopped to help and discovered she was homeless, dirty and hungry with no family or friends. He decided on the spur of the moment to extend this lifeline to her. It might even reassure those at the clinic that he's got no idea what they're really up to. They can hardly turn her away without tipping their hand to him. Are you sure you're up for this, Hannah? There's absolutely no shame in saying you've changed your mind, you know.'

'I wish you would,' said Jean, clearly worried about the risk Hannah was taking and frustrated she wouldn't be in the clinic herself to keep an eye on her.

'It's fine,' said Hannah, with a grin, eyes shining in excitement. 'I suggested doing this way back, didn't I?'

'Your main task is to try and locate our client and then we can pull both of you out of there. Any other information you come across is a bonus.'

'If they believe that Eliza is really Beth, how do you think they'll have reacted when they find she's healthy if they were monitoring her before?' asked Jean.

'I'm hoping they'll get really excited thinking that she's recovered therefore potentially their treatment has worked,' said

Grace. 'At any rate, as long as her real identity hasn't been discovered she should be safe enough. Eliza's a smart cookie.'

'I still can't believe you're going to be in the catering team,' said Jean with an unmistakeable snigger.

'I can cook,' said Grace, indignantly.

Jean and Hannah looked at each other with eyebrows raised.

'Of course, you can,' said Hannah. 'I don't have to eat there, do I?'

'Very funny,' said Grace, smiling. 'Angus managed to nobble one of the kitchen staff and has sent her off for a couple of weeks with a healthy increase to her bank account. She nominated me as her replacement whilst supposedly off sick.'

'I take it Ben still hasn't been in touch?' asked Jean. 'It would be better if we had more information about what's going on in there before you go.'

'He phoned me last night. He's taken leave from his job to work on this full time. Their computer defence systems are extremely robust and have defeated all his efforts so far. He's quite beside himself with worry, but knows to phone Jean the minute he has a breakthrough.'

'He must really love her,' said Hannah wistfully.

Grace and Hannah exchanged covert looks. Hannah had apparently had a bit of a tiff with Marek. She hadn't said much about it, but had looked a bit down in unguarded moments. Grace was momentarily thankful she was happily single. She glanced at her watch – it was time.

'You're not going to love this, Hannah, but needs must,' she said, removing a bottle of strong cider from her bag. She also produced some filthy jeans, underwear and a threadbare jumper from a sealed plastic bag and a pair of smelly scuffed trainers.

Hannah and Jean screwed up their noses. Harvey sniffed ecstatically.

'That is rank!' Hannah exclaimed. 'How did you get my clothes so smelly?'

'Harvey may have helped,' smiled Grace. He pricked up his ears on hearing his name and gave the clothes another delighted sniff.

'Are you sure it's okay to still use your first names?' asked Jean.

'Yes, it's easier that way. We've taken different surnames, but our first names are fairly common,' replied Grace.

'Who are you calling common?' asked the irrepressible Hannah with mock outrage as she went off to change. She walked back in after a few minutes looking wretched, her hair greasy and hanging limply around her face. Even her body language had changed. Grace remembered that Hannah had excelled in drama at school, and she was clearly already inhabiting the part she'd have to play. Grace handed her the bottle of cider. 'Take a couple of slugs just to get your breath smelling,' she said. 'Your clothes should help as they've been dabbed with cider, too.'

Hannah did as she was told, grimacing as the liquid burned its way down her throat. 'This would be a lot more fun if I was out clubbing,' she complained, pulling a face.

'You've agreed a back story with Angus,' Grace said. 'He'll fake your blood work where necessary and make sure you don't get given any experimental substances. Any problems that you feel you can't handle, get yourself out of there. If all goes according to plan, you should be able to contact me every meal-time. Once you're inside, Angus will pass you a burner phone, which I've given him with my own number already programmed in for another burner. Jean's new burner number is in there, too.'

'Don't worry, I can handle it,' said Hannah, sticking her chin in the air.

'What did you tell your mum?' asked Jean.

'I told her I was on a course in London to gain a qualification needed for my work. She grumbled a bit, but I told her Brodie and Jean can help out with Jack if needed. It's only for two weeks max, hopefully a lot less,' said Hannah, sounding determined. 'Our client needs us.'

Grace had felt bad about having Hannah lie to her mum and Brodie about what she was up to, but given the attitude of the police towards the clinic she thought it best not to share their plan until she was sure they could be fully on board with things.

'Come on then,' said Grace. 'I'll drop you off at the university library, so Angus can pick you up from there. I wouldn't put it past his bosses to have a tracker on his car. That way his story about where he encountered you will check out.'

Half an hour later, Grace pulled into Buchanan Street. Angus's car was already parked further down the road on the opposite side. The tinted windows meant she couldn't see who was inside it. She turned to Hannah who was in the passenger seat and chalk white.

'You're sure you want to do this, Hannah?' she said, scrutinising her carefully. 'It's not too late to back out, you know. We can find another way.'

Hannah looked back at her, fire in her eyes. 'I'm ready,' she said. 'Those bastards aren't going to get away with this.'

She opened the door and walked across to the car. The driver's window slid down. Angus raised his hand in acknowledgement then spoke to Hannah. She got into the back seat, and they drove off. Grace watched the car until it was out of sight, her insides squeezed with dread. If anything happened to Hannah, she would never forgive herself. Feeling sick to the stomach she turned the key in the ignition and pulled out. Her small team were going to give it everything, but they were up against the might of a massive pharmaceutical company and right now she didn't fancy their chances.

# THIRTY-ONE

Grace presented herself at the clinic at ten o'clock for her interview. She'd invented a fictitious CV and her stepfather, Brian, who was on the committee at a golf club, had agreed to be her referee after a lot of arm twisting. The trouble was her family had no faith in her cooking skills. Mind you, they were probably right. She was someone who ate to live rather than lived to eat. The catering manager, Angela Broadfoot, a tall angular woman, read her resume and sighed.

'Normally, I would be looking for someone more experienced but since you've been referred to me by Paula Black to cover while she's poorly and we're in quite a bind, I suppose you can start right away, if that suits?'

Grace nodded eagerly. 'Thank you, I won't let you down,' she said, though she cringed inwardly as she knew that she probably would.

'Lunch is served at twelve. The woman that you're replacing was one of the servers and also did food prep in the kitchen when required.'

'No problem,' replied Grace, hoping no one developed food poisoning. 'How many people do we cater for?'

'There used to be loads, but these days we only have around twenty rehab patients and thirty staff.'

'How come?' asked Grace, her heart sinking.

Angela shrugged. 'Good at what they do, I suppose? The patients stay with us a long time, but their success rate is second to none, so I believe.'

'Is this the only canteen for staff and patients or do we need to deliver food to patients' bedsides as well?' asked Grace.

'Mealtimes are staggered so that the medical staff get to relax without being bothered by patients and vice versa,' Angela replied. 'However, we do take food through into the restricted area for any research staff who can't leave their experiments or for any patients who are proper poorly and confined to their beds for whatever reason. The head nurse, Frankie Garcia, informs us each morning what's going to be required.'

'Got it,' said Grace with a bright smile, not wanting to be seen to ask too many questions about the rotas for fear of arousing suspicion. 'Are the patients allowed to eat and drink what they like?'

'Of course, it's a rehab facility, not a prison,' Angela replied with a frown. 'We don't serve any old rubbish here. The food is healthy, and the menu plans are devised by our resident nutritionist.' She glanced at her watch. 'We need to get busy, the first sitting will be down in forty minutes.'

Grace felt suitably anonymous swathed in her tunic and trousers with a large wraparound white apron. Her hair was swept underneath her disposable plastic cap. She sniffed the air appreciatively. No boiled cabbage here. As the kitchen staff brought through the metal trays and she helped put it out for serving, she could feel her mouth water at the sight and smell of pork tenderloin and apple sauce with mash and an array of steamed vegetables, grilled chicken breast stuffed with cheese, and salmon fillet with a honey glaze. Not a burger in sight, and certainly no chips unless they were so healthy as to be unrecognisable.

The door to the canteen slid open and a few doctors and nurses walked in. Grace noticed Angus amongst them, alongside a beautiful woman with a glacial expression. This must be Carina, his wife. He whispered something to her, but she shut him down, hissing angrily in his ear. Angus looked alarmed and shot Grace a sideways look. She ignored it, hoping he wasn't going to blow her cover. She'd only been in the door five minutes. Had he already ratted her out to his wife? She forced her eyes away from them and focused on serving the queue building up in front of her. The medics seemed glum and distracted, barely acknowledging her. It felt a bit like the police canteen after a major incident. Had something happened? She hoped that her client was still alive and well, but had no way of knowing. Angus's wife was sticking to his side like Velcro and the contemptuous look she gave Grace was enough to scorch her out of her shoes.

'You're new here,' said a cultured American voice, as she bent to put the empty tray under the counter and replace it with a full one.

Startled, she jumped up, bumping her head hard enough to make her eyes water. It was Dr Walker. He was tall and angular with fierce grey eyes and thin lips.

'Hello, yes.' She smiled. 'My name's Grace. I've been drafted in as a replacement for Paula whilst she's sick.'

'I see,' he said, his eyes coldly assessing her. She kept her body language open and friendly.

'What can I interest you in for lunch today?' she asked.

His eyes suddenly glazed over as though he'd decided she wasn't worth bothering with.

'I'll have the pork,' he said, taking it from her without so much as a thank you.

A nurse who she recognised from Jean's photo as being

Frankie Garcia appeared at his side. She pulled him away and started to speak, sounding agitated. All that Grace heard were the words, 'It's happening again.'

Walker held up his hand to silence her.

'Not here,' he commanded and, dumping his full plate on the serving hatch, he took off with Garcia at speed. Some people in the queue looked nervous and nudged each other, but others continued their chat oblivious. Grace noticed that Angus's wife had peeled away from his side without a word and followed the other two out of the door. Grace felt her heart beating faster and carried on serving as before. Something was wrong and she fervently hoped it had nothing to do with her client or Hannah.

# THIRTY-TWO

Hannah was a bag of nerves. Angus had assured her that he would be the one managing her medically during her stay at the clinic. He'd personally hooked her up to a saline drip when she was admitted and Heather Kelly, a friendly, bubbly young nurse, had run her a bath afterwards in her private ensuite, washed her hair and given her a clean nightgown to wear.

Hannah had taken to Heather and felt that she could maybe appeal to her in an emergency. There was no way she could be involved in harming patients. She radiated kindness. Hannah's bloods had been taken, but Angus had said he would switch them for those of another patient with alcoholism to avoid suspicion. Even so, she felt her position to be precarious and hoped that she could leave soon. She also found she was missing Jack already. The weird thing about being a mother, she had come to realise, was you always fantasised about having a break from your kid then when you got it you did nothing but miss their warm little bodies. That had been twenty-four hours ago, and she was now feeling trapped and a bit stir-crazy.

Heather bustled across to her. 'How are you feeling?'

'Like I want a drink,' snapped Hannah, determined to stay in character.

Heather laughed as though she'd just said the funniest thing. 'Tea, coffee or juice?' she asked.

'Hot chocolate?' asked Hannah.

'Coming right up.' Heather bustled off at top speed and Hannah swung her legs out of bed and went off to explore, IV stand in tow like an unwanted dance partner. The room was luxurious, more like a hotel than a hospital. There was a comfortably upholstered chair beside a round table with a vase of fresh flowers. A well-stocked bookcase was full of the latest in books and magazines. No TV though. She picked up a menu of beauty treatments and massages. Another beside it included painting and pottery classes, along with a host of other opportunities. There was also a leisure centre with a pool and an exercise studio. Hannah had to admit, they weren't exactly torturing people here. Was it possible they'd got it all wrong? She walked over to the door and tried the handle. It was locked. So much for that. Annoyed, she went back to her bed, just before Heather returned with a tray of hot chocolate and a warm blueberry muffin.

'Are you my gaoler as well as my nurse?' Hannah asked, her voice tragic.

'No! Of course not,' Heather replied, looking horrified. 'The door is only locked for the first forty-eight hours to make sure that you're medically stable and over the worst of the withdrawal symptoms. It's for your own safety, I promise. You'll be able to join the other residents tomorrow.'

'S'pose,' sulked Hannah. In the car on the way in, Angus had briefed her on how to act as though she was detoxing. He'd given her a salt-water spray, a battery hand warmer and shown her some footage of real patients. She'd shuddered. It looked terrifying. She'd accessed them yesterday whenever the nurse was expected. Her obs were taken at regular intervals so it was fairly easy to predict when the nurse was close to entering her room. Her props made it look as though she had a slight temperature and was sweating. She'd also trembled as much as she could – hard to do when you were faking it – and had a few convincing delusions involving locusts crawling over her. The terror with which she had reacted was not entirely fake.

Heather took her temperature, looking a little surprised and Hannah was cross with herself for trying to get out of the room instead of using the stuff Angus had given her before Nurse Kelly returned. She couldn't afford to let her guard down.

'Your obs are much better today,' she said. 'You're doing very well for someone this early in detox.'

'I'm still craving a drink,' whispered Hannah, putting every ounce of longing she could imagine into her voice. 'Maybe just a little one to steady me? That won't hurt, will it?'

Heather's kind round face crumpled into worried lines. 'I'm so sorry, but we have to get you on the other side of this and I'm afraid total abstinence is the only way here. Just hold on to the fact that you're going to feel so much better soon,' she encouraged, patting her arm.

Hannah turned away from her and faced the wall, feeling guilty. You've nothing to feel guilty about, she told herself fiercely, but she would bet that Heather was one of the good guys.

Heather left again then returned a few minutes later with some liquid medicine in a cup. 'Just a little sedative to help you feel more comfortable,' she said.

Hannah hadn't counted on that and had clearly overplayed her hand. With the nurse's full eyes on her she had no option but to take it. To her intense frustration it started to take effect more or less right away and with a disgruntled sigh her head sank down into the pillow.

## THIRTY-THREE

After the medics finished lunch there had been a sitting for those patients undergoing rehab. There were around twenty of them. They'd been a relaxed, healthy-looking bunch with good appetites and wearing an assortment of fitness gear and casual clothes.

Once they'd eaten and were starting to leave, Grace turned to Angela Broadfoot. 'What about the people who are just beginning treatment? Do we deliver their meals to them on a trolley? I take it they can't come here?'

'No, some of them are too ill to eat if they've been chucking up too much. The doctors sort them out until they're stronger. Those that can eat but aren't up to getting to the canteen have their meals delivered to them. In fact, that's where I'm going right now,' she said, plating up meals and putting metal containers over them to preserve the heat.

'Would it be possible for me to shadow you?' asked Grace. 'I don't know how long I'll be here but you're going to need a day off sometime so it's probably best if you show me the ropes in case I have to do it myself.'

Angela deliberated, her lips compressed. Grace waited with

bated breath, continuing to wipe the counter surfaces with a cloth. Finally, she spoke.

'They don't usually like temporary staff to go into the clinic proper, but I guess on this occasion it makes sense. Stay by my side and don't speak to the patients beyond the barest essentials,' she cautioned. 'Are we clear?'

'Crystal,' said Grace. Angela passed her the list of who required what then disappeared into the kitchen to bring out some more trays. Grace hurriedly took a photo on her tiny burner phone. She was relieved to see that Beth and Hannah were both on the list. Hopefully her client would have the sense not to give the game away when she saw her with the trolley. She was desperate to see Hannah with her own eyes after she'd spent her first night as a patient. A few minutes later they set off, the lunch crowd having abated to the extent that the remaining server, a taciturn woman in her forties, could deal with it.

Grace's heart sank as they moved through the clinic as it seemed that different areas were segregated from each other. It reminded her of the sensation of moving through a prison even though the facilities were luxurious and there was artwork on the walls. How could the inmates bear to be cooped up in here away from the real world for so long? Mind you, given the state they would have been in before, living rough and in the throes of the most desperate addiction, she could understand why they liked living in such a warm, supportive cocoon. Their first port of call was the ward that Hannah was on.

'Keep your wits about you in here,' warned Angela. 'This is for those recently admitted. They'll be in withdrawal, possibly even hallucinating, so approach with caution. Plastic cutlery only. They're prone to self-harm. You'd think some of them had been dragged here by force the way they go on rather than being admitted to one of the best rehab facilities in the world. Take no notice of what they say. In a few weeks they'll be as happy as clams.'

There were six patients on this ward. Hannah was in the end room. All of them were young, which Grace thought was suspicious in itself. A legitimate rehab facility would have a varied age range. Obviously, they wanted a population they could return to optimum health before irreversible damage had been done to their internal organs. The faux healing vibe made Grace feel sick to her stomach. The first room they approached was locked and contained an angry young man pacing up and down. He was shouting at someone or something that wasn't there. When Angela entered to deliver his food tray, he dashed it from her hands and she ran back out again, muttering swear words under her breath. She turned to face Grace, her hands shaking.

'Sorry, I should be used to it by now. In another forty-eight hours he'll have calmed down and his door can be opened so he can access the recreation facilities. This is the worst ward for disturbed behaviour. It's not their fault, but it's hard not to take it personally sometimes. The demon drink, eh? It certainly puts you off when you see what it can do.' She reached for her radio and informed housekeeping of what had transpired.

The next two rooms contained young women who were quiet and listless and pulled their trays towards them with no real interest. Their heavily lidded eyes gave away that they were still heavily medicated. Grace felt worry cramp her insides at the thought of how Hannah would be faring. Angus had promised that apart from saline she would be kept drug free, but what if something went wrong? Finally, Angela unlocked Hannah's room. Grace hadn't realised Hannah would be locked in her room. She should never have agreed to this.

'Well, you're looking brighter today.' Angela smiled. 'Can I interest you in some Balmoral chicken with boiled potatoes and carrots?'

Hannah pulled herself to a sitting position. 'Yes, please. Any chance of a glass of wine with that?' she asked cheekily.

'I think you know the answer to that,' replied Angela, 'but I can give you a can of Coke?'

'Fine,' sighed Hannah. She waited until the older woman was occupied serving her meal then asked for help in going to the bathroom as she was still feeling very dizzy.

'I can take her,' offered Grace. 'It's just across there, right?'

Angela nodded. 'Very well, as she doesn't need nursing assistance. Don't lock the door, just in case.'

They made their way across with Hannah swaying a little once or twice and gripping on to Grace's arm. Once the door was closed, they were able to whisper.

'My door gets open from tomorrow and I'll be able to talk to people and roam around a bit,' said Hannah. 'Have you seen Eliza?'

'No, but Beth's on the lunch list so I should see her soon. At least we know she's still alive. Remember, don't allow them to give you anything other than saline or paracetamol.'

'Easier said than done,' Hannah sighed. 'I was given a sedative last night, but at least it knocked me out till morning.'

'That wasn't meant to happen,' said Grace, worried. 'If things take a dangerous turn text me at once and I'll get you pulled out any way I can, even if I have to call the fire brigade.'

Hannah flushed the toilet and washed her hands. She then sprayed some air freshener. Then Grace opened the door. To her surprise, Angela was on the other side, staring at them suspiciously.

'You took your time.'

'What can I say?' groaned Hannah. 'The earth moved.'

The tenseness in Angela's body relaxed. 'Back to bed with you now before your meal gets cold.'

Hannah obliged, with a little dizzy spell on the way there. Grace was impressed by her quick thinking under pressure.

Their next stop was the High Dependence Unit. Grace felt herself tense. Was Eliza in here?

'There's only two in here that are well enough to eat regular meals,' Angela said. 'They're going to be moved to the recovery ward tomorrow, all being well. The rest are receiving their nutritional needs from drips.'

'I thought people just came here to dry out,' said Grace. 'How come they're so ill?'

Angela shrugged. 'You should see the state of some of them when they first come in. You can't always tell if they've got other stuff going on health-wise as well. They work miracles here, so they do.'

Definitely a fan then, thought Grace, resolving to watch her step. The ward here was larger and contained twelve beds, six of which were occupied. Four patients were unconscious, their vitals being monitored by a cacophony of beeping machines. Head Nurse Frankie Garcia was evidently stationed here all the time and welcomed them in with a smile.

I only need meals for Beth and Tom, who're both well on the mend now after their recent surgeries.'

'Coming right up,' said Angela, pulling out the trays after consulting her list. Grace took them from her, desperate to ascertain if it really was Beth or if Eliza had successfully impersonated her twin. To her consternation, the young woman perched on the bed betrayed not the slightest flicker of recognition. Was it Grace's client or her sister? There was no way to tell. Mind you, they did have an audience. Even so, Grace had hoped if Eliza was in here that she might have found a way to let Grace know. Maybe it was Beth after all? Had Eliza succeeded in penetrating the clinic or had something terrible happened to her before she even got here? At least she'd established that Tom was still alive. His partner Ryan would be relieved. But what kind of surgery could they have had? That was worrying. The magnitude and risk of the task she and Hannah had taken on was starting to really hit home.

Their final stop was at the door to the research complex. Angela had plated up meals for the doctors who had peeled away from the lunch queue.

'Does that happen often?' asked Grace as they waited for someone to come to the door.

'It's been happening more and more,' she said. 'I don't know what they're working on through there, but from what I can gather it's reaching a critical stage. There was never meant to be a rehab facility here. It was purely a research lab to start with, but Dr Walker got lost in Edinburgh one night after going to the theatre. He was shocked to the core by the levels of homelessness and addiction he stumbled upon that night and decided to open up the rehab side as a charitable endeavour. He's a saint, that man,' she concluded, going quite misty-eyed.

The worst kind of sinner more like, thought Grace, though she managed a polite smile. The door suddenly opened with an angry buzz and a white-coated lab assistant came to take the trolley from them. She looked pale and distracted, muttering a forced 'Thank you' before closing the door in their faces. Grace was disappointed. She'd hoped for the opportunity to do some snooping around. Angus still hadn't managed to get the entry code from his wife, though he was working on it. She needed to get in there and see exactly what was going on before someone else died.

# THIRTY-FOUR

Jean was in the office, but couldn't settle. Harvey was watching her curiously, head on one side as he tried to figure out what was going on. She stooped to make a fuss of him, knowing he was missing Hannah but especially Grace. 'They're going to be alright, boy, you'll see,' she murmured. At least Grace got to leave at night after dinner was served. They'd given her address as a small, terraced house in Duns that Grace had discovered from a local lettings company was being rented to someone currently on holiday. The thought of Hannah locked up there with those crazy doctors was keeping Jean awake at night. She wasn't cut out for the amount of stress that this job entailed at times. She'd been told not to contact Grace or Hannah by text unless it was a dire emergency. Hopefully, she'd get an update tonight as Grace had said she'd drop in on her at home. She'd had an arrangement to go to the theatre with Patrick, but he'd understood. Jean was growing very fond of him, and she hoped the feeling was mutual. It was such a revelation after wasting those miserable years with Derek. Patrick treated her with warmth and respect, and, despite her age, she felt quite weak at the knees when she saw him coming towards her. He was interesting, and interested in her and what she might have to say. It was early days yet, but she was daring to dream that they might build a life together.

A loud bark startled her from her musings. She glanced up as Brodie opened the door.

After stooping to pet Harvey, he straightened up. 'Is Grace around?' he asked.

'No, she's out on a job,' said Jean. 'Can I interest you in some coffee?'

'Go on then,' he said with a smile, settling down in one of the comfortable easy chairs. 'This job she's out on, it's not anything to do with that clinic up at Whiteadder, is it?'

'Yes,' said Jean. 'Why do you ask?'

He looked worried. 'I really can't say, Jean, but there's stuff going on behind the scenes she might not be aware of. There's a bit of a power struggle going on in the police about this case.'

'And what side are you on, Brodie?' she asked, staring directly at him as she handed across his coffee.

'The side of the angels, Jean,' Brodie said with a twisted grin. 'I don't suppose there's any of your legendary tray bake to go with that, is there?'

'Give him an inch,' she said, reaching for the tin.

'And he'll take a mile,' said Brodie, fishing out the biggest piece he could find. 'I'm looking forward to having Jack to stay over tomorrow night.'

Jean looked at him, eyebrows raised. 'I gather Julie finds Jack a bit much at the moment,' she said.

Brodie looked uncomfortable. 'She gets more tired because of the pregnancy, that's all it is,' he said. 'Even so, I must arrange to see Jack on my next day off, maybe take him to the Links family park near Dunbar. He loves feeding the llamas and going round on the train.'

'I'm sure he'd love that.' Jean smiled. Grace had told her

what a piece of work Julie was underneath all that scatty charm. And her boss wasn't one to take against another woman. Looking at Brodie now, she could see that he was far from happy. He was putting a good face on, but everyone had unguarded moments, and she'd seen enough of his to know that he still loved Grace. It was very sad.

'How's Hannah getting on with her course in London?' he asked suddenly.

'Er, she's enjoying it,' said Jean, sliding her eyes away from his.

Brodie stood up. 'They're both embroiled with the clinic, aren't they? You might as well tell me, Jean. If you don't, I'll need to go up there myself.'

Jean sighed. It was difficult to know how much she should say. Eventually, she decided to go with her gut.

'Okay, fine, they're both at the clinic. Grace had no choice. She tried to involve the police,' she said with a glare. 'But got nowhere. For some reason the clinic seems untouchable. Our client got the same message loud and clear because next thing we know, Eliza has presented herself at the clinic pretending to be Beth, gambling on the fact Beth hadn't mentioned that she was a twin. She didn't tell Grace, as she knew she wouldn't have allowed it.'

Brodie ran his hands through his hair and stood up explosively. 'I knew it!' he exclaimed. 'So, Grace has gone in to try and extract her, is that it?'

'And Hannah,' said Jean. 'Grace will come home every night, but Hannah has been admitted as a patient so can't leave.'

'I can't believe I'm hearing this,' said Brodie, shaking his head. 'Have you guys ever heard the words Risk Assessment?'

Jean drew herself up to her full height. 'Don't you take that tone with me, Brodie McKenna. Grace tried to ask for your help with this, but you sent her away with a flea in her ear.'

Brodie collapsed into his seat again and adopted a more

reasonable tone. 'Look, I know, you're right, but I'd no choice. There are things going on that I can't share with you. Even at work, it's hard to know who I can trust.'

'Yet you expect us to share everything with you?' said Jean, rather surprising herself, as she didn't usually manage to be this assertive.

'It's complicated,' he snapped.

'So this has nothing to do with Julie warning you off from helping us?' said Jean.

'What?' he asked, looking surprised. 'No, of course not! Her father is a different kettle of fish though.'

'What do you mean?' demanded Jean.

'Nothing, forget I said anything. Look, what do you need to know anyway?' he asked, looking like she was extracting too great a price for some tray bake.

Jean floundered. What did she want to know? She would likely only get one chance at this. What would Grace most want to know?

'Have you identified the dead girl yet?'

'No. No one seems to have reported her as missing.'

'Have the police consulted an oceanographer to ascertain where she was put in the water?'

'Yes, but it doesn't help us. She could have been dumped in the water anywhere on the east coast as far as the Scottish Borders and still wound up at Portobello. Nothing to tie it to the clinic. Now, I really do have to go, Jean.'

'One more question,' she begged.

'Go on then,' he sighed, looking at her with hollow eyes.

'Why are the police stonewalling on this investigation?'

'Honestly? I wish I knew,' he said with a mirthless smile as he turned to leave, giving Harvey a pat on the head before he walked out the door.

Jean sighed as she settled down at her desk again. At least

she hoped she'd now lit a fuse under Brodie. If the police were stalling for whatever reason, he wouldn't stand for it now that he knew Grace and Hannah had put themselves in the firing line. She had to hope that would be enough to make him stick his neck out.

# THIRTY-FIVE

Hannah fished out her burner phone from under the mattress and memorised the code Grace had sent her for access to the High Dependency Ward. After bunching up her extra pillow to look like a body under the covers, she quickly slipped into the ubiquitous scrubs worn by the nurses and doctors together with the white tennis shoes she'd been allocated. She also put a mask on and scraped her long hair up into a bun in the manner favoured by a few of the nurses she'd already seen. Time to go on the prowl.

She already had a good idea of the layout of the facility as she'd memorised the map that Angus had sent her. Opening her door, she could hear the sound of the two nurses on duty gossiping about their boyfriends. The lights had already been dimmed for the night. The only other sound was a rhythmic snoring from another girl further along the corridor. Slipping out, she made her way to the end of the corridor and quietly slipped out through the ward doors. She stopped for a minute, listening hard, her heart thumping, to see if she'd been spotted. Nothing stirred.

She was now in the recreation zone which she would be

allowed to join tomorrow. Glancing at the noticeboard she was impressed by the wide range of activities on offer, everything from art therapy to bungee fitness. The décor in these areas was far from institutional and the vibe seemed to be more upmarket spa than hospital. They also had a large pool, and hair and beauty salon. On the surface it was a great place if only they weren't hiding a maggoty secret, she thought. Her aim for tonight was to try and get into the recovery ward to speak to Eliza/Beth, who Grace had said had been moved there after lunch. It should be fine if it was Eliza, but if it was Beth and she didn't know about her and Grace she'd have to proceed with caution in case the girl reacted badly and caused the nurses to come running.

The recovery ward was on the other side of the clinic and needed an access code to get in. Fortunately, it was included amongst those Grace had managed to send her after her lunch rounds with the dinner lady. Her heart in her mouth, she keyed in the code. Moving through into a restricted area was the most dangerous part as she could run into someone on the other side without any chance to hide away while she scoped out the lie of the land. This time, she got lucky and was able to slip into some kind of store cupboard beside the ward staffroom. She could hear the murmur of voices and kept the door open a crack so she could hear what was going on. As the voices grew louder whilst clearly trying to remain quiet, she recognised Angus's voice. He was speaking to a woman, and he sounded upset. She strained to hear what they were talking about, setting her phone to record the conversation, just in case.

'How can you cover up for them now that you know what they've done?' he demanded. 'I feel like I don't even know who you are anymore.'

'Why can't you see the bigger picture?' the woman pleaded.

It must be his wife, Carina, realised Hannah. It sounded

like their whole marriage was on the verge of imploding over this.

'You sound like a Nazi,' Angus said in disgust. 'When individual lives are regarded as mere collateral damage it's a price that's too high to pay. How can you not see that? Those young people had everything to live for and we killed them? I'm not sure I can live with that knowledge. How can you?'

'Stop being such a boy scout,' she shot back, her voice laced with contempt. 'I'm a scientist and therefore I have to look at the greater good and that means weighing up the evidence and the cost benefit ratio.'

'We're talking about actual human beings here!' he shouted, only to be hushed by his wife.

'People are living longer and longer, but what good is that if your last twenty or thirty years are spent in cognitive and physical decline? The drugs we're developing here not only increase longevity but could ensure a good quality of life within that lifespan. Old people often say they feel young inside. Imagine having the benefit of a youthful body with all that experience and wisdom? Who wouldn't choose to live like that? This research could benefit the whole planet. What's the death of a few youngsters compared to that? Nothing, in the grand scheme of things. Also, don't forget, these kids were on the verge of checking out before we even got to them. Another harsh winter would probably have finished them off, if the drugs and alcohol didn't. At least we gave them a shot. All your work does is put a sticking plaster on the wound. Admit it!'

'My work got them healthy and supported them back into society. It wiped the slate clean so they could begin again as functioning members of their community. I thought that was the beginning and end of it. I was lured here under false pretences. How could you do that to me, your own husband?'

'I'd have told you all about it if I thought there was a chance of you growing a pair,' she snapped.

'Why did Conrad have to do it this way? To obtain proof of concept by experimenting on humans without their knowledge and consent is morally bankrupt and commercially insane. It'd take just one voice to blow this whole operation sky high and set longevity research back decades,' he said, a note of despair in his voice now.

'You've not got some romantic notion of becoming a whistle-blower, have you?' she asked, her voice shrill with anger.

'Of course not,' he soothed. 'I'm just trying to persuade you round to my way of thinking.'

'We could end up in prison,' Carina said. 'Nobody intended for any of this to happen. But, now that it has, we need to keep a lid on it. Despite the problems, our research data has put us years ahead of our rivals. Conrad has promised me a seat on the board of Magnum Pharmaceuticals. We just need to complete this final round of experiments, then we can pull out and no one will ever know. Once I'm on the board, we can start a family like you wanted. Our futures will be assured.'

Angus sighed. 'You make it sound so easy,' he said.

'We'll get through this, I promise,' she said, her voice softer now.

Hannah pulled a face and switched off the recorder, hearing smooching sounds. She did not need to hear this.

Since they were now otherwise occupied, she slipped from her hiding place and continued along the ward. There was a nurse at the desk halfway along, busy working on the computer. Hannah's shoulders went back, and she tried to look as though she belonged there. The nurse glanced up as she walked by but seeing that she wore the clinic lanyard and was dressed in scrubs, she merely nodded and went back to her work. Hannah looked at the name outside each of the single rooms she passed until she came to the one with Beth on it. Slipping inside, she adjusted her eyes to the dimmer lighting and approached the bed. The young woman lying there looked like their client, but

Hannah had no way of telling if it was her or her twin. Why couldn't one of them have dyed their hair or something? She hovered uncertainly by the bed.

'Eliza,' she whispered. No response. 'Eliza, wake up, it's Hannah,' she hissed, more forcefully this time.

The girl in the bed opened her eyes and cringed away from her. 'Get away from me!' she cried.

There was no recognition in her eyes, but she'd only met her in passing a couple of times so that was hardly surprising.

'Listen, Grace sent me to help you get out of here. I need to know if you're our client Eliza or her sister Beth?'

The young woman's eyes filled with tears. 'I think Beth's dead,' she whispered. 'I came here to rescue her, but I haven't been able to find her. They're calling me Beth and haven't challenged me at all, but I have a feeling they know who I really am. They've taken away all my links to the outside world. I'm not allowed a phone or computer access because they say it will put my recovery in jeopardy. I'm effectively a prisoner here.'

'Have you asked to leave?'

'Not yet. I was still clinging on to the hope of finding my sister. I should have thought things through better. All the areas are isolated from each other. I thought I'd be able to sneak around and find her, but I haven't been able to leave the ward.'

'You were on the High Dependency Ward yesterday. What were they doing to you?'

Confusion clouded her eyes. 'No, I wasn't. I've only ever been on this ward.'

'That must have been... Beth!' said Hannah. 'Don't you see? She's here, after all!'

'She is?' gasped Eliza. She started to swing her legs out of the bed, but Hannah stopped her.

'Cool your jets! We need to get you both out of here. It won't be easy. We need to be smart about it. Grace has a plan,' she announced, hoping that was true.

'Let me go!' Eliza said, shrugging off her restraining arm. 'If Beth is here, I need to go to her!'

Hannah rocked on her heels. It had been a long day, and she was exhausted. She needed to convince her client to leave the clinic. They must have twigged by now that she was lying to them, which meant that she was in grave danger. They were hardly going to let her run amok with wild allegations about them at such a crucial stage in their operation. Who knew what they had already done to her without her knowledge and consent?

'Eliza, you're not thinking straight. Your life is on the line here. A woman washed up on Portobello Beach recently. She'd already had a post-mortem performed on her. All of her organs, even her brain, were missing. We think the clinic is responsible. You have to get out now. Ben's worried sick about you. Think of him!'

Eliza opened her eyes wide. 'Hide!' she hissed. 'Someone's coming.'

Hannah slipped into the ensuite, hiding behind the door, her heart hammering in case she was discovered. Her disguise wouldn't pass close scrutiny.

'Having trouble sleeping?' a sympathetic voice asked.

'No, I've been asleep, just been to the bathroom,' she heard Eliza say.

'I'll just complete these obs, then I'll give you something to help you drift off,' the nurse replied.

Hannah then heard the sound of the blood pressure cuff inflating.

'Hmm, it's a little high,' the nurse said. 'I'll check it again in an hour. In the meantime, take this. Doctor's orders. It'll help you get fit and well again.'

After a pause Hannah heard the sound of the nurse's squeaky shoes leaving and peered out from behind the door. She'd gone. She ran over to the side of the bed, but Eliza was already fast asleep. The nurse must have given her a fast-acting sedative. Frustrated, she stifled a yawn and when the coast was clear she returned to her room and texted Grace in relation to what she'd discovered so far.

*Be careful*, her boss texted back. *The main thing is to extract Eliza and Beth then I'm going to find someone I can trust in the police and get them to blow this whole thing wide open.*

Hannah was shocked. What she clearly meant was that for some reason Brodie was compromised in relation to this case. But how could that be? She'd never had a male role model before he came into her life. Surely he, too, wasn't going to let her down? She dashed away a tear and snuggled down under the duvet.

# THIRTY-SIX

Grace unfastened the painted wooden gate and walked up the path to Jean's front door. The moon was a creamy orb, high in the sky tonight, and the bitter chill almost took her breath away when she left the warmth of the car. It was already ten pm, but she knew that Jean would still be up. A loud woof from inside announced her presence without her needing to knock and Jean came to the door with Harvey who was overjoyed to see her and knocked over the umbrella stand with the force of his wagging tail.

'Come in,' cried Jean, trying to restore order to the doggy chaos.

'Sorry it's so late,' said Grace. 'I wanted to wait until I'd heard from Hannah.'

Jean led her through to the cosy sitting room where a log fire blazed. Harvey flopped down by her side. 'Tea?'

'Please, if it's not too much trouble,' Grace said. She settled back in the comfortable easy chair, relaxing for the first time that day as the warmth of both the stove and the welcome stole over her.

Jean was back in a flash with a loaded tray. 'I'd already

boiled the kettle,' she said as she poured the tea out of a pretty teapot and gestured to the cold plate of home-made quiche, salad and cherry tomatoes. 'I thought you might be hungry,' she added. 'If you don't want it, I can box it up for lunch tomorrow.'

'No way,' said Grace, 'I'm starving! Thanks so much, Jean.' A few minutes later, warm and fed, she drained what was left of her tea and placed her empty plate back on the tray.

'Hannah has managed to locate Eliza,' she said. 'She's in a recovery ward under Beth's name. I've already let Ben know.'

'Any sign of Beth?' asked Jean.

'She's alive though very poorly. We haven't been able to get to her yet. Obviously, the clinic must now know that Eliza snuck in under false pretences. They're going along with the pretence for now and haven't challenged Eliza.'

'If the dead girl that washed up on the beach came from the clinic, do we know if she died of natural causes or because of something they did to her?' asked Jean.

'Impossible to know at this stage, though I guess the person who performed the post-mortem will know. If only we could get our hands on those results,' said Grace, grinding her teeth as she started to tense up once more.

Sighing, she rose to her feet to depart. Jean held out her hand to stop her.

'I had a visit from Brodie today,' she said.

Grace's heart missed a beat. 'What did he want?'

'He confirmed the police still have no idea as to the identity of the girl who washed up on the beach. The oceanographer couldn't help narrow it down much either.'

'I was hoping she could be connected to the clinic, which would mean they'd have grounds to get in there,' said Grace.

'I'm not sure even that would be enough,' Jean said. 'He more or less admitted to me that the police are stonewalling on the clinic, and he has no idea why. You should've seen him,

Grace. He looked thoroughly fed up and demoralised. Not like himself at all.'

'As long as he's not colluding with it,' said Grace. 'That's what's worrying me. Does his loyalty to Julie extend all the way to her father? I'm as sure as I can be that Superintendent Blair is involved up to his neck in any cover-up. How extensive the rot is it's impossible to say.'

'I'm sure Brodie will come through for us if the chips are down,' said Jean. 'He's as decent as they come.'

'He certainly used to be,' said Grace. 'These days, I'm no longer so sure.'

Grace heard the sound of the toilet flushing upstairs.

'Jean? Have you got company? I'm so sorry! I shouldn't have just turned up out of the blue like that.'

The older woman flushed to her roots. 'That's Patrick upstairs. We've become rather good friends. He's, er... staying the night,' she whispered, looking both happy and terrified in equal measure.

'I'll get out of your hair then,' whispered Grace back to her and they both laughed.

'Come on, Harvey,' she said in a normal voice, quickly gathering her things.

'Bye, Patrick!' she called up the stairs, getting a cross poke in the back from Jean as she headed out the door. She put Harvey in the boot and drove round to her usual parking spot near the office. Still with a smile on her face at the cheering news of Jean's autumn romance, she took him down to the beach for a last romp around before turning in for the night. Maybe there was hope for her yet?

## THIRTY-SEVEN

Grace woke up to the sound of her phone ringing. Blearily she felt around her bedside table with her hand before accepting the call. Her eyes widened when she saw it was only five in the morning. It was Ben. He sounded wired.

'I've managed to get into their systems,' he said. 'It wasn't easy, but I found a backdoor through some of their more basic systems like supplies and maintenance and burrowed deeper and deeper. Can you come over here now?'

'Sure,' said Grace, clawing her way out of sleep with a struggle. 'Stick the coffee on. I'll get there as quick as I can.' She threw on her work clothes, grabbed a banana to take with her and ousted a reluctant Harvey from his memory foam mattress. He looked at her like she'd taken leave of her senses, and she wasn't the only one with bed hair.

'Come on, boy, I know it's early,' she said, clipping on his lead, 'but if I don't take you out now, you'll be crossing your legs longer than you'd like.' He gave her side eye but lurched out of his basket and stretched before staggering to the door.

The wind was whipping up the sand, blasting them both in the face, so she turned away from the angry beach with the sea hissing and spitting, and headed for the park. It was a wild one today. Even there, the wind was blowing litter around from an overflowing bin. Harvey barked crossly when a crisp packet attached itself to his face and trotted off to perform quickly, his shoulders hunched in displeasure. Once she'd cleared up after him, she walked him to the boot of her car where he snuggled down amongst his blankets and pointedly closed his eyes. She'd brought his breakfast along for later. On the way to Ben's flat at Leith Walk she stopped off at a supermarket to buy some pastries. She didn't do her best thinking on an empty stomach.

At six fifteen she was buzzed up to the flat, having left a sleepy Harvey in the car. Ben welcomed her at the door and held out a mug of steaming coffee which she gratefully accepted. He looked as bad as she felt and had obviously been up all night. His clothes were crumpled, and his skin had a sheen of sweat. This case was exacting a high toll on them all. She thanked him and followed him through to the lounge. He pushed some papers off the settee onto the floor and motioned for her to join him there so they could both look at his laptop together.

'Okay,' he said, taking a slurp of his own coffee, 'the clinic actually opened eight years ago but didn't start taking in patients for rehabilitation until five years ago.'

'What was it doing for the remaining three years then?' asked Grace.

'Pure clinical research, it would appear,' replied Ben. 'I've cross-referenced their raw material orders and done a search on the individual ingredients that they seemed to be using the most. Then, I used these items in a combined search and found they had been applied in research into conditions such as progeria or accelerated aging in children.'

Grace thought back to the before-and-after pictures she had seen of Beth, and also those the friends of the other two missing young people had seen. Was that it?

'Could they think they've stumbled on some kind of elixir of youth?' asked Grace.

'I guess they might think that was worth killing over,' Ben said. 'It would be the biggest medical discovery the world has ever known. Any pharmaceutical company which cracked the code for that would be rich beyond price and it would forever change the future of the human race.'

'So, they're in a race to establish proof of concept then,' said Grace. 'Even so, why not simply go about things in the normal manner? Why all the shortcuts?'

Ben shook his head. 'If this got out, all the big rival companies would be in on the act. Money would be no object.'

'The main thing they have going for them is secrecy, I suppose,' said Grace. 'The minute news of what they have potentially achieved leaks out, their employees will be paid life-changing money to spill the beans then it will be a filthy race to market. They're trying to perfect it without anyone cottoning on to what they've been doing so they're so far ahead no one can touch them.'

'These drugs have been making healthy people sick, haven't they?' said Ben, his voice tight with worry. 'How have they been able to get away with this? Why haven't the police stopped them?'

'Partly lack of evidence,' said Grace. 'This clinic has big pharma behind them and the type of fancy lawyers that can topple institutions. I imagine that tying up the whole Scottish legal system and laying waste to those that challenge them would only be the start. Careers would be wrecked by association, and everyone forced into bankruptcy. A battle that's impossible to win.'

Ben slammed his fist down on the table in frustration, causing the coffee cups, now empty, to jump. 'I don't understand – why wouldn't Eliza let Hannah help her out of there?'

'Because Beth is still alive,' she said, 'though very seriously ill.'

'This is all my fault,' he groaned, tugging on his hair as though he intended to pull it all out. 'If I hadn't turned Beth away that night she came to our door, then she might not be fighting for her life, and Eliza wouldn't have put herself in such danger to try to save her.' His voice rose in anguish.

Grace felt for him. Even though he'd been bang out of order in what he did, it had had such far-reaching consequences. At the time he'd no doubt thought he was protecting Eliza from being dragged down by her alcoholic sister on another bender. He wasn't to know she was clean, given the ravages the experimental drugs had wrought in her body.

'We need to make a concerted attempt to get Eliza out of there today and find some way of safeguarding Beth and the other remaining patients. If she refuses, Ben, I'm going to have to pull Hannah out of there anyway. I can't put her at risk if Eliza insists on remaining.'

'I understand. That's only fair, I guess. How long do you think the clinic intends to keep going?' he asked. 'If they get wind of us being on to them, they may just pull the plug and run back to the States.'

'That's what I'm afraid of,' said Grace. 'If that happens, I doubt very much they'll leave anyone alive who can expose what they've done. The situation is highly volatile.'

'What do you need from me?' asked Ben. 'I'm all in.'

'Keep trying to get hold of patient records for everyone they've had through the door, and particularly any that have been readmitted. We know that the drugs have harmed some patients, but they may not have harmed everyone. Any patients we can trace will probably need their health monitored for the rest of their lives in case there is a ticking time bomb inside their cells. I also need pathology records of any patients who have died and the post-mortems on their deaths. You'll need to be so careful, Ben. If they get any notion that someone is snooping around in their tech, that might cause them to abort the whole operation and press the kill switch.'

'No pressure, then,' he said with a feeble attempt at a smile.

'As soon as we have concrete proof that the police can't ignore, let me know and I'll come running.'

'How will that help if they've got to the police in Edinburgh?' he asked.

'I'll find a way to get the message to someone who has the clout to act,' she said. 'But for that to be effective, I need something tangible.' She stood up to go, draining her second mug of coffee.

'Get some rest, Ben. You're going to need to be operating at optimal capacity to pull this off.'

He nodded, his eyes heavy with fatigue.

'I'll see myself out,' she said.

# THIRTY-EIGHT

Grace checked her watch. It was still only eight. She headed back through the city to the coastline, dropping Harvey off at the flat on the way to Angus's house. She'd cautioned the doctor against trying to get through to his wife. From what Hannah had told her of overhearing their conversation she doubted he would be successful. His wife sounded like a zealot, and he was clearly the weaker partner. She was more likely to rat him out to the others than anything else.

It was still pitch black as she left the main road and wound her way up through rural villages into the hills leading to Whiteadder Reservoir. Even though her car heater was going full blast her hands were like blocks of ice. She shivered, whether from the cold of the icy morning or the monumental task ahead of her, she couldn't say. As she didn't have a four-wheel drive, her tyres struggled at times to find traction on the icy roads and by the time she slithered to a halt near Angus's cottage every muscle in her body ached with tension. She parked opposite the cottage but concealed by trees leading into the woods. Pulling on her gloves, she exited the car.

The lights were on in the cottage so at least one of them was home. The question was, which one? Given the isolated location she could hardly rock up announcing she was the Avon Lady. Approaching from the side she could see that both cars were still in the driveway. Drat. She'd hoped to catch him on his own before he went to work. She waited for a few minutes, by which time her body was so numb with the cold she wasn't sure she'd be able to move. Just as she was on the verge of giving up and driving off, the front door spilled golden light out into the darkness, and she heard the sound of brisk footsteps before a car engine started up, sending a whoosh of engine exhaust into the cold frozen air. Grace stifled the urge to cough, listening to the sound of a scraper being applied to the windscreen.

A man's voice came from the open doorway. 'Want any help with that?'

'Too bloody late,' the woman barked back before getting into the car and driving off. Grace had no choice but to launch herself determinedly through the hedge to avoid being seen. She scraped herself off the ground and trudged to the front door, watching Angus's face sag in disbelief.

'What are you doing?' he stuttered.

'What does it look like?' she snapped. 'I was trying to catch you on your own. I couldn't have your wife see me.'

'You'd better come in,' he sighed. 'Your hair is full of twigs.'

She followed him into the charming farmhouse kitchen, and he poured them both coffee then sank down at the table, placing his head in his hands. Clearly this was all exacting a heavy toll on him but the longer he covered it up, the more culpable he would appear.

'I can't do this,' he said, raising his head and looking at her with soulful brown eyes. 'You're asking me to destroy my own wife.'

'Because...' Grace prompted.

'She's destroying the lives of others,' he groaned. 'I would never have believed she could be so cold-hearted. The worst thing is she's convinced she has right on her side. They're all delusional. Mad as hatters. How could I have been so blind?'

Grace thought for a minute. 'Well, if she won't come round to your way of thinking maybe she has to think you're the one who's had the change of heart.'

'What?' he asked, looking bewildered.

For someone who was incredibly smart he didn't half need someone to take him by the hand, Grace thought. He'd spent too long in a lab and lacked common sense.

'Think about it,' she urged. 'If you've discovered your wife is up to her neck in illegal and unethical drug trials on patients who haven't given their consent, she may well have flagged you up to Dr Walker and Dr Campbell as being a weak link in the chain. What do you think those two are likely to do to someone who might blow a lid on the whole operation?'

His face drained of colour. 'What can I do?'

'I'm not just saying this for my benefit, I'm saying it for yours, too,' she said, more gently now. 'Show her you're coming round to her way of thinking. You can admit you feel concerned about the lives lost but if these drugs actually work, they'll save countless lives and that you've zoned out to see the bigger picture. Say it'd help if you were able to understand more about the science behind it all and involve yourself intellectually rather than caring exclusively for those who have become sick. Perhaps it was that which was disrupting your perspective.'

'You really think it'll work?'

'If you're convincing enough, then yes, I do. Hopefully, you'll then get access to the whole protocol. What I need you to obtain are records of all the experiments along with the names of those guinea pigs. We need to know if there was a control group of people who weren't given the drugs as well. Once you can safely access the files, get it all on a memory stick then get out of there and get to this address in Portobello, day or night. We can then take it to someone in the police who isn't in their pocket. The sooner the better, but don't jump the gun. Wait until the right moment presents itself, am I clear?'

Angus nodded, looking more determined now. 'I'll do it. This can't go on. I became a doctor to save people and, until recently, that's what I thought we were doing.'

'I'm going in today to try to convince Eliza to leave. Hannah discovered that Beth is in the High Dependency Ward. Obviously, Eliza's ruse failed as they must know perfectly well that she's not her twin,' said Grace. 'Were you aware Beth had been readmitted?'

Angus shook his head. 'No, I wasn't told. Generally speaking, I'm only on the rehab side. I don't have access to the High Dependency Ward. Another team looks after that. That's where the head nurse, Frankie Garcia, works. She's in cahoots with all that lot as well.'

'I rather gathered that,' said Grace.

'They won't just let Eliza walk out of there,' he said. 'The only reason they must have taken her in at all is to enable them to do baseline comparisons on her. If the drugs have had a catastrophic effect on Beth, then they'll be desperate to hold onto her to try and work out what went wrong and counteract it somehow. That means Eliza's in real danger.' He was starting to panic again. 'But how can I leave Hannah to go and work in the labs when another doctor might push all their poisonous shit into her?'

Grace thought for a minute. 'Jean has pretended to be Beth's mother before. Maybe she can visit and demand to be let in. As they clearly now know that Eliza is Beth's twin, she can demand that Eliza be released into her care. They wouldn't want to make her suspicious, so might well cave. Also, if they feel the girls' mother is still sniffing around, they might be more wary and less likely to make rash decisions. The three of us will work together and try to get her out today come what may. It won't be easy but if we all keep our heads and play our allocated roles, hopefully by the end of today we'll be in a position to present real evidence to the authorities.'

Angus looked out of the window. The sky was lightening over the hills. He glanced at his watch. 'I'd best get going. I'm known for being a creature of routine.'

'I can't force you to do this, you know,' said Grace as they left the house together. Angus took a last lingering look around the cottage as he went out, clearly anticipating he might never return.

'I know that,' he said, 'but thank you for saying it. I won't let you down, Grace. It's the right thing to do.'

Grace watched his taillights recede up the hill then phoned Jean and explained what she needed her to do. She felt sick at the thought of the risks they were all taking but she couldn't abandon her client or her sister now. She wound down the window, despite the cold, looking to distract herself but all she could hear was the sound of silence as mist rolled in from the hills and blanketed the sounds of nature. She had a feeling that this case was going to test her team as never before.

After half an hour she switched on the ignition and bumped down the dirt track before turning left and following Angus up to the clinic.

# THIRTY-NINE

Hannah had woken up early when the nurses turned on the light and started bustling about doing obs. Grace wasn't part of the breakfast staff so she most likely wouldn't see her until lunch. After breakfast she threw back the bed clothes, quickly showered and changed then, now that she was allowed into the recreation facilities, she set out to see what she could learn about what was going on.

There were a number of young people ranging from late teens to mid-twenties scattered around the rec room. You could hazard a guess at where they were in recovery just by looking at them. There was no sign of Eliza though, which was frustrating as Hannah was aiming to persuade her to leave with help from Grace. A couple of girls were sitting on their own far away from the rest, their eyes shuttered, hunched over and seeming miserable. Heather Kelly, the cheerful nurse, was trying to convince them to have a go at an art class or check out the gym or spa. There was an exhaustive and exhausting list of activities on the notice board: some optional; others, like group therapy, compulsory. There were just under twenty others who had clearly been here some time. They looked healthy, fit and happy, split off into different friend groups, munching on toast and drinking coffee from the Nespresso machine. This welcome dose of normality reassured her a little and she took a deep breath and pulled a mug off the shelf, filling it with a latte before looking for a way into conversation.

First, she drifted over to a girl sitting on her own in an easy chair by the window. Her face was drawn and tense and she was twitching slightly.

'Hey, I'm Hannah,' she said. 'I'm new here, too, mind if I sit?'

'Suit yourself.' The girl shrugged, looking daggers at her. 'I'm Ruth.'

Hannah sat down and waited a few minutes before saying anything. 'How have you been finding it so far?' she asked. 'I don't think I can go through withdrawal again. I reckon it's now or never for me. Not sure which way I'm going to jump to be honest, but don't let on to Pollyanna over there.' She jerked her head towards the nurse at the other end of the room. 'This your first time?'

The girl nodded, weighing her up. 'I was sleeping rough. I'd spent my last few quid on some booze to numb me for the night. It was so damn cold I doubted I would survive and couldn't have cared less. I was done, know what I mean?'

Hannah nodded. At least no matter how tough things had been she'd always had a roof over her head and people who loved her. 'So, what happened? I mean, how did you wind up here?'

'This guy was going round giving out extra blankets, warm drinks and stuff. He sat down beside me and we talked. He said he could get me help, more than just a bed for the night, he could get me into free rehab for as long as I wanted. He really sold it to me, the spa, the chance to get qualifications, supported housing afterwards. I knew inside that this would be my only shot. Next stop was the city morgue. I let him drive me there that night.'

'Any regrets?'

'Plenty,' the girl said with a twisted smile. 'I could murder a voddy right now. They had me sign some stuff when I came in even though I couldn't see straight. It means I'm stuck here for months. I'm not allowed to leave until they say so. Bit shite, that. Still, it'll tide me over the winter.'

'Yeah, me too,' said Hannah. 'Who was the guy who brought you up here? Had you seen him before?'

'Good looking, maybe that's why I agreed,' she said with a sly smile. 'He was tall with black hair and high cheekbones. I'd seen him before that night. He'd been round a few nights beforehand with some skinny bitch in a purple hat.'

Hannah felt lightheaded. That skinny bitch had been her, which meant Marek had been in cahoots with the clinic all along. How could she have been so blind?

'Well, we're here now. Like you say, it's better than freezing our bits off on the street,' said Hannah. 'Might as well make the best of it.'

She wandered off, shaking for real now. Was Marek simply taking a backhander to get the rough sleepers into an ostensibly good rehab facility? She could just about live with that idea. Or did he know the people he was helping were being used as caged lab rats for their off-book experiments? If it was the latter, she would gladly lock him up and throw away the key herself. Forcing herself to calm down and remember why she was here, she hovered on the periphery of a mixed group in their twenties who were arguing over a film they'd watched the night before. When there was a lull in the conversation caused by two of them getting up for a coffee refill, she piped up.

'Hey, my name's Hannah. I'm new here. Mind if I join you?'

Two of the girls, Queen Bee types, rolled their eyes at each other and said nothing but a third one glared at them.

'Play nice, you two. We were all new once. Take a seat,' she said, shifting over to make room for her. 'I'm Bex, this grumpy twosome are Celine and Dana. Bit rough at first, isn't it?'

'You can say that again,' said Hannah. 'Drying out is the pits. I think I'm over the worst of it now, but that's not to say I couldn't murder a drink and I don't mean coffee! This place is different to other places I've been. Usually, it's get you dry and ship you out.'

They all laughed.

'And don't let the door hit you in the butt on the way out,' added Bex. 'No, this place is completely mental on how far they're willing to go to get you clean and keep you that way. The reason they make us stay so long is to set us up for success in the outside world. I'm due to leave next week and I've got a nice flat in a good area with subsidised rent waiting for me. I'm due to start college in September to get some Highers, then I want to apply to be a nurse. For the first time I'm excited about the future.'

'Will you keep in touch in the outside world?' asked Hannah.

Regretfully, Bex shook her head. 'No, it's part of our contract. They're worried that if one of us has a relapse she'll take the others with her like a sort of contagion, so we can never contact each other again once I walk out of that door.'

The others hugged her and Hannah excused herself, feeling like she was intruding. On one level what the girls said made a degree of sense, but she also wondered whether the real reason might be so that if any of them broke down physically as a result of the experimental drug regime they were on, then the others wouldn't raise the alarm.

A tinkling bell rang and everyone apart from her and the two new girls melted away to their classes, activities or therapy sessions. It felt very quiet without their chatter. The others sat apart looking stormy, so Hannah curled up in a chair and mirrored them. The rather awkward silence was broken a few minutes later by Nurse Heather Kelly's smiling face poking back round the door.

'How are we doing in here?' she asked, sitting amongst them. Her warm manner caused tears to spring to Hannah's eyes. The stress of being cooped up in here was really getting to her. At least it was in character, she thought, still rather embarrassed and wiping them away. Nurse Kelly sat beside her and patted her hand which made her feel even more like bawling her eyes out.

'I know this feels incredibly tough, but you'll never again feel as bad as you feel today, I promise you,' she said. 'Although we've given you medication to control the worst of the shakes, you're still going to feel a bit fragile for a few days. That's completely normal. You've probably not being eating much in the weeks leading up to your admission here, but we employ a wonderful chef who's going to turbo charge every delicious meal with the nutrients your body and mind needs to heal.'

Hannah nodded. 'What happens now? Am I free to just wander about? I don't feel ready to join in with classes and stuff today.'

The nurse looked at her, head on one side assessing. 'You can have one more day. Too much time on your hands to brood isn't healthy, but if you promise to visit the spa and perhaps have a nice relaxing massage or facial then we have a deal. Agreed?'

'Agreed,' said Hannah. She felt the urge to giggle at the thought of her swanning about in a spa. She'd never even been to one before.

'That goes for the rest of you, too,' said the jolly nurse. 'If you all come with me, I'll show you the way and our spa staff will give you a tour and take it from there.'

Hannah trailed behind her with the others, looking through the windows on the doors as she walked by to see what other people were doing. Suddenly she stopped frozen in her tracks, unable to believe what she was seeing. In a room full of easels, Julie, Brodie's partner, was teaching a class. As Julie glanced towards the door, Hannah dropped to the floor, pretending to adjust a shoelace, her blood thundering in her veins.

# FORTY

Grace was up to her elbows in food prep for lunch in the large stainless-steel kitchen. As she was far from a domestic goddess it was a bit of a shock to the system. Impatient to go poking around for answers and also to try and smuggle Eliza out, she felt the pressure of the ticking clock. She could understand her client's blind devotion to her sister, but given how ill Beth had appeared to be in that ward, there was no way they could reasonably get her out, too. Their best chance was to smuggle Eliza out and then she could take her client and Angus to someone high up in the police that she could trust.

It rocked her to the core that she no longer considered that person might be Brodie. There was a female officer in Edinburgh that she had worked with on cases before who had now achieved high rank in Edinburgh. She'd also done a long stint in internal affairs so wouldn't automatically go on the defensive at the thought of a cover-up going on within police headquarters. Her name was Superintendent Alis Gray, therefore of equivalent rank to her old nemesis, Superintendent Blair.

Angela interrupted her reverie, her face set in a frown,

hands on hips. 'Hurry it up, will you, Grace? We haven't got all day. Cook needs all that stuff pronto before the hungry hordes descend and there's nothing to feed them.'

'Will do,' she replied meekly, increasing her chopping speed. At this rate, I'm going to end up losing a finger, she thought mournfully, as Angela stood over her until satisfied that she was working fast enough. 'This is taking multitasking to a whole new level,' she muttered behind her boss's departing back.

Finally, she was done, and it was time to wash up and don her serving apron. Swathed in plastic and with her hair stuck up in a disposable plastic cap she felt almost invisible which suited her fine. Angus's wife, Carina, came in with Dr Walker and Frankie Garcia. Once they'd been served, their expressions blank and disinterested, they went over to the furthest table and began talking in low voices, their gestures gradually becoming more animated. As the queue had died back for the time being, and she was working with another server, Grace took the opportunity to slip out with the trolley to clear tables, working her way to the back corner where the three of them were sitting, food pushed to one side, conferring in low voices. Approaching as quietly as she could, Grace took a cloth and wiped the adjacent table, straining her ears to hear over the clatter of tins and the scattered chitchat around her in the cavernous canteen.

'How do we know we can trust him?' said Dr Walker, his expression glacial.

'Because I trust him and you trust me.' She smiled, but with her chin tilted in defiance. 'He's a brilliant researcher, you know that. If it wasn't for his treatment protocols, we wouldn't have been able to cure the patients of their addiction and get their bodies healthy and receptive for use in the trial. It's far riskier to leave him on the outside than to bring him in to the inner circle. He's already asking questions about what we're doing.'

'I doubt he's got the stomach for it,' Walker said. 'Always struck me as a squeamish sort of guy.'

'That's simply not true,' Carina said angrily. 'Frankie, what do you think? You've known him forever.'

'He's a brilliant doctor and a top researcher, but I doubt his mindset is sufficiently flexible,' Garcia said.

'Leave it with me,' said Walker. 'I'll think on it.'

'Are you finished with that?' asked Grace, approaching now. They looked startled that she was so near, but meekly handed over their used trays for her to clear away. It sounded like Carina was struggling to get Angus admitted into the inner circle. Their relationship was under so much pressure she doubted it would survive. The time for serving lunches was almost over now and she hadn't seen Hannah come in. She was always reluctant to place Hannah in any danger due to misplaced maternal feelings, but she usually managed to resist trying to wrap her in cotton wool. She was a young professional now, intent on building a career at the agency and she knew it wasn't fair of her to try and hold her back or limit her exposure to difficult situations.

'Right,' said Angela, coming up behind her. 'You've shadowed me delivering the lunches. Fancy doing it on your own today? We're a staff member down so I need to help with meal planning with the dietician. It's not that difficult. The meals all have a label with the patient's name, ward number and date of birth. The codes to enable you to access them are on this laminated card which you need to return to me once you're done. They change every day, so yesterday's is no good to you now, even if you did remember it.'

Grace nodded, trying not to look too eager. This was an unexpected bonus. The trolley was waiting ready stocked for her, and Angela held the door open for her as she manoeuvred it out of the dining room. To her frustration, she saw Hannah jogging along the corridor hoping to catch some lunch as she left. The frustrated look she sent her probably meant she'd uncovered something important. It would have to keep. They couldn't be seen talking in such a public place.

She headed for the wards, punching in the code. It was only patients who were confined to bed rest who received meals so most of the beds were empty.

She'd hoped that she'd be able to persuade Eliza to leave with her and had a spare set of scrubs under her own clothes she could pull off and give to her, but Eliza was not in her room despite a meal having been supplied for her. Her bed had been stripped and her chart was missing. They'd taken her somewhere. But where? Had they moved her into the High Dependency Ward with her sister? If so, she would bet that they'd no intention of ever letting her live to tell the tale. A set of identical twins would be incredibly valuable in their illicit medical experiments. The pretence was clearly over. Time was now of the essence.

She searched the room and ensuite in all the places she could think of to see if Eliza had been able to leave her a message. Conscious of the time, she was on the verge of giving up when she noticed the smoke detector had a piece of paper poking out along one of its edges. Jumping up on a chair she carefully unscrewed it and pulled out a piece of roughly torn paper.

HELP ME. They're moving me, I don't know where, but I suspect I'm not getting out of here alive. Tell Ben I'm sorry and I love him. I'm scared, really scared.

Grace's mind swung into overdrive as she tried to figure out how to get her out of there. It seemed impossible unless the police stormed the building and took it by force, but it looked like the cavalry wouldn't be coming. She thought about phoning

Brodie but reluctantly put the phone back in her pocket. It was down to her and Hannah.

Mindful of the time, she flushed the toilet in case anyone queried why she'd been in there with the door closed and left the room. She raced along to the High Dependency Ward, which was on the other side of the building. Putting her mask on she went into the rooms one by one for those who were able to eat. Most of the young people in the beds were drowsy, clearly drugged, but she asked everyone who was alert enough if they knew where Eliza or Beth were as she had meals for them. It was horrifying seeing them so unwell and knowing that this sickness had been caused by doctors deliberately experimenting on them for financial gain and prestige. Her blood boiled with fury. As she entered the last room on the ward, which had been empty the last time she had been round, she came across the missing girl, Lorraine Kerr. She was skin and bone and her eyes were huge in emaciated sockets. Moving closer, Grace saw that she was alert with her eyes tracking her movement across the room. She helped her to sit up and made her comfortable. The girl groaned in pain as though even her bones rasping against the starched sheets caused her pain. Too weak to feed herself, Grace helped feed her. The door opened suddenly. Frankie Garcia stood there, her shrewd eyes raking over the scene before her.

'That's not your job,' she said dismissively. 'I'll do it, you can go now. And for future reference, leave the door open at all times. These patients are very unwell and we need to be able to see them at all times.'

'Of course,' said Grace humbly, looking down. 'Oh, er, I also have a meal for someone called Beth, but I haven't been able to find her.'

'Leave it with me,' Garcia said, stretching out a well-manicured hand. 'I'll make sure she gets it.'

'Thank you,' said Grace obsequiously, trundling her trolley

away while allowing her feet to shuffle and with downcast eyes. Glancing back as she left the room, she could see that her ploy had worked, and Garcia had already dismissed her from her mind. She desperately needed to find Angus. They had to act now to see if any of these ravaged bodies could be saved.

# FORTY-ONE

Jean stood at the door to the clinic holding on to her courage which was threatening to desert her at any moment. It was a lot more terrifying going in there this time, now that she knew just how cavalier they were with human lives. The door buzzed and she stiffened her spine, nailing a look of outrage to her face.

It was Lily, the nice girl from reception, who appeared and took her through. This time, though, she looked rather subdued and the smile on her face didn't reach her eyes. She looked scared, Jean thought, recognising the feeling.

'If you take a seat, I'll tell Dr Campbell you're here,' she said, picking up the phone.

Jean noticed that her previously manicured nails were bitten down to the quick. Why was she so nervous? Surely, even though she was Dr Walker's daughter she didn't know what went on here, did she? Perhaps she could be amenable to pressure if she did, thought Jean, feeling mean to be thinking like that.

The door opened behind reception and Dr Campbell stood there, not a hair out of place, with a warm smile on her face.

'Mrs Anderson. Please come this way,' she said, ushering Jean into her magnificent office.

'I've come for my daughter, Eliza,' Jean said, setting her face in uncompromising lines. 'I know she's here. I'm taking her home with me now.'

'I'm afraid you're mistaken,' Dr Campbell said smoothly. She leaned towards her with a look of fake compassion that made Jean uncharacteristically want to smack her. 'Eliza has never been a patient here, only her twin sister Beth.'

'How'd you know they're twins then, if you haven't met Eliza? Answer me that,' demanded Jean. 'Beth told Eliza she hadn't let on she'd a twin when she got out. I suppose Beth is back here, too. You've got no right to keep them here. If you don't give me my girls, I'll be back with the police, so I will.'

Dr Campbell's mask was beginning to slip off her face like melted butter and her anger shone through. 'How dare you come in here making wild accusations and dragging me away from our patients! All I've ever tried to do is help your daughter Beth conquer her addiction and get the support she deserved to live a meaningful life. Support, I might add, that was evidently severely lacking in her own home life. If you want to point the finger at anyone, point it at yourself. For the last time, neither of your daughters are here. The most likely explanation is that Beth has fallen prey to her addiction again, despite our best efforts. As to why you think we have your other daughter, I can only imagine you are not quite in your right mind.' She buzzed through to reception. 'Call security. Mrs Anderson is leaving,' she said in a voice that brooked no argument.

'Fine, I'll go,' said Jean, standing up. 'But if I find out you've been lying to me...'

The door opened and two muscle men arrived with ugly scowls on their faces. With as much dignity as she could muster, Jean walked between them until the door to the clinic closed behind her with a bang. Shaking, she walked to her car. Hopefully, now that she'd confronted them, they wouldn't dare harm the two girls further. Of course, it could have the opposite effect. Jean shuddered. Grace and Hannah were on the inside. They would figure something out. They had to.

Once she was back at the office, she used Grace's key to let herself into the flat and took an exuberant Harvey for a walk through Figgate Park, taking care not to slip on the ice. It was a glorious day with the winter sun high in the sky. Teenagers were kicking a football around on the grass and some mums were shivering by the pond with their toddlers, feeding the ducks. It was too cold to linger though. She'd already lost the feeling in her feet. After a meet and greet with several other dog walkers she headed back for the office, settling Harvey down with a chew bone in his basket.

Putting the fan heater on, she checked her phone for messages. There was just one from Patrick asking her to have dinner with him tonight. Normally that would have made her heart sing, but she didn't think she could manage it with everything going on. He knew she worked at the agency, but it felt awkward when she couldn't talk about her day with him. She would reply to him later.

Sighing, she bent her head to apply herself to catching up on her backlog of employee vetting for a private school to distract her mind from what might be going on at the clinic. Hannah must be missing little Jack. She'd never been away from him for more than a night before. Her mind drifted to Brodie. She couldn't figure out what was going on there at all. It was so unlike him to back away from a case like this. There's no way he was corrupt. She refused to believe it. But what other reason could there be for his reluctance to check out the clinic after everything Grace had told him? They'd all but giftwrapped it with a bow, but it still wasn't enough. She looked down as a furry paw landed on her knee. Harvey made a little noise in his throat. He'd picked up on her mood. She stroked his big head and he thumped his tail.

'It's all going to be fine, boy,' she soothed, although she wasn't sure who she was trying to convince.

# FORTY-TWO

Hannah threw herself down on her bed. She was so annoyed she had missed the chance to talk to Grace. She was desperately worried that Eliza had been placed out of their reach. It was unlikely they'd simply be able to spirit her out of the clinic now. She also needed to warn Grace about seeing Julie.

There was something else niggling her about the glimpse of Julie, but she couldn't put her finger on it. Maybe she'd just changed her hairstyle or something? Hannah was feeling slightly sick about being away from Jack for another night. She missed his warm cuddly body. She hadn't realised just how far the clinic were prepared to go. She needed to get out of here – it was getting too risky. Her son had already lost a father. She had a responsibility to him to stay alive. It was time to find Angus. He'd promised he would make sure she was safe and that nothing dodgy would be put in her body. She hadn't seen him today at all yet. He clearly still had strong feelings for his wife. What if he'd decided to throw his lot in with her after all and rat them out to Campbell and Walker? A rising tide of panic gripped her insides and affected her breathing. Not another panic attack, she groaned, her breathing becoming laboured and her vision fading at the edges. She strove to regain control, but it was no use. She groped for the call button but knocked her book onto the floor instead.

Fortunately, a friendly face in the shape of Nurse Heather Kelly arrived, alerted by the book landing on the floor. Immediately, she took in the situation. By now Hannah was gasping for air, her eyes bulging with terror, desperate fingers clawing at the bedclothes.

'Oh, you poor thing,' clucked the nurse, rushing in to help her. 'Here, let me help you.' She took one of Hannah's hands in her own to measure her pulse.

'You're having a panic attack, Hannah. Look at me and try to breathe with me. In for one, two, three, four, five... and out for one, two, three, four, five...' Her soothing voice kept repeating the instructions until Hannah was able to bring her breathing back under control and the symptoms subsided.

'Well done, you've got this,' Heather said, releasing her hand gently once she was sure the attack had subsided.

Hannah burst into tears as she often did when this happened. 'I'm sorry,' she gulped. 'Everything just got too much for a bit there.'

'Nonsense, don't apologise, you're under a lot of stress. Detoxing is never easy,' soothed the lovely nurse, who only looked to be in her late twenties. 'We've so many things here to help you with that: yoga, art therapy, hot stone massage, energising facials.'

'Everything but walking with llamas,' quipped Hannah.

Nurse Kelly smiled. She got up to leave.

'Can't you stay a while?' Hannah asked. 'I just need someone to talk to. I don't know anyone here yet.'

'Sure,' the friendly nurse replied. 'I've got some time until my next round of obs.'

'Have you worked here long?' asked Hannah.

'Five years,' she replied. 'The clinic has been here longer than that, but it wasn't used for rehab back then.'

'A few of the others have been scaring me,' said Hannah in a small voice.

'Why? What have they been saying?' asked Heather, looking concerned.

'They said that some people who come here for treatment get really sick after they get out and are hidden away in another ward. They heard that sometimes they even die. I don't want to die,' she said, her eyes filling with tears that weren't so hard to conjure up.

'Oh, bless you. Is that what's been worrying you? Look, I'm not really supposed to tell you this, but it's true. We have both an Intensive Care Ward and a High Dependency Ward that are off limits to all but those people working there.'

'But how can rehab make people sick?' she asked, retaining a wobble in her voice.

'It doesn't,' Nurse Kelly replied. 'However, you've got to bear in mind that when people come to us off the streets, they're usually very poorly. Most have prioritised alcohol over food, so their bodies are severely malnourished. Any infections or diseases have been allowed to run through their bodies unchecked. All of this can ultimately cause organ damage. It takes a long time to reverse and restore optimal health. That's what makes this place so special,' she said with quiet pride. 'We never give up on our patients. It's a commitment for life.'

'When I first came in here, I met a girl called Beth. She was a bit older than me and I kind of hoped we'd be friends but now she's gone, and I'm worried about what might have happened to her,' she said, the tears spilling over again. 'Is there any way you could possibly find out for me? It would make me feel so much better if I knew she was okay.' Hannah felt terrible manipulating the kindly nurse, but she had to use everything at her disposal if she was to help Beth and Eliza before it was too late.

'I'll see what I can do if it will put your mind at rest,' the nurse said. She glanced at her watch. 'Now, I suggest you go to the coffee lounge and drop in to one of the activities scheduled to start at four pm. That will keep you occupied until dinner.'

Hannah fell back on her pillow. Her task seemed hopeless. What was she even doing here? Now that Eliza had been moved to a secure area, she was powerless to help her. She would stay until tomorrow and then that was it. She was out of here. There was no knowing what they would do to her if they found out she was a plant. Exhausted, her eyes grew heavier. There'd been something bugging her about Julie. What was it...?

## FORTY-THREE

Grace raced home at the maximum speed she dared as her car wound its way down through the hills on the way back to Portobello. She had the strongest feeling that the researchers were getting ready to cut their losses and flee back to the States. What this would mean for those in the Intensive Care and High Dependency units she could only imagine, but her gut told her their main priority would be to dispose of any evidence connecting them to their unethical experiments, leaving behind only the respectable face of the clinic's rehab arm. There was no way she could bring the case to a successful conclusion without back up from the police. Her phone pinged with a text from Hannah.

Julie is working as art therapist at clinic.

Grace slammed the wheel in frustration. Could Brodie be more compromised? This was insane. What possible hold could the clinic have over his boss? Just how complicit was Brodie in looking the other way if his partner was actually working there? The fact that Julie was working at the clinic also compromised the integrity of the investigation. If she came across Hannah or Grace, she wouldn't hesitate to blow their cover out of the water and take pleasure in doing it, too. Presumably, she would be contracted for so many sessions per week. Hopefully, Hannah would have managed to work out her schedule so they could both give her a swerve. She would speak to Hannah tomorrow. It was time she pulled her out of there. The risks were just too great.

She needed to speak to Angus and lay it on the line. It was time for him to choose a side. He either came with her to the police prepared to testify about everything he knew, or he would get permanently stuck on the wrong side of the story. She knew how hard it must be for him with his wife's career hanging on the outcome of his decision. It mirrored what seemed to be going on in her life in relation to Brodie. She was still desperately hoping for a way out from under this in relation to her former partner and the love of her life. Angus was in exactly the same bind, but she couldn't let him put it off any longer. Nor could she allow her feelings for Brodie to stop her doing the right thing in relation to this investigation.

Tomorrow would be her final day at the clinic. If she could get Eliza out and persuade Angus to step up, then she would go and lay it all out for Superintendent Alis Gray. It would be up to her then what further action was taken and what the consequences would be for Brodie and, more particularly, his boss. Another text pinged up on her screen.

> Eliza moved to High Dependency. I don't know what to do. Angus not been to see me. Not seen him all day.

Grace's heart sank. They couldn't wait any longer. She couldn't risk Hannah's safety any further in this highly volatile situation.

> Hang tight until tomorrow. Will get you out then.
> Stay in your room.

Troubled, she put the radio on to distract herself from the incessant worries gnawing away at her. After a few minutes of inane chatter, the six o'clock news came on. Horrified, she listened as she heard that another body had been pulled from the sea. It had washed up at Dunbar. The person had yet to be identified. A jolt of electricity shot through her body, and she struggled to suck in her next breath. What if it was her client or her sister? She put her car in gear and pulled out, tyres spinning in the dirt as she continued downhill, the lights of the city twinkling now just a few miles away.

Suddenly, something rear-ended her car, taking her completely by surprise. Her seatbelt dug into her ferociously as her body slammed forward, causing her neck to slam back against the seat. Whoever it was must have been travelling without lights or she'd have been warned of their approach. This was no accident. Striving to regain control of her car she steered into the skid and spun her car round to try and cling on to the narrow one-track road. The vehicle that had driven into her reversed at speed, gearing up for another attack. She moved furiously, her brain calculating how best to get away from them. Tyres squealing, she pointed the nose of her car downhill once more, no match for the heavier vehicle behind her that she guessed was some type of armoured jeep judging by the way it had rear-ended her car.

A number of laboured noises were coming from under the bonnet of her car. Her rear tyres were clearly burst but she had to try. She lurched further along the road, which had a steep drop to one side. There was a village half a mile down the road. If she could just get there, she'd be safe. Time stood still as she heard the powerful engine roaring behind her. She was out of options. Flicking her lights off at the last minute she unclipped her seatbelt and rolled out the driver's side seconds before impact, hoping and praying that they hadn't seen her. The jeep shunted her crumpled car over the side of the road and down onto the rocks below. She heard it bouncing off the rocks all the way down and shuddered at how close she had come to being in it. There was no way she could have walked away from that.

Rolling over to the opposite side of the road, keeping her body low, she managed to find cover in a thicket of gorse, surmising that they wouldn't be looking for her on this side. Although she knew that she must be injured, the adrenaline was keeping her from feeling the pain. She ducked her head as a powerful torch swept over her, hearing the blood roaring through her veins. There were two men in the roadway now, peering over the edge where her car had somersaulted down. Apparently satisfied that she hadn't survived, they got back in their massive gas guzzler and turned back up the hill. Grace popped her head up and managed to read the licence plate as it reversed towards her. It confirmed her suspicions. Someone from the clinic was on to her. She had seen that vehicle before in the clinic car park.

She lay there concealed by the bush until she could hear it no longer. Her body was trembling uncontrollably, and she felt a wave of sickness rise up in her throat as she vomited. The temperature had plummeted and frost glittered on the road. She had to get moving or she would die of hypothermia out here. Struggling to her feet, she felt herself all over for broken bones and figured in the circumstances she'd got off lightly. She was bruised and battered but nothing a hot bath and some Epsom salts couldn't fix. As her phone was in her car at the bottom of the ravine, she couldn't call for help, so resigned herself to having to travel to the next village and ask someone to call her a cab from there. Feeling very small and insignificant beneath the black panorama of stars she set off, feeling the loneliness of the hills seep into her very soul. She had lived to fight another day.

# FORTY-FOUR

Jean let Patrick into the agency. Harvey barked at him, but he had come forearmed and soon got round him with a couple of treats and a few kind words.

'Still no word from Grace?' he asked, giving Jean a hug before sitting down opposite her.

'Not a dickie bird,' she replied. 'I've a horrible feeling something's wrong. She'd never leave Harvey here with me this long without checking in. It's nearly eight o'clock. Did you manage to cancel our reservation?'

'Yes, not a problem,' he said, his kind eyes supporting her. 'You haven't told me about this case you're working on yet.'

'I know,' said Jean. 'I'm sorry, confidentiality goes with the territory in this job.'

'Is it dangerous?' he asked, looking concerned.

It felt good to have someone worry about her for a change. Patrick couldn't be more different from her selfish and demanding ex-husband.

'It can be,' she replied honestly. 'Most of the time we do fairly routine stuff, credit checks, employee vetting, cheating husbands, that sort of thing. Every now and again we get a case that challenges us. This is one of those cases.' She spoke quietly.

'You don't mean people might try to harm you?' he exclaimed.

'If we stand between them and what they want, that's perfectly possible,' she said. 'Anyway, let's not dwell on that tonight. Sorry that our dinner's a bust. I'll quite understand if you want to get off home.'

'Why don't I order us a takeaway to the office?' he said. 'You have to eat sometime. I dare say, Harvey here wouldn't object to a spare rib or two.'

Hearing his name, Harvey got to his feet and padded over as if to say, *Now you're talking my language!*

Jean laughed. 'I can hardly say no, now you've got his hopes up.' Harvey put his head on her knee and his brown eyes stared up at her trustingly. 'Okay, that would be great. Mine's a satay chicken with fried rice, and we'll all three of us share a portion of ribs. Maybe order something for Grace? She's got to come back some time.'

Patrick went into the other room to phone it through, and Jean tried Grace's mobile again without success. It went straight to voicemail. Frustrated, she hung up. Everyone seemed to be ignoring her today. She hadn't been able to raise Hannah either. She had to confess at times she felt a teeny bit taken for granted as she was always the one left manning the office when the other two went under cover. Although, to be fair, she was generally quite happy to leave them to it as her nerves couldn't take the stressful situations she had at times found herself in.

Twenty-five minutes later they sat down to eat. Jean suddenly realised she was ravenous. Her clothes had been looser recently as she was so busy she sometimes forgot to eat. Suddenly the door to the office opened, ushering in a gust of freezing air. It was Grace. Harvey raced over to greet her, and she bent over to make a fuss of him, wincing in pain as she did so.

'What's that on your face, boy?'

'Spare rib sauce,' supplied Jean. As Grace stood up Jean looked at her and gasped. 'Grace! What happened to you?' Her boss's clothes were ripped, and her face had a couple of large bruises breaking out against the pallor of her skin. The way she was holding her body seemed off as well.

'I'm fine, no need to fuss,' she said, trying to make light of it but Jean wasn't fooled.

'Hi, I'm Patrick, Jean's friend. I'll plate you up some food. Why don't you both go through to the other room? You'll be more comfortable there.'

'Hi, Patrick, that would be great,' Grace said with a tired smile, walking on through. Harvey remained with Patrick to supervise the food allocation.

Jean squeezed his hand on the way past. It was so thoughtful of him to give them a chance to catch up in private. Grace lowered herself onto the couch, clearly very sore. Once the food had been brought through, Patrick made an excuse and retired next door to wait for Jean. Harvey polished off his ribs then lay on Grace's feet with a contented sigh.

'He seems lovely,' said Grace. 'I reckon you've got a keeper there.'

'Oh, early days yet,' said Jean airily, though she felt her face colour in pleasure. 'Anyway, stop deflecting. Tell me what happened.'

'I got run off the road on the way back from the clinic.'

'That's terrible!' exclaimed Jean. 'You mean it was deliberate?'

Grace nodded. 'Very much so. My car ended up down a ravine. They think I'm in it. My phone, bag, coat, everything is down there. I'm going to need another phone, Jean. Can you sort that for me?'

'Of course!' She looked at Grace. Her face was a horrible colour and she looked utterly exhausted. 'First thing in the morning I'll sort you out with a hire car as well. Are you sure you shouldn't see a doctor?'

'Nothing a hot bath and a good night's sleep won't fix,' Grace said.

'What about the police? What you're talking about is actually attempted murder.'

'No police,' Grace said, her voice slurring with fatigue. 'Not yet anyway.' She slowly and painfully got to her feet and clipped on Harvey's lead.

'He's been walked so you don't have to worry about that,' said Jean as she escorted her out. Grace headed up to the flat. Jean watched her go sadly. She had never seen her boss look so defeated. She cut a lonely figure. Patrick put his arm around her, and she leaned into him.

## FORTY-FIVE

Hannah had tossed and turned all night. She'd sent a number of texts to Grace but not had any reply. She was worried; it wasn't like her. She never turned her phone off when a member of her team was in the wind. Her phone pinged from its hiding place. She reached under her mattress and pulled it out. Talk of the devil, it was Grace, but she was texting from a different number.

> Hannah, old phone gone. Long story. In shortly for breakfast. Need to talk. I'll find you later. Be careful!

Hannah sent a thumbs up. She didn't want to tell her what she'd discovered about Julie until she was sure. It was too early for breakfast. She waited until Nurse Heather trundled in for obs pretending she was only now stirring.

'What are you up to today then?' the nurse said with way too much cheerfulness for this early in the morning.

'I was thinking about trying art therapy. Is the woman who does it any good? Has she been here long?'

'Nearly a year, I believe,' she said. 'She's only part-time, but

I think she's in today so you might be in luck. The patients seem to enjoy her classes.'

After the nurse left, Hannah threw on some clothes and headed for the rec room. As she expected it was still in darkness. She opened the door leading to the therapy rooms and the spa. These were left unlocked as a gesture of trust to those who were deemed to have recovered sufficiently to use them. Only the pool was out of bounds until the lifeguard came on duty and was covered by a tarpaulin. Entering the art therapy room, she searched Julie's desk but found nothing of interest. Of course, she wouldn't put anything secret in there because other different therapists got to use it, too. She had to find a way to get to Julie's locker. Or maybe her car would yield the prize she was looking for. Sighing, she retraced her steps. She couldn't risk Julie seeing her as that would give them away completely and Julie would be beyond happy to land them in it. There was no appealing to her better nature. She didn't have one.

As Hannah opened the door into her room, she jumped to see Grace emerge from her ensuite. Her mouth opened in horror at the sight of Grace's battered and bruised face which even her makeup hadn't fully concealed.

'What happened to you?' she exclaimed, urging her to sit down on the chair by her bed as she drew the curtains to her room and closed the door. No one should bother them for a bit.

'I got run off the road by the two security goons that work here,' replied Grace. 'The car tumbled down the ravine. They thought I was in it. Hence new phone number.' She gave a lopsided grin. 'What I don't know is who instructed them to do it.' Her expression turned serious. 'They think I'm dead, so they haven't bothered to cancel my pass. Obviously, whoever instructed them to go after me won't have broadcasted it to everyone so we have a small window where I can still move around the clinic. We need to get Eliza out of here today. I suspect her sister could be too ill for us to move but we have to try, and we should be able to get Eliza out with Angus's help.'

'What? The invisible man, you mean?' said Hannah. 'I didn't see him around at all yesterday. The other doctors could be filling me with all sorts of dodgy stuff. I thought part of the deal was he was meant to keep an eye on Eliza and me and protect us from the other medical staff? Luckily Nurse Heather Kelly has been watching out for me. I'm sure she has no idea what's really been going on.'

'That's rather worrying,' said Grace. 'Either they've got to him via his wife and he's back in their pocket or something has happened to him. Something bad.'

'You mean, murder bad?' asked Hannah, feeling contrite and hoping it wasn't true.

'Possibly,' said Grace, her voice grave. 'This has to be our last day in here, Hannah. We either get one or both girls out by the end of the day or we walk out of here without them and go straight to the police.'

'You mean to Brodie?' asked Hannah, feeling wretched as she anticipated what her boss might say.

'No, not this time, Hannah,' said Grace. 'I'm just not sure where Brodie's head is, at the moment. He has a lot of conflicting loyalties. I'd rather not put them to the test.' There was a slight catch in her voice. 'The nature of his involvement will eventually become clear.'

'But how are we going to transport the twins?' asked Hannah. 'I mean, I assume you've hired another car but even so...'

'My courtesy car is parked in the staff car park. It's a Peugeot Rifter so plenty of room in it. The clinic also has a fully kitted out ambulance there. What I don't yet have is the key for it, so I'm going to have to try and track that down unless you find it first.'

'But... even if we manage to steal them out of the High Dependency Ward, what if they're too sick to travel?' Hannah said. 'What if we rescue them only to kill them on the way to the Royal Infirmary?'

'Best case scenario, Angus will be with us to provide medical support. I don't have all the answers yet, Hannah, but we need to do something,' said Grace. 'I take the lunches into High Dependency at two pm. Once I've ascertained where both girls are and the state of them, I'm going to dump the trolley and change into the scrubs I'm wearing beneath this uniform. You have your own set. On my text make your way there, fully masked up. I'll put the code number in the text. I'll be issued with it to take the meals round. See if you can find a couple of wheelchairs and stash them close to the patients. I've brought some elastic luggage straps in case they're unconscious or can't support their own weight. We could also wheel them in their beds as another option.'

'You need to pull them backwards, not forwards,' Hannah said. 'Nurse Kelly showed me when I held the door open for her once.'

Grace glanced at her watch and stood up. 'I'd better go. I'll be needed in the kitchens. Keep your head down where possible and wait for my signal after lunch. Be ready to move.'

'Got it,' said Hannah, buzzing with adrenaline.

'Oh, and Hannah? If anything goes wrong and I can't get myself or the girls out, don't hesitate, get the hell out of here. Run like the wind and don't look back. Promise me!'

'Promise,' said Hannah, crossing her fingers behind her back just in case. It was only when Grace had left that she remembered she hadn't told her what else she'd discovered about Julie. It wasn't the kind of news she wanted to deliver via text. In any event, they were hopefully going to be away from here by the end of the day. Odds were that they wouldn't even come across each other. Julie was the type to bring a packed lunch over-flowing with lentils. She'd never even seen her in the canteen. It would be fine.

# FORTY-SIX

Grace swallowed some painkillers and drained a cup of black coffee from the machine in the staff locker room. She was so stiff and sore but now was not the time to wallow. She noticed a coat hanging on the hooks and thought it looked vaguely familiar but couldn't remember where she'd seen it. 'Get a grip, Grace,' she muttered. Now was hardly the time to be thinking about fashion.

She'd just put her kitchen mask on when the door swung open and in marched... Julie in one of her floaty hippy dresses. Grace almost gagged on her coffee. Pulling her plastic cap way down on her forehead she closed her locker and, giving a polite nod whilst avoiding eye contact, left the room. Julie's gaze slid over her, but nothing registered. A couple of minutes earlier and she would have had nowhere to hide. It made sense that if Superintendent Blair was on the take, he might have used the connection to get a nice cushy little number here for Julie. Disgust roiled in her stomach. She was going to bring that man to his knees but, first, she had a job to do.

Stiffening her spine, she marched into the canteen to begin serving breakfast, keeping an eye out for Angus who was nowhere to be seen. His wife came in and sat by herself rather than joining the other doctors. She had a paper with her as an excuse not to engage but turned the pages listlessly as though she wasn't actually reading it. Grace studied her covertly. Her cheeks were bleached of colour, and she had two odd shoes on. The style was the same but one was brown and the other was black. Her hair was greasy and scraped back in a bun. She'd taken a bowl of cereal but pushed it aside after one mouthful. There was still no sign of Angus. Grace was starting to worry that they'd got wind that he was against what they were doing and therefore considered him a security risk. She had no doubt that they would silence one of their own to avoid exposure. They were so steeped in criminality by now that there was no turning back. Grace approached with her trolley.

'Morning,' she said cheerfully. 'No sign of Dr Angus today? Haven't seen him for a couple of days. Such a nice man. I hope he's okay? There's a lot of bugs going around at the moment.' She wiped the table with her cloth.

The doctor didn't answer, continuing to stare into space as though locked in her own vision of hell. Abruptly, she pushed back her chair and rushed out of the room, her hand to her mouth as if she was going to be sick. Grace quickly glanced around. Everyone was deep in conversation, no one had noticed. Pushing her trolley to one side she slipped out of the canteen after her. Racing along the hallway she saw the end of a white coat disappearing round the corner, evidently heading for the ladies' toilet. Opening the door quietly, she listened. She could hear the sound of stifled sobbing coming from one of the cubicles. Grace weighed up her options and based on her gut she decided to take a risk.

'Carina, let me help you,' she began.

The sobs stopped. 'I'm fine. Go away,' came a defiant voice. 'My cat died. That's all.'

'Look, I know your husband. He's a good man. A good

doctor. He's concerned about what's been going on here. Aren't you?'

The crying started up again. 'Leave me alone. You know nothing,' she said through her sobs.

'Why did you become a doctor?'

'To help cure the sick, of course. Why are you asking me questions? Leave now.'

'But that's not what's going on here, is it?' Grace persisted. 'Young people are being harmed. They put their trust in you. You're treating them like lab rats. Yours is supposed to be a noble profession. Something has gone terribly wrong.'

There was a pause. 'Who are you?' Carina demanded, her voice regaining some of its previous hauteur. Grace heard the sound of the bolt being drawn and the door slowly opened. Her eyes widened in surprise when she saw Grace standing there.

'You're the dinner lady?' she said. 'I don't understand. How do you...?'

'I'm a private investigator,' Grace said. 'I was instructed to find out what happened to one of your patients. I know what's been going on here.' She took a gamble. 'The body that washed up on Portobello Beach, that came from the clinic. Someone, perhaps you, had performed a post-mortem on it.'

Carina collapsed into a chair beside the vanity unit as if all the air had been knocked from her lungs. 'We had to do that. Otherwise, her death would have been in vain. We had to learn from what had gone wrong to prevent it happening again. We're not the monsters you seem to think we are,' she said, seemingly on the defensive now.

'Then what's happened to your husband?' Grace asked. 'Is he missing? If they've harmed him, are you still prepared to carry on like nothing's happened?'

'He didn't come home last night. I didn't see him at the clinic yesterday or today. They won't hurt him,' Carina snapped.

'Why not? They've hurt other people. *You've* hurt other people. Why on earth wouldn't they kill him if he threatened to expose what's been going on here? Experimenting on the vulnerable in society – who does that remind you of?' said Grace, her voice dripping scorn.

Carina was clearly distressed, her worry about Angus a palpable thing between them. Grace knew there was a risk she'd overplayed her hand, and that Carina would call security and have her removed from the clinic, or worse. But she had a feeling that, despite her clinical approach to research and lack of empathy, she really did love her husband.

'Look,' said Grace, 'is there anywhere we can go to talk properly where we won't be overheard?'

'No,' Carina replied. 'The clinic has listening devices everywhere. Put your number in my phone.' She keyed in the code and passed it across. 'I need time to think about things, to process where I stand in relation to recent developments. Wait a minute, you say you're a private detective... that means you have a client. Who instructed you?'

Grace hesitated. Her client and her sister were both under the control of the clinic. She couldn't risk naming Eliza whilst they were in such a vulnerable situation. Equally, she had to tell this woman something to convince her she was on the level.

'I act for someone vulnerable and under your care,' she said. 'For obvious reasons I can't tell you who. The police are also aware of my investigation and that I've penetrated the clinic with a view to obtaining evidence,' she added, trying to sound as though she was working hand in glove with them. On this occasion, it couldn't be further from the truth.

'I need time to think,' Carina said, recovering her customary abrasiveness. 'I'll contact you when I'm ready to talk. In the meantime, if you happen to come across my husband...'

'You'll be the first to know,' Grace promised. Although, privately, she had a feeling that the news might not be good.

Angus had now been missing for at least forty-eight hours. If he wasn't at home and wasn't at the clinic, then where was he? After all, if they'd been prepared to unleash those goons on her last night, what lengths might they be prepared to go to against betrayal by one of their own?

# FORTY-SEVEN

Time was weighing heavily on Hannah's hands. She couldn't wait to be out of the clinic for good although her stomach churned at the thought of what she was going to have to do to get there. To distract herself her mind drifted to Julie who she felt had really taken a wrecking ball to their lives since she'd announced her pregnancy. Grace had never come right out and said it, but Hannah knew that she had Brodie had nearly got it together at the end of their last case. She had desperately hoped that they could all be a family but, not only had Julie's pregnancy announcement forced Brodie's hand, Julie had also been treating her and little Jack like they were cuckoos in her nest. It made her blood boil.

She wandered back out until she found the corridor with the door leading to the staff locker room. There was no one around. She consulted the day's codes sent to her by Grace and punched in a four-digit number. The door opened with a click and she entered. Hardly anyone on the staff knew her by sight except for Angus and Nurse Kelly. She'd noticed from the daily schedule that Julie was teaching still-life sketching that morning, so the coast should be clear.

The medical staff had their own separate changing rooms, as did the staff who worked in the spa, so there weren't many in here. She also looked at the row of coats hanging up. The lockers were only small so most people seemed to leave their outdoor coats there. She noticed one she recognised as belonging to Grace. There were another six and one that Hannah remembered seeing hanging in Brodie's house. It looked as though it was two blankets stitched together and just screamed Julie at her. Hopefully, she stuck her hands in each pocket hoping to find her locker key. No such luck. She would have no scruples about picking Julie's lock, but she drew the line at doing it to someone else and there was no way to know which was hers.

Hearing the door open, she dived into one of the two toilets and slid the bolt across. Standing on the seat, she reached up and peered over the top. It was Julie! She must have finished her class. Reflexively ducking down at first, she heard the door to a locker open. Daring to peer over the top again she saw something that confirmed her worst suspicions. Part of her longed to burst out and challenge her there and then but she knew there was too much at stake for her to do that. Instead, she bided her time until she heard her leaving then quickly made her way back to her room to await the call to action from Grace.

After a few minutes, Nurse Kelly poked her head round the door.

'Not feeling up to sitting with the others?' she asked, coming in to perch on the end of her bed.

Hannah stifled her annoyance. She needed to get rid of the well-meaning nurse pronto.

'It's not that, just pacing myself, you know? Don't want to get too caught up in other people's drama while I figure stuff out.'

'That makes sense, I guess,' Nurse Kelly said, leaning back in her seat as though determined to keep her company.

Hannah felt as though her teeth were about to crack due to the growing tension in her jaw. She was expecting a text from Grace at any time now.

'Actually, I'm planning to go swimming later this afternoon,' said Hannah. 'Just thought I'd grab a bit of shut-eye before then. My energy levels still aren't as good as I'd like them to be.' She faked a yawn as a convincer.

Nurse Kelly lumbered to her feet. 'I'd best leave you to it then.' She smiled. 'I'll check in on you later.'

Hannah smiled her thanks and lay down on the bed, her face to the wall. The nurse closed her blinds and left, shutting the door behind her. Hannah waited until she heard the sounds of her shoes squeaking down the hall then sat bolt upright. Hastily, she arranged a couple of pillows under the covers to look like a sleeping body to a casual glance. She rushed to the ensuite and donned the scrub set Grace had given her, complete with stethoscope and fake ID. Squinting at it she saw she was Staff Nurse Paige Barclay. If challenged, she was to say she was an agency nurse arranged by Angus due to staff sickness. It would also explain why she didn't know where everything was already. It was the flimsiest of covers but they had no intentions of lingering. It was a case of busting in, acquiring their target patients and straight out the door to the waiting car. Hannah desperately hoped that was how it all went down. Her real fear was getting trapped there and put in an induced coma or worse. She thought of Jack waiting for his mum to come home and was nearly undone. Hurriedly, she pushed that traitorous thought away. She would be seeing him soon enough.

Her phone pinged. It was time. She peered out into the corridor. It was empty. She closed the door behind her and started walking. She came to the door to the High Dependency Ward and with a confidence she didn't feel she started keying in the number. Too late, the hairs on the back of her neck prickled a warning. She felt a jab in her arm and tried to spin round and face her attacker but, as she did so, her vision blurred, and the world tilted as she collapsed into their arms. As she fell unconscious, she was dimly aware of being wheeled away in a wheelchair. Her last thought was of Jack.

# FORTY-EIGHT

Grace was dressed as a doctor, her white coat flapping as she strode along the corridor. Hurriedly she pressed in the same code she had inputted earlier when bringing the lunches to those patients deemed too sick to visit the canteen. Hannah would have preceded her by thirty minutes so had hopefully located and positioned the two wheelchairs in the patients' rooms. It was unfortunate that both girls were in separate wards, but she had assigned Hannah to grab Eliza and she would take Beth. Hearing angry voices coming from an office on the ward she slowed to listen, making notes on the fake chart she was carrying to avoid attracting suspicion. There was a nurse's station further along the corridor but the nurse sitting there was busy typing notes on her computer and didn't even glance up at her. It was Dr Walker and Dr Campbell.

'Are you crazy?' he snapped. 'What on earth possessed you to do that? You've made things ten times worse. There's no way we can bring him round to our point of view now. Also, how's Carina going to react when she finds out what we've done to her husband?'

Grace's heart nearly stopped. This was bad. Very bad. She

slipped into the open supply cupboard adjacent so she could continue to listen without being seen.

'She's not going to find out,' Campbell replied. 'His expressing interest in the research side was clearly a ruse so he could snoop around unfettered. I caught him interfering with the twins' medication, trying to lighten their sedation. We've worked too hard and long on this to be brought down by a bleeding-heart liberal. He's a top-notch doctor but he doesn't have the guts to make the hard decisions research needs.'

'But still... couldn't you just have used that as an excuse to place him on gardening leave? We've got so many loose ends to tie up as it is before we ship out. Carina's an essential part of the team. We need to take her with us both literally and metaphorically. It was... imprudent.'

'We can still rescue this situation,' she said. 'All Carina knows is that he's disappeared. I arranged for his car to be removed from the car park and hidden in a remote location to buy us some time. Perhaps a car accident? The area by the ravine on the descent to the village might be a possibility.'

Grace's blood boiled as she recollected their hired goons' attempt to place her in that exact same spot.

'Not at the moment,' Dr Walker muttered. 'I noticed that dinner lady was taking too much of an interest in our conversations. I told our security to deal with her so I suspect the ravine may be... er... occupied.'

'Isn't that a bit extreme? Even for you?' asked Dr Campbell.

'We cannot have any more mistakes,' snapped Dr Walker. 'This whole operation has cost a fortune to set up and implement. Our initial results have been promising but we need to see if the damage caused to a small minority of participants can be reversed. Only then will our parent company be prepared to launch massive clinical trials and bring it to market.'

'I agree. Nothing must stop us taking our place in history. I'll do as you suggest.'

'Are you sure we can trust our operatives?' he said.

'For what we're paying them they'd lend us their own grandmothers to experiment on,' she said with a cruel snigger. 'I can't wait to leave this miserable place and return to Boston. I'm sick of this exile.'

'Not long to wait now but I must urge the greatest caution. If word of what we've been doing here gets out then the only Boston we'll see will be the inside of Massachusetts Prison whilst wearing an orange jumpsuit,' said Dr Walker. 'Is it possible someone put Angus up to this?'

'Who could be pulling his strings?' said Dr Campbell. 'Definitely not Carina.'

'What about the police?' asked Walker, suspiciously. 'So far, they've been content to look the other way in exchange for the retirement of their dreams. But what if someone else within their ranks has got wind of it? Could someone have nobbled him or do you think he was acting alone? We could ask him but, wait... no, we can't, because he's bloody unconscious,' he finished sarcastically.

'Fine, point taken,' she snapped. 'He won't be out for much longer. I've locked him in a basement storeroom nobody uses. He's bound and gagged for now. Anyway, I've just done my rounds. The twins are stable and so is everyone else for the time being, though there seems to be nothing we can do to stop the deterioration long term. We need to map the genomes of the ones who have accelerated aging to see if we can find the gene mutation that our protocol activates.'

'It's actually a good thing Eliza wound up in here,' said Walker, his tone more conciliatory now. 'It's such a gift to have an identical twin to study. Of course, we'll learn even more during the post-mortems but I'm confident we're going to be able to bring this to market at an accelerated pace once we work out how to prevent these adverse outcomes.'

*Post-mortems?* Grace could hardly believe what she was hearing.

'Anyway, I'm heading back to the lab,' announced Dr Campbell. 'You might like to see my latest results. They're encouraging to say the least.'

They exited the room together, their voices receding down the corridor until she heard the fire door at the end close behind them.

She had to get those girls out of there without delay, whatever it took. She also needed to secure the release of Dr Angus. He'd clearly been trying to help their client. His predicament might sway Carina to their cause, but it might do just the opposite. Her temple started to throb. How on earth were they going to pull off this rescue and ensure these unscrupulous monsters were never allowed to practice again?

She heard the sound of someone keying in the code at the entrance to the ward. The door buzzed to let someone through who she desperately hoped was Hannah. She'd seen no sign of her so far and she was supposed to be in the ward before her. There was no way she could manage to spirit the two girls away on her own. When she heard steps go by, she peered out, but it was just an orderly – there was still no sign of her.

She waited another hour by which time her muscles were stiff from the enforced lack of activity. It was no good, she wasn't coming. She didn't even dare go to visit her client as if she was discovered there, she wouldn't have the freedom to make another attempt.

Perhaps the best thing she could do was try to get down to the basement and locate Angus. If she could get him out, then surely he would agree to come with her to the police now? There was no way he could carry on at the clinic as if nothing had happened. If only the police hadn't been compromised, she could call Brodie and he could mobilise reinforcements. She had never before faced such overwhelming odds.

# FORTY-NINE

Hannah forced her eyes open. She had a pounding headache. The room was dark and the curtains drawn. Her heart missed a beat. She was confused. It was night-time? The last thing she remembered was...

A rustle from the chair beside her bed alerted her to the fact she wasn't alone. Turning her head with difficulty she expected to see Nurse Kelly, but she could tell immediately it wasn't her. This woman was taller and skinnier with a hard, narrow face like a fox.

'What happened?' asked Hannah, her voice croaky. 'Water?' She was parched and her tongue felt stuck to the roof of her mouth.

The nurse ignored her request for a drink, leaning forward instead to speak to her, her mouth set in an angry line. As she came closer, Hannah recognised her from Jean's photos and her heart sank. It was Head Nurse Frankie Garcia, and she was involved up to the hilt in the unsavoury goings on at the clinic.

'Who are you?'

'Why are you asking me that? You know who I am.'

'Why were you impersonating a nurse?'

'It was just a bit of fun,' muttered Hannah, rolling her eyes. 'Lighten up. One of the others dared me to do it.'

'Save the pantomime for Nurse Kelly. I'm nobody's fool. What are you doing here? I knew there was something off about you from day one when you waltzed in with Dr Angus Macdonald.'

Hannah was terrified but felt she had no option but to stick to her story. 'I was sleeping rough, necking booze, when that posh doctor saw me. I was freezing my bits off and hadn't eaten for days. He got me a burger and said I could come here if I wanted to get off the drink. It's not my fault he dragged me here, lady. It's getting old anyway. Time I bounced.' She tried to swing her legs out of the bed and was horrified when nothing happened. What had this bitch done to her? Suddenly she received a stinging slap to one side of her face that snapped her head to one side and made her bite into her tongue. She tasted blood and felt a wave of nausea roll over her.

'You'd better tell me what you're really doing here or I'm going to make you wish you'd never been born,' the nurse said, her voice full of malice.

Hannah's mind rifled through her limited options. She knew that mentioning Grace or revealing her real identity was impossible. For all she knew, Grace had been successful in getting at least one girl out and was now on the way to the police with her and Dr Angus Macdonald. She had to believe that help was coming. The alternative was unthinkable. She could try to find Julie and beg for help, but she realised that she didn't trust Julie not to throw her to the wolves. Her only option was to convince this fearsome woman that she was just a harmless grifter working on her own.

Throwing herself into character she rolled her eyes. 'Look, you got me, okay? I got that sad-sack doctor to bring me here. I wanted a bed for a few nights, fresh clothes, decent food. I even thought I might score some uppers and downers. That's what I was up to when you stabbed me with that needle. I figured the good stuff might be on the other side of that door.'

'How did you get the code?' Garcia asked with narrowed eyes.

'I didn't. Just thought I'd have a few tries. Nothing ventured, nothing gained, right?' Fortunately, she'd been one digit away from success when Garcia had jabbed her.

'You look too healthy to have been living on the streets, despite your initial blood work. Why are you really here? Who are you working for? Who is your contact in here and what's their agenda?'

She removed something from her pocket and held it up. Hannah was hard put not to groan. It was her phone. Fortunately, she'd erased her texts as she went, including incoming ones. Her mind raced as she remembered that her phone had pinged just as she was keying in the number to the door. Only Grace, Jean and Dr Macdonald had the number to her burner. She just had to hope that the text had given away nothing important.

Hannah shook her head and looked mutinous. 'I'm telling the truth. Just fix me up and get me out of here. Looks like I've overstayed my welcome. This place is a shithole anyway.' Hannah's eyes widened in alarm as Garcia stood up and injected something into the drip that Hannah belatedly noticed was attached to her left hand.

'Hey, what are you doing? You've got no right—'

Her voice tailed away as the ground slipped from under her once more.

# FIFTY

Grace was in the bowels of the clinic looking for Angus. It was already late afternoon and she'd heard nothing from Hannah, which was concerning, although they had agreed to keep texts to essential use only. There was no reception down here, so she had no option but to put Hannah out of her mind and focus on locating Angus Macdonald. Although Campbell and Walker were still nominally weighing their options, she had a strong feeling that they'd decide he was expendable. He knew too much and was clearly burdened with a conscience which made his position here untenable. Probably the only reason he was still alive was because they needed to come up with an explanation for his absence that would satisfy Carina and keep her firmly on board. Campbell and Walker had no moral scruples whatsoever.

Grace shivered. They clearly didn't bother keeping this level heated. It wasn't only cold but felt damp and inhospitable as well. The lighting came from dull low-energy bulbs, which were on a motion-activated timer and only dimly lit the way as she advanced along the narrow corridor. She could hear pipes and ventilation shafts clanging and whirring above her head.

The pipes unnerved her as they sounded as though they could pull apart at any moment, showering her with goodness knows what. The annoying thing was that as she moved along the corridors the lights behind her winked out, meaning she couldn't see back the way she had come or determine whether anyone was creeping up on her or not. As she moved further and further down into the interior of the clinic, checking all the doors for signs of the missing doctor, she could feel the walls closing in on her. Was it her imagination or was there not as much oxygen in this stale air? Her head swam as she fought off a feeling of panic. Their last case had left her with a visceral fear of enclosed spaces. *One step in front of the other, Grace. That's all you've got to do. Keep it together.* She hoped she didn't have to descend to the next level after this one. It felt a lot like being buried alive.

The thought of Angus alone and immobilised in the dark spurred her on. She had to get to him before they did. His testimony would be vital in bringing the unethical doctors down and making sure they didn't visit such terrible suffering on others. Something furry ran over her feet in the darkness and she stifled a scream, her stomach churning with revulsion. Still two doors to check. Surely, he'd be in one of them. She got lucky as she turned the handle of the last one, and flipped the light on as she walked inside. At first, she thought what she was looking at was simply a roll of old carpet alongside metal shelving but suddenly, the carpet moved, and she realised it was Angus's prone body wrapped in a sheet and bound with masking tape. Only his head was free and he had duct tape over his mouth, too. When he realised that someone was there, he started trying to struggle and guttural groans escaped from behind the tape. Grace stepped over immediately and stooped to rip off the tape from his mouth. He cringed away from her in terror.

'Don't hurt me!' he yelped. 'I won't tell anyone, I promise.'

Hmm, this didn't bode well, she thought, viewing him in consternation.

'Angus, it's Grace McKenna,' she said, cutting his bonds with the small penknife she always carried. 'I've come to get you out of here. Stop fighting me. I'm here to help you,' she snapped as he tried to jerk out of her way. Eventually, her words started to penetrate, and he simmered down.

'I thought I was done for,' he muttered. 'They're planning to kill me.'

'I know,' she said.

She helped him stagger to his feet then supported him until his legs were strong enough to bear his weight. At first, she'd thought that if she found him, she might be able to persuade him to go back upstairs with her to try and spring the girls, but she could see from looking at him that he was too far gone, too crazed with terror to be of any assistance.

Hurriedly she weighed up her options, none of them good. She wanted nothing more than to get Angus out and flee with him to the police, but she was also concerned about how quickly Campbell and Walker would react to discovering that such a loose cannon, from their point of view, had managed to escape. They had the means to dispose of the evidence quickly and flee the country back to the US where, no doubt, they had already arranged fake identities to step into.

Every decision she could make carried danger for someone. Despite her internal anguish, Grace was able to weigh up her options with the cool logic she had practiced while in her previous position with the police. She would call Jean who could be here in thirty minutes and get her to collect Angus from the car park and take him to Grace's flat. He would be safe there until she'd managed to escape with Hannah and hopefully her client and Beth as well.

'Right, Angus, here's the deal. Take it or leave it. I'm prepared to get you out of here now, and have Jean pick you up and transport you to my flat. I'm going to need you to surrender your phone and promise not to contact the police for twenty-four hours or until I tell you it's safe to do so. Some of the local police are on the take and I need to find someone I can trust and who will be receptive to what we have to say.'

'What about Carina?' he asked. 'I can't just leave her behind.'

Grace sighed. 'I understand, really, I do, but right now I've got no option but to view her as complicit in everything that's been going on. The only way forward for her would be to seek a deal with the prosecution in exchange for partial or complete immunity. Right now, I have to focus on getting Hannah, Eliza and Beth to safety.'

'Fine, you've got a deal,' he sighed, handing over his phone.

Grace's phone pinged. It was Jean.

On my way.

Grace felt flooded with relief. At least one of her staff was present and accounted for. She couldn't understand the radio silence from Hannah. Something must have gone badly wrong. After waiting twenty-five minutes, with her assistance, Angus made it out of the basement entrance to the hospital and running with his body low and hugging the boundary, he arrived at the car park. Grace stood just inside the door and felt a tug of regret as she saw Jean's cheerful lilac car set off down the hill. If only they were all in it. She was starting to feel it would take nothing short of a miracle for them all to escape this one unscathed. Her heart heavy, she closed the door and was swallowed up once more into the bowels of the clinic.

# FIFTY-ONE

Jean looked across at Dr Macdonald as they wound their way down the hill as fast as Jean dared, which wasn't all that fast given the hairpin bends and sheer drops on the right-hand side of the road. She was fighting a major impulse to drive him straight to the police station in Portobello High Street and blab her guts out to anyone who'd listen. The weight of responsibility sat as heavily in her stomach as a clootie dumpling.

It was the not knowing that was the worst. If this was how they treated one of their top doctors and researchers, they were hardly likely to hold back when it came to Hannah, Grace or their client. For the first time since she'd been working with Grace, she doubted whether she was doing the right thing. She couldn't help but wonder if Grace's feelings about Brodie were clouding her judgement. Whilst she was no fan of his boss, Superintendent Blair – from what she had heard about him – she couldn't conceive of a world in which Brodie himself might be capable of looking the other way for a kickback, financial or otherwise. Admittedly what Grace had overheard between him and his boss a while back sounded suspicious, but he'd been challenging Blair at the time not just blithely going along with things. Jean sighed, frustrated. She knew she wouldn't go behind her boss's back. Not yet at least.

Glancing in her rear-view mirror again she was satisfied they weren't being followed. Just in case, she took a circuitous route to the flat in Portobello, parking in her usual spot in a street facing the sea. It was still bitterly cold. She'd flipped the sign on the office door to closed when she rushed out to collect Angus. As she walked along the Esplanade with him on the way to the office, she realised she would have to sit with him in Grace's flat. Although she was tempted to stash him in the back room of the office so she could get some work done, if anyone came after him, he stood a better chance in the flat with its door phone entry system and the very strong locks on Grace's flat door itself.

'How are you with dogs?' she asked, inserting her key in the door adjacent to the agency.

'Not good,' he said, looking anxious.

He really wasn't good for much, thought Jean uncharitably, before suffering a pang of guilt. 'Grace's dog Harvey is a sweetie,' she said. 'You'll not need to worry about him. I've never heard of anyone being mauled to death by a Golden Retriever.'

Apparently, giving the lie to her words, her voice was almost drowned out by Harvey's barking as they started to climb the stairs. Angus went pale and she noticed a sheen of sweat on his forehead. He dropped further behind her.

'It's only me, boy,' she soothed the dog as she opened the door to the flat. Harvey was clearly conflicted as he was delighted to see her but not at all happy about a strange man being ushered into his space. He rushed around him sniffing and growling deep in his throat until he judged him not to be a threat.

As Jean told Angus to take a seat, Harvey positioned himself between Jean and Angus and sat down, never talking his eyes off the visitor. There had been no further word from either Grace or Hannah and Jean was now beside herself with worry. She couldn't just hole up here with Dr Macdonald for all eternity. At some point she would need to take matters into her own hands, irrespective of what Grace had said. She couldn't storm the place single-handed. What was she going to do? Stab them with her knitting needles? She needed back-up.

'Coffee?' she asked with a sigh. As she was unable to do much else at the moment, she might as well make them both some sandwiches. Mind you, she wasn't all that confident in Grace's food supplies. Unlike her, Grace didn't care much about food and her cupboards were never that well stocked. However, Jean managed to rustle up something and took them through with a cafetière of strong coffee to find Angus and Harvey having a staring contest.

'Right, Angus,' she said, pouring the coffee. 'Since we're stuck here until I hear from Grace or Hannah, I think we should use the time to take down your statement so that we can present it to the police as soon as possible.'

'The police...' he gulped, his eyes widening in alarm.

'Yes,' said Jean firmly, offering him a sandwich then picking up her notepad and pen. 'Where else did you think this was going to end?'

'All I wanted to do was help people,' he said in a low voice. 'I grew up as the son of an alcoholic. I saw the depths of depravity it was possible to sink to with my own eyes. I also knew that I had an inherited predisposition to addiction and monitored myself constantly. I tried to focus this propensity through a constructive lens. I became obsessed with exercise, then academic endeavour, but ultimately, I realised I wanted to focus my energies on treating addiction.

'I'd lived and studied in the States since I won a scholarship there as an undergraduate. Eventually, I set up my own clinic in Boston. I treated wealthy clients with my bespoke programme. This programme addressed the whole person, physically, metabolically and psychologically. In the earlier stages, I made extensive use of aversive therapy which was developed uniquely for each person. I also experimented with judicious use of psychedelics to summon up elements from the patient's own unconscious mind to help them in achieving sobriety. The treatment protocol was longer than the usual period of time and, crucially, supported that individual when they returned to their normal lives. They would have family therapy, support into new hobbies and interests and ongoing contact with a dedicated pastoral worker.'

'Sounds expensive,' said Jean, looking up from her notepad in which she was scribbling furiously in shorthand to keep up with the torrent of words.

'It was exorbitant but incredibly effective. I had leveraged everything I owned to create a massively appealing programme to attract the wealthiest elite. Then, when I started turning a profit after a few years I created a sister facility and started inviting those who were addicted and homeless, applying the exact same pillars of treatment but with the luxe downgraded to comfortable. I employed dedicated social workers who ensured that when they left us our patients were assisted into housing and jobs or study routes. Any relapses, and there weren't many, were treated with immediate follow-up.'

'Sounds laudable,' said Jean then narrowed her eyes as she glared at him. 'So how did we end up here?' she said pointedly, sitting back, wiggling her cramping fingers.

Angus sighed, passing a trembling hand across his white face. 'Greed, I suppose you might say. Oh, not greed for more money. I've never been particularly fuelled by that except what benefits it can produce for my patients. Greed for acceptance amongst my peers, more clinics, more accolades. Just more... I guess. Growing up, I was a bit of a social outcast, what with my dad's very public drinking and my mother leaving us for a new life in another country when I was ten.'

'She left you?'

'She said she wasn't going to sit and watch me turn into my dad,' he said bitterly. 'She wasn't prepared to lose the prospect of her shiny new life over me.'

Jean felt the stirrings of sympathy but cautioned herself to remain objective. She had a job to do here. 'How did you meet Carina?'

'I'd been invited to a few seminars at Magnum Pharmaceuticals. They'd reached out to me saying they were impressed by my work and made a sizeable donation. Like a few of the more progressive pharmaceutical companies, they have a philanthropical arm and they were particularly interested in my work with the homeless, which had formed the basis of a few well-received peer reviewed papers. I met Carina at one of these events. She was a brilliant research scientist, and I found her passion for curing society's ills very compelling. We were engaged within a year and then we were made an offer it was hard to refuse that would advance our work to a new level. It wasn't a hard sell. Two years later we were in the wilds of Scotland.'

'Did she tell you what she was working on?'

'Only in the most general terms. For obvious reasons there was a firewall between the two projects. It was an exciting time for both of us.'

'When did you realise things were not as they seemed?'

'I didn't at first. There were so many success stories. Almost too many. Although my results were outstanding in comparison to other rehab clinics, I became aware that rather than simply being readmitted because they'd fallen off the wagon, several patients were being brought in who were seriously unwell. I was also being side-lined from their treatment. At first, I had access to them, but I became extremely concerned when I discovered that some of them were suffering from the effects of untypical illness in the form of tumours and also cellular break-

down. These patients seemed to have been exposed to something that had made them catastrophically unwell.'

'Did you find out what it was?'

'Well, naturally, I assumed that something had gone wrong
at my end, but I couldn't imagine what as none of the drugs I
had administered were experimental. I was working day and
night to find an explanation. I was haunted by the worry that it
was something to do with my treatment protocol at the clinic.
One night, Carina found me weeping at my desk in the middle
of the night. She took pity on me in a rare moment of weakness
and said that what happened to the patients was nothing to do
with me. It was something else. Despite my pleas, she wouldn't
elaborate. I pretended to let matters lie but I was determined to
find out the truth.'

'What about Beth? What happened to her?'

'Such a lovely girl,' he said sadly. 'I thought she was one of
my biggest success stories at first. When she was first brought in
from the streets she was in a pitiful state. Her spirit had been
completely broken and she was indifferent as to whether she
lived or died. It was only when our psychologist started probing
into her art that we realised she had an identical twin, and that
knowledge began to drive the engine of her recovery. She was
determined to get out and reconnect with Eliza.'

'Did you share that information with anyone on the
research side, your wife for example?' asked Jean.

'No. Like I said, there was a wall between the two sides of
the clinic and the implication was we would each stay in our
lane and not interfere with the other's work. The mere fact that
big pharma had prioritised a free rehab clinic had completely
reassured me of their ethical boundaries.

'I remember the morning that Beth left. She was glowing
with health and energy. I thought that she'd a bright future
ahead of her. Then, a few months later, her assigned social
worker, Talia Edwards, sought me out and said that she'd

noticed a marked deterioration in her health and had been wondering whether she'd become involved with drugs as she wasn't exhibiting any signs of alcohol abuse. Beth completely denied it but kept getting worse. Then she started ranting and raving that the drugs we had given her had been making her sick.'

'Had you prescribed drugs for her on release?' asked Jean.

'I hadn't prescribed any ongoing treatment for her. Why would I? When she left the clinic, she was perfectly healthy. Then Beth disappeared and Talia reported that her apartment had been broken into. At that stage the scales slowly started to fall from my eyes, and I realised she'd been admitted in a critically ill state to the clinic hospital but no one had seen fit to inform me. It was shortly after that that I first contacted you thinking you were Beth's mother.'

'So, what is your take on what's been happening?' Jean asked.

'I believe that vulnerable young people are being recruited into the clinic and, on their release, experimented on with drugs that are not even close to being approved for clinical trials on humans. This takes place without their knowledge and consent.'

'What kind of drugs?' asked Jean, horrified to be confronted by the reality of their suspicions.

'I believe they're working in the field of regenerative medicine, experimenting with drugs to increase healthy longevity. I was able to access my wife's computer a few nights ago while she was in the bath. They've been building on the early work of Yamanaka, the first scientist to demonstrate the ability to turn normal cells into stem cells in fifty days by introducing four key molecules, which became known as Yamanaka particles. It appears that some patients have suffered cellular disintegration and advanced aging. They're desperately working on finding a way to reverse it but have been unsuccessful so far.' His voice dropped. 'So far there have been five fatalities.'

Jean paused. 'How many people have been given the drugs?'

'I wasn't able to discover that information. There wasn't enough time. She came back into the room and closed down her computer. I think she suspected that I'd been snooping and told them. That no doubt accounts for why they came after me,' he said, his voice bleak.

Jean sat and thought for a few moments. 'Grace and Hannah are up there along with our client and her sister. I can't sit idly by while they're in such terrible danger. I have to do something.'

'You can't go there again as Beth's mother,' Angus said. 'They most likely wouldn't let you in. In fact, I wouldn't even go back to your house if that was the address that you gave them.'

Jean gulped. She should have thought of that. Never mind, she could stay here for the foreseeable. Someone would need to take care of Harvey if Grace didn't make it out tonight. If she couldn't get in and Angus had been rumbled then there was only one person who could help them: Angus's wife, Carina. But would she?

# FIFTY-TWO

Grace crept out of the basement to the lower ground floor where she imagined the mortuary was located. The complete silence was unnerving, and her soft-soled shoes made no sound. She was still dressed in her fake ID and scrubs. She suspected that the clinic didn't employ a pathologist or mortuary staff but carried out their own post-mortem investigations, storing the bodies of these unknown young people who had no one to lay claim to them.

Pushing open the door to the mortuary she paused, half-in and half-out, to listen but all was quiet. Encouraged, she closed the door behind her and penetrated deeper into the interior. She swallowed hard as she saw the stainless-steel slab had a body on it covered by a thin white sheet. Terrified that it would be one of the twins she forced herself to approach, every nerve in her body demanding she flee and not look back. Lifting a corner with a shaking hand she felt sick to her stomach.

It was Lorraine Kerr, the girl who had turned her life around and had so much to live for. Her face was mottled, and her skin was wrinkled. Her hair had turned white at the roots but the magnificent auburn mane she remembered from her photos still reached to her waist. A howl of anguish caught in the back of her throat, causing her to swallow hard to avoid her anger and outrage escaping into this sterile space. If only she'd figured things out more quickly, she could perhaps have saved this young girl.

She heard the outer door open and the sound of voices approaching. Frantically, she looked for somewhere to hide. There was staged seating at one end, and she ran up the few stairs and lay flat on the ground, her pulse racing as the door to the mortuary swung open. All she could see were their feet through the bottoms of the seats which probably meant if they thought to crouch down that they would be able to see her prone body. A woman's voice spoke. It was Carina. She sounded hesitant, a lot less sure of herself than Grace remembered. Clearly the strain was getting to her.

'When I started all this, Conrad, I felt sure that the ends justified the means,' she said. 'But now I'm not so sure. I mean, look at her! If we'd just let her be, she might have had a good life.' Her voice trembled.

'Don't go soft on me now,' scoffed Dr Walker. 'You're romanticising the situation. Let me remind you that if we hadn't plucked her off the streets in the first place, she would likely have been dead in the gutter in days. That was the whole point of the rehab facility. Get them in, restore them to health then use them to test our hypothesis.'

Grace felt sick. This wasn't a situation that had spontaneously evolved. It had been chillingly planned from the outset.

'I know that,' Carina replied. 'But it's still heartbreaking when it comes to this.' She pointed to the girl on the slab. 'It's just as well that Angus doesn't know the whole truth. It would break him.'

'He doesn't have the scientific objectivity or, indeed, the

stomach for it,' he retorted. 'I never quite understood your choice,' he added, turning to stare curiously at her. 'Far too emotional by half. I should have thought you would want someone more like...'

'You, you mean?' She choked back a laugh. 'I felt that my kids should have at least one parent who wasn't a monster.'

'Carina, where's this coming from? You seem completely out of sorts?'

'My husband's missing!'

'And you think I had something to do with that?'

Grace held her breath. The silence elongated until Carina sighed and turned away.

'Of course not, Conrad, don't be ridiculous. We've been rowing a lot lately. His mental health isn't strong. He's most likely just taken off to the Highlands for a few days to clear his head and do some walking.'

'I'm sure you're right.' He turned to the dead girl. 'Shall we get started?' He pulled down the sheet and in a cold voice devoid of all emotion, he began dictating his notes. It seemed that Carina, too, had flicked a switch into professional mode.

Grace gritted her teeth. The smells were bad enough, but it was also the range of sounds in a post-mortem that made her queasy. At the sound of the hammer and chisel being employed on the skull, she shivered, wishing desperately to be anywhere else. The snip of the scissors was next as the body was forced to relinquish its secrets one by one.

Eventually, Dr Walker sighed and flung his scalpel onto the used instrument tray.

'Just like the others. I don't understand it. I thought our modifications would have improved the outcome. Yet she's showing the same accelerated decay as the others. We're so damn close! If only we had more time, I could crack it completely, I know I could.'

'The two bodies they found in the sea...' said Carina. 'It's only a matter of time until the authorities come knocking. We can't go on like this. Even the staff in the clinic are starting to talk amongst themselves. They're becoming suspicious. We can't control the narrative anymore. We need to get out from under this while we still can.'

'Those girls, the identical twins, they could make all the difference. I must have that information before winding this operation up. When else will we get such an opportunity? I'm on the very threshold of a breakthrough that could revolutionise medicine. The greatest scientific discovery of our generation. I have to see it through. To do otherwise is unthinkable. Surely you can see that? Stay with me, Carina. Help me.'

'But those girls are still alive,' faltered Carina. 'The others died, so we were simply making sure that their deaths weren't in vain. That they, at least, advanced medical science. You surely don't mean to suggest that we *kill* them?'

'The needs of the many outweigh the needs of the few.' His voice was persuasive, reeling her in. 'If we manage to iron out this defect in the protocol, then it will revolutionise aging and indeed the whole of society. Imagine, everyone able to age with grace and dignity. No more cell senescence outside controlled parameters. Think of the burden aging places on our over-stretched society, not to mention the emotional cost of people stretched so thinly they snap trying to care for elderly relatives who are dead in everything but name. It's a utopian vision and it's within our reach. I'm convinced of it! You're with me, right?'

'Of course,' said Carina. 'Always! It's just hard sometimes.'

'No pain, no gain,' intoned Dr Walker.

'Well, now you just sound like Jane Fonda,' Carina said, with a small laugh. 'Anyway, I'll let you head off and consider your notes. I'll clean up here and put the body away.'

Grace heard the door swing shut behind him. She stretched

her neck, but she could no longer see Carina's white tennis shoes. Where was she? Her heart sank and she twisted her head.

'You can come out now,' said Carina, who had noiselessly crept up the stairs and was now standing staring down at her.

# FIFTY-THREE

Grace was left with no option but to scramble to her feet and face her. Carina's face was expressionless. 'Not here,' she snapped.

With that, Grace was dismissed, and Carina walked away from her, gathering up the various instruments used and placing them in the steriliser.

Grace glanced uneasily at the body on her way past. but it had already been covered up with the sheet and there was nothing to see. Carina completely ignored her as she slipped past, carrying on with her work as though there had been no interruption.

One cool cucumber, thought Grace, feeling nervous turning her back on her in case she threw a scalpel at her. Hurriedly, she sought a linen supply cupboard on the floor above and found a concealed corner to hide in while she regrouped. Carina could be looking for a way out. Perhaps murdering the twins in cold blood was too much, even for her. On the other hand, depending on when she spotted her in the mortuary suite, her apparent reluctance could all have been a pantomime for her benefit. Carina couldn't have overpowered her on her own but perhaps she was walking straight into a prearranged trap. Maybe they both wanted to pump her for how much information she knew and ascertain how many people she'd told. Regardless, Grace had to hope her concern for her missing husband would be enough to win her over to her side. It was a gamble she had to take. In the meantime, she had to locate Hannah and find out why she wasn't answering her texts. She also needed to hatch another plan to extract the girls before they were murdered by Dr Walker.

The pressure of her predicament made her head feel like it was trapped in a vice, but she ignored it and forced her body to calm down by taking deep diaphragmatic breaths. The pain lessened and she set off for the floor where Hannah's ward was located, the one above this one. Fortunately, she was intimately acquainted with the layout of the clinic by now, due to taking the meals trolley round. She headed for the staff changing rooms first which, as she hoped, was empty at this time of day. She quickly pulled on her dinner lady uniform over her scrubs, merely removing the white coat and bundling it up in her locker. When she pulled the cap on over her face, she felt invisible once more. She also grabbed a stash of menu cards and a pen to take with her as a rationale for being on the floor.

Hearing someone come in she momentarily froze but then simply locked her door and turned towards the exit. What she saw in front of her nearly stopped her heart. Not again! It was Julie! However, her nemesis simply walked past her with a blank smile, scarcely registering her presence. She had on her usual hippy layers and artful makeup. Grace carried on walking. It was only when she reached the safety of the stairs that she realised she'd been holding her breath. The woman was haunting her. She carried on up the stairs, composing her face into a blank slate on the way. Entering the ward, she greeted Nurse Kelly pleasantly, waving the menu cards.

'They forgot to hand these out earlier,' she said. 'Are all the rooms occupied today?' There were twelve rooms on each ward. Those whose withdrawal was complete slept in bedrooms on the other side of the rec room.

'Only five still on the ward,' Nurse Kelly said. 'Three have been moved over to the other side as they're doing well. One has gone to High Dependency.' Her face clouded over.

'Oh, who was that?' asked Grace. 'That's unusual, isn't it?'

'It was young Hannah,' she replied. 'I don't understand it. They were all doing so well. Then the Head Nurse, Frankie Garcia, came along and Hannah apparently had a bit of a turn. She was unconscious when they shipped her out. I've not heard anything since. I was on my break at the time.'

Grace felt a wave of rage almost lift her off her feet. If they'd harmed her in any way all bets were off as to what she'd do to them.

'You know her?' asked Nurse Kelly gently.

'Yes,' Grace said. She looked hard at the friendly nurse, trying to assess her character. Hannah had clearly felt she could be trusted. Deciding to take a chance she moved closer. 'Is there anywhere we can talk privately?'

The nurse looked alarmed at first but then nodded. 'We can go in the office. Nobody will bother us there.' She led Grace to the other end of the ward and into a small office with a window facing the front of the building. 'Okay, so tell me, what's really going on here?' she said, turning to face Grace and folding her arms.

'I'm a private investigator,' Grace said, pulling off her cap and stuffing it into her pocket. 'Hannah is working with me. She's not an addict and was completely healthy when she was admitted. Dr Angus Macdonald, who's helping with our investigation, was assaulted and imprisoned but has now been placed somewhere safe.'

'But... what are you investigating?' asked the nurse, completely astonished at this turn of events.

'Our client instructed us in connection with her missing sister. The trail led us here where we discovered the clinic is dishing out free rehab to get hold of young people who can be nursed back to full health and then, without their knowledge or consent, form part of illegal drug trials. These drugs have caused severe harm to some, if not all, participants. After post-mortems, their bodies have been dumped in the sea.'

The nurse's legs gave way, her face a mask of horror as she collapsed into an upright chair.

'But that's...'

'Monstrous?' said Grace. 'Indeed, it is. I take it you didn't know?'

'Of course not! I only support the withdrawal phase and nursing them back to health. I've been uneasy since I heard that Beth was back but terribly ill. I asked to go and see her, but they said she was in isolation. She'd been so well when she left. We'd become quite close over the time that she was here. I initially thought that she'd simply had a relapse and would be pitching up back on my ward, but she was still in High Dependency with no visitors. I couldn't understand it. Then, a few weeks later, Beth was moved to my ward for a week. But she had no recollection of me. She'd clearly lost her memory. I suggested to them that she might have had a stroke.'

'That wasn't Beth, it was her twin sister, Eliza,' explained Grace. 'She posed as her sister to get in here and get answers, not realising they still had her sister imprisoned here.'

'The head nurse, Frankie Garcia, is involved in whatever's been going on,' Nurse Kelly said. 'It was after she visited Beth, I guess I should say Eliza, that she suddenly deteriorated and was moved to High Dependency. The same happened to your colleague yesterday.' She bit her lip.

'You weren't to know,' reassured Grace. 'These people are fanatics and highly dangerous. They've already shown that they view any deaths as merely collateral damage. I need to get the two girls and Hannah out to safety then I'm going straight to the police to close this operation down.'

'Why not call them first? The girls will need urgent medical care. They could bring ambulances and storm the building, take them by surprise.'

'That would be my preferred option,' said Grace grimly, 'but as they've bought off some of the local police, I'm no longer sure of who I can trust.'

'I can't believe I'm hearing this,' said the shell-shocked nurse before making a determined effort to pull herself together. 'Tell me what you need from me. I want to help. They've made me complicit in what has been going on.'

'Can you access the hospital records for those in High Dependency and Critical Care? I need to find out the location of Beth and Eliza as well as Hannah,' said Grace.

The nurse shook her head. 'I don't have access to that information on my computer terminal,' she said. 'They said it's for patient security, though I thought it odd at the time.'

'Does the lift in the High Dependency ward go all the way down to the mortuary level?' asked Grace.

'Yes,' replied the nurse. 'They can't go careering all over the hospital with dead bodies.'

'That's how we'll get them out then,' said Grace. 'Do you ever take patients from here to the HDU?'

'Sometimes, but usually they send their own staff through.'

'Here's what we'll do,' said Grace. 'If you get me a hospital gown I can lie on a trolley, and you can say I've been transferred if we're stopped. Then, I'll find Hannah and you can locate the twins. The twins can double up on a trolley to look like one person and we can take a trolley each down in the lift to the mortuary level where we go out through the fire door and get everyone into my car. Then we drive like the clappers straight to Edinburgh Royal Infirmary.'

'You make it sound so simple,' the nurse said, her face full of doubt. 'What if something goes wrong?'

'Then, I will say I deceived you and take the consequences,' said Grace firmly.

'You'd do that?'

'Of course,' said Grace with a warm smile. 'You can also squeeze into my car and come with us if you prefer?'

'I only wish I could,' the nurse said, welling up and looking away. 'I can't run out on my patients. They need me.' She went out into the corridor and came back with a gown. Grace followed her into an empty room on the ward and quickly changed. She was not a fan of the gap at the back. It wasn't ideal for what she had planned, but needs must. She got up on the bed and lay down under the sheet. Nurse Kelly took off the brake.

'Ready?' she asked.

'Ready,' confirmed Grace. Her heart rate rocketed as they set off. The ceiling was all she could see as they made their way along the corridor to the lift to go up a floor.

'That's us,' said the nurse, sounding nervous.

As she opened the lift, the nurse's phone rang. Hurriedly she snatched it up out of her pocket but not before Grace had seen the distinctive cover. The phone was Hannah's. Grace sat bolt upright but it was too late. There were two masked and gowned figures waiting for them. A hypodermic syringe pierced her arm. It was over. As she slid into unconsciousness, she managed to turn her head to look into the eyes of the nurse who was leaning over her now, holding her down. Her eyes sought Nurse Kelly's for an explanation. The nurse stared back at her, blank and unfeeling no longer wearing her mask of benevolence. The world went black.

## FIFTY-FOUR

Jean woke up stiff and sore after a night on the couch with Harvey who had a kick like a donkey when he was after more space. Her hair was like a bird's nest when she looked in the mirror. Harvey woofed behind her back.

'Yes, I know, you need a walk,' she murmured. That meant Dr Macdonald coming with her as she wasn't letting him out of her sight. She knocked on the door to the spare room where he was perched ready on the edge of the bed, looking as rough as she was.

'Right, Angus. First order of business is walking and feeding Harvey, then we need to call the police.'

Angus stiffened in terror. 'But how do you know we can trust them or which ones they have bought off?'

'I don't, but no matter what, there is one officer I do trust. He's Grace's ex-husband and he would move heaven and earth to prevent anything bad happening to either Grace or Hannah. I'd stake my life on it.'

Harvey trailed listlessly along the beach. He was clearly missing Grace and wondering when she was coming back. After a short walk to let him do what was required, they turned back towards the flat.

'Carina's not a bad person, you know,' he said as they waited on Brodie's arrival. She hadn't told Brodie what it was about, just said that she needed to speak to him urgently at Grace's flat and to tell no one.

'Good people can do bad things but if they keep doing bad things it changes them,' she said.

He sighed but nodded his agreement. 'I don't see how we can move on from this. I would never have believed she could deliberately harm people in this way.'

The doorbell rang and she buzzed Brodie up after telling Angus to go and wait in the bedroom with Harvey until they were done talking. As soon as she opened the door to the flat, Brodie burst in, his face creased with worry.

'Where's Grace?' he demanded.

'She's in trouble, Brodie, and so is Hannah.'

'What do you mean? What's happened?'

His whole body radiated tension. She needed him to calm down and take a more measured approach. 'I'll make us some tea,' she said in a voice that brooked no argument. 'Take a seat, I won't be a moment.'

He opened his mouth to protest but stopped himself, clearly realising he needed to calm down and focus.

In a few minutes, she came back with a tray and had also opened the bedroom door to let Harvey out before closing it on Angus's anxious face. She was going to see what Brodie had to say before letting on that he was here with her. Harvey was ecstatic to see Brodie and sat staring up at him, making soft noises in the back of his throat with a meaty paw on his knee. Brodie stroked him.

'I've missed you, too, boy,' he whispered.

Jean cleared her throat and handed him a cup of tea. It felt strange to be hosting in Grace's flat and she wished with every fibre of her being that her boss was here to take all this heavy responsibility off her.

'Grace and Hannah are in grave danger, Brodie. I need you to level with me. Have key people in the police been paid to look the other way in relation to Whiteadder Clinic? Have you?'

'Don't be ridiculous—' he began.

'Brodie, Grace overheard you talking to Superintendent Blair. She knows he's on the take. She's just not sure about you. I need to know if I can trust you, or if I need to go elsewhere?' She studied him intensely as she was talking.

'Grace thinks that of me...?' he said, the hurt in his eyes unmistakeably genuine.

Jean shrugged, hardening her heart.

'Okay,' he sighed, leaning back. Harvey jumped up beside him as though to give him support. 'I admit things have been difficult of late. What I tell you can't leave this room, Jean, but I need you to tell me exactly what's been going on in relation to the clinic. Grace and Hannah could be in real danger. These people are completely without scruples and likely to become more so as the net closes in.'

'So, there is a net then?' asked Jean, her voice sceptical. 'I was beginning to wonder if they had some kind of get out of jail free card.'

'It's not what you think. Well, it is what you think in some respects,' Brodie said. 'You're correct. The clinic has bought influence at the highest police levels, including Superintendent Blair. I went to Internal Affairs when my suspicions were raised. Since then, I've been working for them trying to gather solid evidence of the corruption whilst seemingly becoming a part of it. I currently have a very healthy bank balance and have been seen flashing the cash, though of course I have to account for every penny to the investigative team.'

Jean's head was reeling, but she was relieved that she hadn't misjudged Brodie. 'That's all very well but then who's actually investigating the clinic?'

'Another team entirely, led by Superintendent Alis Gray. They've been trying to gather sufficient evidence to obtain search warrants to blow the place wide open but still don't have enough.'

'They do now,' said Jean quietly. 'If you'd only told us the truth earlier. Grace has been trying to manage the whole investigation on her own and now, I fear, she and Hannah are trapped inside the clinic completely at the mercy of the rogue doctors and scientists there.'

'She should have trusted me,' he ground out in frustration.

'You can't exactly blame her,' said Jean, banging her mug down on the table. 'You didn't want to know when she first tried to interest you in our missing client. It's also complicated with Julie being the Super's daughter. How was she to know where your loyalties lay? Julie even works there, for goodness' sake.'

'What? No, she doesn't,' he replied, startled.

'Art therapy apparently, three mornings a week.'

'She told me she was working for Women's Aid,' he said, his tone flat. 'Anyway, you've evidence linking the clinic to the young people who have disappeared?'

'Yes,' Jean said, making a decision. It might be the wrong decision. She had no way of knowing but right now it was hers to make. 'I have one of the clinic doctors with me now. He's only recently worked out exactly what's been going on as he was on the rehabilitation side. His wife, Carina, is a research scientist and implicated up to the hilt. He's willing to talk in exchange for immunity.'

Brodie's face cleared. 'This is the break we've been waiting for. I won't let you down, Jean.'

She rose to her feet and brought Dr Macdonald out to meet him.

'I'm going to need to call my boss, Superintendent Gray, to

obtain authorisation but I'm sure she'll ask me to bring you in voluntarily to make a statement. If you're able to confirm the illegal operations at the clinic, then she'll no doubt be prepared to speak to the Prosecution service on your behalf requesting immunity from prosecution.'

'I can certainly confirm it,' Dr Macdonald said, looking Brodie straight in the eyes.

'What about Grace and Hannah?' Jean asked. These people are dangerous. They ran Grace off the road deliberately last night and left her for dead in a ravine up in the hills.

'As soon as we've taken the statement, I'll get a search warrant and assemble a team to go and extract them, Jean. I won't let you down, you have my word. In the meantime, if you hear anything, anything at all, text me on my work phone right away.' He passed across his card with all his contact details.

Jean walked over to watch them from the bay window as they walked along the Esplanade and out of sight, their bodies bent against the wind. Time was not on their side. Although she knew that Brodie would move heaven and earth to rescue Hannah and Grace, it was clearly going to take hours to arrange a team and get everything aligned. She turned to Harvey and bent down to his level.

'Looks like it's down to you and me, boy,' she said, her heart heavy with dread. He solemnly gave her a paw and she shook it before standing upright with renewed determination.

'Come on, boy, let's go.' She clipped on his lead, grabbed her jacket and a scarf from the hook and walked out the door.

# FIFTY-FIVE

Hannah woke up slowly. The winter sun shone brightly through the window. She had no idea what day it was, and felt weak and disorientated. Without moving her head, she tried to see what she could of the environment she'd been placed in. There were three other occupied beds in the room. She relaxed a bit when she realised there were no medical staff in with them.

Next, she wiggled her fingers and toes. To her relief everything seemed to be in working order. She remembered how horrific it had been to feel paralysis sweeping over her in a wave after that injection. Fortunately, the effect had only been temporary. She never wanted to feel like that again. She slid her legs out of the bed, keeping her body low as she investigated who was in the room with her. To her relief, it was Grace and the two girls. No one was awake yet. She crept to the door and looked through the glass window. As she'd suspected, there was a beefy security guard positioned on a chair outside the room. He looked alert and by the bulge at his hip, he appeared to be carrying a gun. His head swung in her direction, and she quickly ducked out of sight, her heart racing. She ran to Grace's bed and shook her urgently by the shoulder.

'Grace, wake up!'

Her boss turned away from her, muttering something in her sleep. She tried shaking her again and grabbed hold of her nose for good measure.

'Ow!' exclaimed her boss, her bleary eyes opening.

'Shhh!' whispered Hannah. 'Grace, get with it, I need your help.'

Grace sat up and stared around the room, fully alert now. She swung her legs over the bed and started towards the door.

'Don't bother, they've a guard as big as a house outside, and he's got a gun,' said Hannah. She looked over at the other two girls. It was hard to tell who was who by sight alone, but she assumed that the one attached to bleeping monitors was Beth. Running to Eliza's side, she woke her up next, with Grace coming up behind her.

'Hannah, Grace!' Eliza's eyes filled with tears. 'Boy, am I glad to see you guys!'

'I wouldn't celebrate yet,' Grace said grimly. 'We came in looking for you and managed to get caught ourselves. There's an armed guard outside the door. I don't know what they've got planned for us yet but I'm guessing it won't be pleasant.'

Eliza's gaze alighted on her sister in the next bed, and she let out a strangulated cry of joy. 'Beth, it's Eliza! I'm here.'

Her sister didn't reply, her face pale and waxy on the starched white pillow. She was so thin she almost looked completely flat under the covers.

Hannah looked at Beth's chart, but couldn't understand the medical terminology. She passed it to Grace who glanced at it and also shook her head. It was clear that she was seriously ill though. Her body was wasting away. There was a drip, feeding various substances into her veins. Her heart sank. It probably wasn't safe to move her but nor was it safe to leave her here.

Grace took charge and Hannah felt weak with relief. She was happy to relinquish responsibility but would back her boss up the hilt. Anything to get them all out of this horrible place.

'Anyone still have a phone?' she asked. The three of them shook their heads. 'What about Beth?' asked Grace. 'As she's unconscious they might have let her keep it as she's not in a position to use it.'

Eliza slipped out of bed and padded across to her sister's locker. 'Nothing,' she reported back.

'You know how Julie works here?' said Hannah.

'Yes, I saw her earlier,' said Grace. 'She didn't see me though.'

'Is there any chance she would help us?'

Grace screwed up her face. 'Honestly? I'm not sure. If her father, and potentially Brodie, are taking kickbacks, I reckon she's more likely to side with them. Too risky in my opinion. No, I'm afraid we're on our own in here. My experience with Nurse Heather Kelly only goes to show that we can't trust any of the staff here.'

'She certainly had me fooled.' Hannah glowered. 'Jean will be working on a plan,' she said, refusing to accept that their situation was hopeless.

'I'm sure you're right,' said Grace with a quick smile. 'But, in the meantime, we need to get past that guard.'

'Even if we could,' said Eliza, tearing up, 'I can't leave my sister. This is all my fault. You wouldn't be in this mess right now if it wasn't for me. Just leave me here, save yourselves! I let her down before. I'm not going to do it again, no matter what the cost.'

Grace sighed but nodded. 'The only thing we can do is overpower the guard and get the lift down to the mortuary level and try to get out that way. Right now, they're probably planning what to do with us before abandoning the clinic, taking their precious research with them. I noticed a sign for a helipad adjacent to the car park. My guess is they'll arrange for a helicopter to collect them and transfer them to a chartered private plane after which they'll fly back to Boston having destroyed all the evidence.'

'Maybe we should just sit tight and do nothing until help arrives then?' said Hannah.

Her boss looked at her, her expression grave. 'I don't think they can afford to leave anyone behind to bear witness, Hannah. They'll evacuate the rehab side as no one there has a clue what's going on, but the rest will be sacrificed.'

They all fell silent for a moment as they contemplated what this might mean for them if Grace was correct. Hannah felt pierced to her soul at the thought of leaving little Jack without his mum. Then, like flicking a switch, she snapped out of it. She wasn't going down without a fight. 'So, what's the plan then?' she said.

'We need to get the guard to open the door and then I will try to disarm him,' Grace replied. 'I can handle myself in a fight as long as we can take him by surprise to the extent that he doesn't have his gun out when he enters. We need to bolster two of the beds so it will look like two of us are still sleeping. Eliza, you need to attract his attention, say that your sister has started fitting or something. Anything to draw him into the room. I'll be behind the bathroom door and as soon as he's past that, Hannah will trip him up and I will attempt to grab his gun from its holster and disable him.'

'It sounds risky,' said Eliza.

'It is,' agreed Grace, 'but I don't fancy our chances if we simply stay here and do nothing. I think we need to take the initiative if we all want to get out of here alive.'

'I'm in,' said Hannah. She pushed pillows down into two of the beds until they resembled human forms then stood back to admire her handiwork.

She then rolled under the bed nearest the door. Grace stood

behind the door to the bathroom to the right of the door. She poked her head out and spoke to Eliza.

'Are you sure you're up to this?' she asked. 'If you're not we can find another way.'

'Hell, yes!' was the fierce response from her client, her eyes turning towards the supine body of her sister.

'Let's do it then,' said Grace.

Hannah curled up in a ball concealed by a chair and trailing blanket ready to shoot her legs out at the right moment.

Eliza began banging on the store urgently. 'Help me! My sister, she's stopped breathing, I don't know what to do! Please, open the door, she needs help!'

The door burst open, and the security guard stood on the threshold as he glanced around. Eliza was bent over her sister's bed, sobbing. They'd placed the monitor on silent and darkened the screen.

Having satisfied himself it was genuine, he rushed forward to check for a pulse at which point Hannah shot her legs out causing him to trip while Grace jumped him from behind, pulling his gun from the holster before he'd even quite worked out what was going on. He went for his radio, but Hannah punched him hard on the side of the head, knocking him out cold.

'Ow,' she yelled, shaking her fist, 'that hurt!'

'I think it hurt him more,' said Grace with a quick grin as she tied his hands and feet with cords removed from the blinds. He was already starting to come round so she whipped off his radio and secured it to her own belt. 'Might come in handy,' she said. 'Help me lift him.'

It took the three of them to deposit his bound and gagged body in the bath, his eyes popping with rage. Grace pulled the shower curtain to conceal him from sight. She then slipped out to the linen cupboard to obtain a fresh supply of scrubs and masks. Once she returned a few minutes later, the three of them changed then disconnected Beth from the monitoring equipment.

'Look confident,' said Grace, after which they opened the door and marched purposefully along the corridor. This ward in the clinic wasn't in regular use so there was no one at the nurse's station as they rolled by. They'd just reached the lift and opened the doors when another security guard pushed through the double doors at the end of the ward.

'Wait!' he yelled, rapidly closing the gap between them as the lift doors opened. Rushing inside, Hannah stabbed the buttons on the lift, but they were painfully slow to close and as he inserted his hand the doors started opening again.

Grace stabbed at his hand with a scalpel she had obtained from the medical supplies room, and he reflexively withdrew it, shouting in pain and anger. 'That's them on to us now,' she said, looking worried. 'I hoped we might have longer. At this rate we might have a reception party waiting for us at the bottom.'

Hannah was terrified. Had they just jumped from the frying pan straight into the fire? The tension built as the lift descended from the fourth floor to the lower basement. Grace positioned herself at the front of the trolley, indicating Hannah and Eliza should stand on either side at the back.

'If we have a reception committee, I'll do my best to tackle them. Then one of you press the button and take the lift to another floor. Do not let them capture all of us. Is that understood?' Grace said to Hannah, her gaze fierce.

Hannah nodded, a lump in her throat. The lift pinged and the doors started to open.

# FIFTY-SIX

Jean pulled into the car park at the clinic then got Harvey out of the boot and clipped on his lead. She had changed her appearance and hoped she would be unrecognizable as her former self. A visit to the British Heart Foundation charity shop and the costume shop on Portobello High Street had supplied her with an auburn wig, hooped earrings and a colourful patterned coat. Gosh, she could pass for Julie, she thought, then rebuked herself for being mean. She'd also borrowed a pet therapy coat for Harvey from a lady she knew in the church. It had cost her wine for her friend and nearly a whole packet of titbits to persuade Harvey to wear it. She presented Grace's scarf to Harvey who sniffed it and wagged his tail. Since their first case, which had shown Grace he had natural ability as a scent dog, Grace had done a little training with him, but even so Jean knew it was a long shot. She bent down to him and stared into his warm brown eyes.

'Harvey, I need you to be a very good boy. Grace is in trouble and so is Hannah' – more wags – 'so we need to get in there and find them.'

He cocked his head to one side, picking up on the gravity of her tone. She presented the scarf again and he sniffed it then looked up at her, puzzled. Jean handed him a titbit and threw the scarf round her neck. She was completely bonkers for even attempting this, but needs must.

Throwing her head back and nailing on a confident smile, she walked straight up to the door and entered, sticking her head into reception. Harvey did likewise.

'Oh, cute dog,' cooed the receptionist, smiling. Fortunately, it wasn't Lily, but she doubted she would have recognised her anyway. 'How can I help you?'

'My name's Gloria' – she smiled – 'and this here is Harvey. He's a therapy dog. We're due on the rehab wing for a couple of sessions. I know my way up, save you the bother. I've been here before.'

'I only work here part-time,' said the receptionist, 'but if you're sure?'

'That must be why we've not met before,' Jean agreed. She glanced at her watch. 'If you could just buzz me through? I don't want to be late for them.'

With a loud click the door opened into the interior of the building and they walked through. She was stopped by a young nurse and also a beauty therapist as she made her way up the stairs. No one found her appearance here odd as Grace had told her they had loads of people coming in to deliver short courses and extra mural activities to prevent the rehab patients from becoming bored. It certainly had the vibe of a spa rather than a clinic with a tiled mosaic floor and rose-pink walls. Even the smell was of essential oils rather than the more clinical smell of a hospital setting. It was like two separate facilities incorporated into one, she thought.

She'd decided she would make her way to the top floor and then check each floor until she found them. She realised that there was no way they could get into the HDU or ICU areas but if she didn't find them in the remaining parts then she would at least know that they were in one of those two places and be able to advise Brodie and his team accordingly.

She decided to keep to the stairs rather than take the lift as she didn't want to encounter a bunch of people she might not be able to get away from. She knew her story could easily be pulled apart. Not everyone was a dog lover.

Jean wandered along what seemed to be the leisure space on the first floor. The young people she met seemed happy and healthy, clad in an assortment of gym clothes and normal stuff. There was even a handful dressed in fencing gear on their way to a class, their voices animated as they waited for the studio door to open. It was time to move to the next level. Making her way back to the stairs she nearly ran slap bang into Julie. The shock almost stopped her in her tracks. What on earth was she doing here? Harvey stopped and growled low in his throat, his ears flat against his head.

'Get that mangy thing away from me,' snarled Julie, backing away. She hadn't recognised Harvey, though clearly he had her number. Although she'd never met Julie, she'd seen pictures of her on social media.

'I'm so sorry,' said Jean brightly. 'We're just on our way to a pet therapy session. The doctors felt it might help some of the patients.'

Julie snorted in disbelief, rolling the whites of her eyes. 'Give them some horrible disease, more like,' she said, stomping past her. Harvey looked like he was tempted to nip her ankles on the way by. 'You and me both, boy,' she whispered as she carried on upstairs.

Finally, huffing and puffing, they were at the fourth floor. I really need to start doing more exercise, thought Jean, her calves trembling like blancmange. 'Steady, boy,' she murmured, presenting the scarf once more, along with a titbit. Harvey would need to go on a diet at this rate, she thought.

'Find Grace and Hannah, boy,' she murmured, 'seek them

out.' Then she opened the door, checked the coast was clear and unclipped his lead.

Harvey loped off, his nose to the ground. Hurriedly, she followed him. Halfway along the corridor he paused then turned and started scratching at a door, whining. Jean tentatively opened it. At first, she thought two of the beds were occupied but as Harvey put his front paws on one of the beds and pulled the covers off, she saw the pillows positioned as a decoy.

'Hannah and Grace have been in here, haven't they, boy?' she said. She did a quick recce of the room, but they'd left her no clues. Then Harvey went over to the closed bathroom door and barked. She opened the door. It was empty. Then she saw the tip of a shoe poking out at the end of the bath and heard a few grunts. Harvey growled, his hackles rising.

'Easy, boy,' she said as she pulled the shower curtain quickly to one side. 'Well, that's not something you see every day,' she said to a bemused Harvey. The security guard glared at her but appeared otherwise unharmed. She pulled the shower curtain across again and moved back into the corridor. It didn't take her long to ascertain that there was no sign of her colleagues on this floor, so she went back down to the rec floor where Harvey was pounced on by everyone he met but endured it with good grace. She also encountered a few support staff there, but no one thought their appearance odd.

'We get all sorts in here,' said one employee. 'It's important to provide a wide and varied experience for our rehab patients '

This was all very well, but she was no closer to finding Grace or Hannah, not to mention their client. Finding the security man had given her hope. She hoped they were still evading capture. If only one of them had managed to retain a phone this would be a lot easier. For the sake of completeness, she also visited the spa level on the pretext of introducing the therapy dog to everyone. No reaction from Harvey except he was getting rather fed up with all the attention by now.

'What's below this level?' asked Jean casually. 'It's our first day so I'm still trying to orientate myself.'

A cheerful young woman called Tracey replied, 'Well, this floor is below reception and is as far as people go. The only thing below us is the mortuary level. Only the doctors have the code for the door, so don't worry, you can't just wander in there by mistake. Even the thought of it gives me the creeps.' Tracey shuddered. 'I think they store medical supplies and all sorts down there as well. Best avoid it. Don't want to give this handsome chap nightmares, do we?' she cooed, prompting pleading eyes from Harvey as she leaned in for a hug. Jean produced a titbit from behind her back and he licked his lips. As she stood up, Jean noticed she'd left a lipstick kiss on the top of his big head.

'Lovely to meet you,' she said, tugging on the lead. Harvey didn't need to be asked twice. 'I'll be sure to steer clear.'

As they left the spa, the more she thought about it the more likely it seemed that Grace and Hannah would head to the mortuary. She didn't know the code but with a bit of luck she wouldn't need one for the lift. The trick would be finding an empty one. She waited in the spa corridor, having called the lift. With a ping the lift doors started to open but fortunately, it was filled with a crowd heading to the spa. Entering after them she closed the door and pressed the button to go to the next floor down. In the lift she once again presented the scarf to Harvey. 'Seek her out, boy,' she whispered as the lift stopped with a clunk. The doors opened and Jean braced herself, but no one was there.

She walked with Harvey into various storerooms, still not hearing a sound. She felt the souls of the dead pressing on her as she entered the mortuary itself. The smell of disinfectant and formaldehyde didn't entirely mask other, more earthy odours. As she pushed through into the interior, she gasped in horror. There was a body on the table. Instinctively, her eyes slid away but then swivelled back, puzzled. The body had a drip attached to it on a stand. Surely that wasn't right. Feeling sick with apprehension, she lifted the sheet only to recognise Eliza. She looked like she was barely clinging to life. Forcing herself to touch her forehead she was relieved to find her still warm.

'Eliza, wake up!' she hissed. 'I'm here to help you.' There was no response.

Harvey meanwhile had stopped outside a door at the back of the mortuary. Jean felt a visceral feeling of dread as she realised that this door probably led into the place where the dead bodies were stored in refrigerated drawers until they were uplifted. 'You've got to be kidding,' she muttered as Harvey sent her beseeching looks across the room and pawed anxiously at the door. Jean walked to the door and paused for a moment, psyching herself up. What if Grace and Hannah had been murdered and stored in there until their bodies could be dumped in the cold North Sea? She just wouldn't be able to bear it. They were family to her now.

With shaking hands, she started opening the drawers. All of them seemed to be empty, thankfully. Then she started to pull out one that was heavier, and contained a body draped in a sheet. Hesitantly, she peeled back the sheet to reveal Hannah, eyes wide open and staring at her.

'Boo!' said Hannah, irrepressible as ever.

'Are you trying to give me a heart attack?' scolded Jean, her heart taking a few moments to resume its normal rhythm.

'Help me out of this thing,' said Hannah, sitting up. 'Grace and Eliza are in those ones,' she added, pointing along the row.

'Eliza?' said Jean, helping her out of the drawer. 'But isn't she next door?'

'That's Beth,' said Hannah. 'She's proper sick so we didn't dare put her in one of the drawers as she's on a drip.'

Hannah patted Harvey who was looking at her as though

she'd lost her mind then quickly opened the drawers that Grace and Eliza were in. They each clambered out with help.

Harvey threw himself at Grace whimpering with joy and she gave him a heartfelt hug.

'I contacted Brodie,' Jean quickly said.

Grace looked worried.

'It's okay, he's on our side. He's been working with Internal Affairs on this one and reporting to Superintendent Alis Gray.'

Grace relaxed and nodded. 'I take it Dr Macdonald has given a statement and they're going to mobilise a team?'

'Yes, I just couldn't wait that long. I was worried sick!'

'They took our phones, Jean,' said Grace.

'But why hide in here?' asked Jean. 'Can't you get out?'

'Unfortunately not,' said Grace. 'They've chained the door and there's bars on all the windows. We can't leave via the front door because we can't remove Beth that way, not without a load of people trying to stop us. I figured you'd find a way to send help.'

'Have you looked in all the drawers?' asked Jean nervously.

'Completely empty,' said Grace. 'That's why we figured they wouldn't think to look there.'

'That's weird,' said Hannah, who was over at the window peering out. They joined her and looked out in surprise. There was a fleet of unmarked white vehicles lined up in the turning circle outside the clinic. People were loading equipment and large boxes into the vans under the supervision of Dr Anna Campbell. Suddenly, she turned and waved at them, her expression a rictus of a smile, her eyes dark with hatred.

'They know we're in here,' said Grace. Suddenly, she ran through into the other room and spotted the lone CCTV camera above the mortuary door. 'Dammit!' she yelled and rushed back through to where the lift was. She pressed the button, but it was completely unresponsive. She then ran up the stairs. They heard her furiously rattling the door then she ran back down.

'They've locked and padlocked the door. It's too solid for us to kick it down,' Grace reported, real fear in her eyes. 'We've played right into their hands. They intend for us to perish in here.'

Jean glanced out of the window and saw Dr Walker dragging his daughter, Lily, by the hand off in the direction of the helipad. She was sobbing and trying to resist but to no avail.

Grace stopped abruptly and sniffed the air. 'Can you smell that?' she asked them. Hannah and Eliza paused, too, looking horrified as their brains registered what they were smelling. Harvey whined and paced up and down uneasily. It was the smell of burning.

# FIFTY-SEVEN

Grace quelled her own rising panic at their situation and took control. 'Jean, give me your phone,' she snapped. Jean handed it over and she immediately called Brodie on his personal number praying he would pick up. Fortunately, he did.

'Excuse me, I have to take this,' she heard him say. 'Grace? What the hell is going on? I can't find Jean either.'

'Listen, Brodie!' she shouted over the noise of an approaching helicopter. 'We're in trouble, big trouble. The clinic staff are loading stuff into unmarked white transits. I can't make out any of the reg numbers but they're going to be leaving the clinic imminently. You're going to have to intercept them. I'm not yet sure which way they're headed. I think the main players will leave by helicopter to go to a private plane, so you need to contact all local airfields.'

He barked out orders to someone immediately. 'Anything else? Are you hurt?'

'Yes, they've set the building on fire. They've evacuated the clinic into coaches which are readying themselves to leave. These people will be largely innocent. As for us, we're trapped in the mortuary. Jean, Hannah, Eliza, Beth and...' her voice broke, 'Harvey. We need fire engines and some cutting gear to break us out.' Again, she heard him yelling out instructions.

'Christ, Grace. Anything else?' he asked.

'I think that about covers it,' she said. The words 'I love you' sprang unbidden into her mind but she didn't voice them. It was too late for any of that.

'I'm on my way, Grace,' he said, his voice gruff. 'You hang tight until I get there.' After a slight pause which might also have contained words unsaid, he hung up.

Grace was damned if she was going to let her team, her client and Harvey be cooked alive in here. She paced around taking everything in about their surroundings whilst Hannah and Jean reported on the goings on outside.

'Look, it's Julie!' shouted Hannah, hammering on the window. Julie heard the banging and looked back as she came down the steps, one of the last stragglers as the bus was now nearly full. She narrowed her eyes, sweeping the building for the source of the noise.

'She's seen us!' yelled Hannah, banging harder and waving. Grace ran over to look out, fully expecting Julie to raise the alarm. Instead, what happened next chilled her to her very soul.

Julie smirked then simply turned her back on them, marched away with a stiff back, and climbed onto the bus which promptly set off down the hill.

'That cow!' exploded Hannah, bursting into tears. 'I can't believe she did that.'

'Never mind that now,' said Jean, giving Hannah a comforting squeeze. 'She'll get what's coming to her.'

'Jean's right,' said Grace. 'We need to save all our energy for getting out of here. I want everyone to gather up anything they consider might be useful or that we can use and meet me back here. There might be stuff in the storage rooms we can use to smash our way out. We need to hurry before the air becomes too smoky.' She stared in consternation at the hazy cloud drifting slowly towards them from the ceiling. 'First off, I need a ladder so I can block off those air vents. That's where the smoke is coming from. I need material and tape.'

Hannah and Jean ran off to search and she looked across at Beth. Eliza stood beside her, tears streaming down her face.

'We need to move her,' Grace said. She knew that even the slightest amount of smoke inhalation could be really serious to someone in her condition.

'But where to?' cried Eliza, taking her sister's cold hand in her own.

'The refrigeration room, where we were hiding earlier,' replied Grace, starting to wheel the trolley away.

'But it's too cold in there. It'll finish her off,' she cried.

Grace knew that she could be right, but help was on the way. At least it would give her a fighting chance. 'Go into storage and find me blankets, sheets, anything at all we can use to insulate her from the cold,' Grace demanded.

Eliza did as she was asked, returning with a big pile of sheets, a pillow and a warm parka that someone had left hanging on a hook in the small kitchen area. Together, they dressed Beth then wrapped her in several layers of sheets, putting the pillow in the middle drawer which was an easy height to access. Watching their warm breath suspended in the air they prepared to lift her up into the drawer. They could hear the sounds of a helicopter approaching as it prepared to land on the helipad.

'What about her drip?' asked Eliza.

'I haven't a clue what it is but we're going to have to take the risk and remove it. Otherwise, we won't be able to seal the door shut. There should be enough oxygen in there to keep her safe until help arrives.'

Eliza nodded her assent and Grace hoped to God she was right about all this. Gently, they lifted her body and placed it inside. Beth was skin and bone. She looked more dead than alive, Grace thought, swallowing hard as she pushed the drawer tightly closed. She could hear the clatter next door of Hannah and Jean returning so she walked back through to find they'd managed to find the items she'd asked for. The smoke was stronger in here now and they were all coughing intermittently. Grace tore up a sheet into strips and soaked them at the sink before handing them out.

'Wrap these round your nose and mouth,' she said. 'It'll help.'

Then she sorted out her own and mounted the ladder. There were four vents, one in each wall, the smoke a toxic cloud enveloping the room. Feeling lightheaded, she blocked off each in turn, securing the strips of material with surgical tape that was handed up to her piece by piece by Hannah. Eventually they were all blocked off but not before the air in the room was nearly unbreathable.

Hannah had found two fire extinguishers, but they weren't small enough to get through the bars to break the glass. Grace also knew that sooner or later the ceiling would give way and fire would rain down on them. Given that help was on its way, she was wary about letting oxygen into the room in case it caused a backdraft once the flames reached them. 'I want everyone to go into the mortuary drawers now,' she said. 'They offer your best chance of surviving until the fire brigade arrives.'

'But what about you?' demanded Hannah, coughing. 'What about Harvey?'

'He'll be fine,' she said. 'I'll look after him. He wouldn't understand. Best he stays with me.'

She walked through with them and got them all settled, memorising the numbers then she lay down on the floor in the refrigerated room with Harvey. She wetted their cloths once more and cuddled him to her. He thumped his tail feebly, already weak from smoke inhalation. She texted Brodie telling him which drawers everyone was located in. She had just pressed send when she heard a huge crash. The ceiling had collapsed next door.

That was it then, it was all over. She cuddled Harvey to her, shielding his body with hers. The last thing she heard apart from the angry hiss and crackle of the fire was the sound of sirens approaching up the hill from the village. Gradually the room faded to black.

# FIFTY-EIGHT

Grace suddenly came to with a start.

'Stand back from the window!' yelled an authoritarian voice. She couldn't wake Harvey, so she opened the door to the mortuary and dragged him over to the other side, away from the window, collapsing in a heap with him on the wet floor. The fire still smouldered but the hoses trained on the rooms above had extinguished the flames. The roof was a blackened jagged hole above them.

There was a loud whirring noise as a circular saw attacked the bars on the window and the reinforced glass was knocked out. Cool fresh air rushed into the room. Brodie rushed forward and Grace passed Harvey to him, refusing to leave herself until her team were extracted. A medical team entered via the window and helped Grace get Hannah, Jean and Eliza out of the drawers. Then they extracted Beth onto a stretcher and gently passed her out to the waiting ambulance. After a quick exam, they wrapped her in a foil blanket and prepared to leave.

'How is she?' asked Eliza, tear tracks washing away the grime.

'She's breathing,' said the kindly paramedic, 'but we won't know how she's doing until she's been evaluated at the hospital.'

'Can I come?' asked Eliza. 'I'm her sister.'

'Yes, jump in,' she replied with a smile. 'We'll check you over, too.' The doors slammed shut and, lights flashing, sirens blaring, it turned away down the hill.

The fire was burning out of control now, the helicopter long gone. Grace, Brodie, Heather and Jean were gathered round Harvey who lay on the ground, unresponsive. One of the fire fighters approached. Grace looked up at him from her position on the ground, cradling Harvey's head in her lap.

'Please, I'm begging you, can you do anything?' she beseeched the tall firefighter with the kind, concerned eyes. 'He's a very special dog.'

Hannah turned into Jean, sobbing as the older woman wrapped her arms around her.

'I can see that,' he said, squatting down. He leaned over Harvey's face. 'He's not breathing.' He felt for a pulse. With Harvey still floppy and unresponsive he turned him on his side and holding the dog's mouth and lips closed he blew firmly into his nostrils. 'Breathe, boy,' he muttered.

After a couple of minutes, Harvey's chest started to rise and fall on his own. His eyes remained closed, but he attempted a feeble wag then his eyes struggled open and he tried to get up.

'Easy, boy,' the firefighter said, giving him a reassuring pat.

Grace cuddled Harvey, tears streaming down her face. 'How can I ever thank you?' she gasped. 'I don't even know your name!'

'I'm Eric. All part of the service.' He grinned, springing to his feet. 'You'll need to get him to the vet right away.'

'I'll take him,' said Jean to Grace. 'You got way more of the smoke than we did. You need to go to hospital and get checked out.'

'Nonsense, I'm fine,' protested Grace, her hacking cough as

the air hit the back of her throat exposing the lie. She stumbled back against the firefighter, and he steadied her.

They turned back to look at the building. It was an inferno now and there had been a few explosions from within. The roof had gone and the whole façade was melting before their eyes. Firefighters were training hoses on the building with water piped from the hydrant at the nearby reservoir. Fortunately, before the fire worsened, they'd been able to sweep the building for people trapped. They'd been the only ones.

Brodie was standing apart from them now, barking orders into his phone. He clearly had his hands full. The firefighter helped her lift Harvey into the boot of Jean's car, where they made him comfortable. He put up no resistance.

'I'll see you soon, boy,' Grace whispered, his big head between her hands as she kissed the top of his head. Then they were off down the hill.

Eric the firefighter turned to Grace and in a voice that brooked no argument he said, 'Right you, into that ambulance now.' Grace opened her mouth to protest but thought better of it and meekly got in. He gestured to Hannah to climb in beside her.

Brodie, standing nearby, turned to him and grinned. 'Wow, that's quite the party trick. This one never does what she's told.'

'Oh, I didn't realise, are you and she...?'

'No, not anymore,' said Brodie. 'Grace!' he shouted. 'I'll be in touch about the case. Keep me posted on Harvey.'

She nodded and attempted a smile then slumped back in her seat, a spent force. The doors were closed with a bang and the ambulance set off, more quietly this time.

'There's something I need to tell you about Julie,' said Hannah. 'She's not pregnant.'

Grace pulled her mask down. 'You mean, she lost the baby?' she wheezed.

'No,' replied Hannah, her lips tight with anger. 'She was

never pregnant. I saw her strap on a pregnancy bump in the changing rooms.'

'Unbelievable,' muttered Grace. Her thoughts immediately flew to Brodie and what might have been, had Julie not so callously intervened.

Now that the adrenaline was leaving her system, she was too exhausted to speak. As she pulled the mask back up and closed her eyes all she could see was Julie's smirking face as she turned her back on her and walked away, leaving them all to burn.

# FIFTY-NINE

A week later, Grace was sitting with Harvey snuggled up on the couch. It was cold out and she stretched out her feet towards the warmth of the stove burning in the hearth. Fire was such a weird thing when you thought about it. It could support life, or it could take it away. After seeing the full brute force it could command, she would always be wary around it. Apart from a hacking cough and a sore throat, she had got off lightly. Harvey had made a full recovery and was loving life being spoiled rotten by them all.

Her thoughts turned to their client and her sister. Beth had recovered consciousness and been stabilised though she was still in hospital undergoing a battery of tests as they tried to work out just what had been done to her, and whether it was possible to reverse it. She had a long road ahead of her, but her sister was a constant presence at her side, supported by Ben.

The buzzer sounded and her body tensed. She'd asked Brodie to come round to update her on the case in so far as the clinic was concerned but also to break the news to him about Julie. It was going to be a tough conversation. She buzzed him up and opened the door, emptying the kettle into the cafetière and bringing everything through on a tray to the coffee table.

He stood in the doorway, his eyes seeking out Harvey who wagged his tail furiously and lifted his head but didn't get down from the sofa.

'I see he's enjoying his new invalid status,' he said to Grace, taking a seat beside the fire. Grace poured the coffee and handed him a cup along with some fruitcake delivered by Jean earlier.

'Positively milking it,' she said, squeezing back on the couch. 'The vet has sorted him out and he's got a clean bill of health, but we came so close to losing him.'

'I'm glad your client found her sister and that she's hopefully on the mend,' he said.

No help from you, she felt like saying but didn't. He read it on her face anyway and looked down.

'I'm sorry I wasn't there for you, Grace. It was... complicated. At first when you alerted me about the clinic I was intrigued and well up for looking into it. I couldn't understand why I was getting so much pushback from the Super. He in turn seemed to be getting grief from his boss and I started to realise it extended all the way up to the top. It didn't help that I was living with Julie, and she was expecting our child.'

Grace said nothing, feeling sick about what she would soon have to reveal.

'Anyway, I started probing deeper and felt more and more concerned. Blair told me that if I kept pushing, it would have an adverse effect on my career. I had no option but to involve Internal Affairs.'

'Superintendent Alis Gray...' Grace said.

'Yes. Since then, I've been working for her, gathering intel on the clinic and finding out to what extent certain officers in the force have been covering up the stink in exchange for massive back-handers.'

'So, you kept your distance,' said Grace.

'I had no choice. I was tasked with rooting out the corruption in the force and working independently to get into the clinic and investigate the missing kids whilst maintaining the illusion that the police weren't involved at all. It hasn't been easy.'

'And you were relying on me to do half the job for you,' she said, her tone studiedly neutral. No matter how angry she was with him, she had to bear in mind the fact that she was about to shatter his world into a million pieces.

'I knew you would get it done,' he said simply. 'Alis Gray is a fan. As you no doubt saw in the news, we managed to arrest them at Leuchars, where they had a private jet fuelled and ready to go. Needless to say, they've lawyered up with the big boys but the testimony that Beth can provide will be invaluable. Angus is also willing to testify and has been granted full immunity. The lawyer acting for his wife is trying to negotiate for a plea deal that will result in a lighter sentence, but I doubt she's going to swing it. We've got enough without her. They deleted the trial information from their hard drives but took some of it with them on portable drives which we managed to recover when they were arrested. Also, Ben has provided us with all the information he managed to obtain by hacking into their systems. It's not admissible as evidence due to how it was obtained but it has helped to inform the investigation. He downloaded screeds of information about their illegal trials and research materials. Lawyers or no lawyers, I reckon we've got them. They thought they were so clever burning the clinic to the ground.'

'What about the two bodies who washed up? Have you managed to identify them now?'

'Yes, there appear to have been five deaths directly implicated in the drug trial. The two bodies recovered were the missing lad you told me about, Tom White, and the girl was a Tamsin Murray.'

'Did you manage to trace their next of kin?'

'Tamsin was reported as a missing person in Grimsby a few years ago. We've managed to track down her family and they'll be arranging a funeral once the body is released. We've drawn a blank on Tom White's family, but didn't you say he had a partner?'

'Yes, Ryan. I'll ping his details over to you.'

'We've also located Lorraine Kerr's mother.' He winced. 'She was heartbroken, but comforted by the fact her daughter could be buried in the family plot in Argyll. The other two we're still making enquiries about, but I'm hopeful someone will claim them.'

They both fell silent thinking about the devastated families at the very heart of this case.

Brodie suddenly turned to her.

'You're very quiet. What is it, Grace? What aren't you telling me?'

Grace took a deep breath. 'Brodie, it's Julie. I have some shocking news.'

'Go on...' he said warily.

'When I was trapped in the midst of that inferno and Julie was leaving to get on the bus, she saw me banging on the window, begging for her help.'

Brodie was aghast. 'Are you sure?'

'Completely,' she said, her voice flat and emotionless. 'She locked eyes with me, smiled and turned her back, getting on the bus without so much as a backward glance. To be honest, it's not the first time she's revealed her true colours to me, but until now I was prepared to let it go if she made you happy.'

'I can't believe it,' he said, his face draining of colour. 'How could she...?'

'There's more, I'm afraid,' she continued, steeling herself. 'Julie is not and has never been pregnant.'

'What do you mean?' he asked, confused. 'Look at her, she's obviously pregnant.'

'No, she's not,' said Grace with a note of finality. 'She was afraid you were going to come back to me, so she came up with something to bind you to her. Hannah saw her strap on a pregnancy bump at the clinic when she thought no one was there. It was all a lie.'

Brodie's face flushed as though he were struggling to hold back tears. She knew how much the thought of this child had meant to him.

'I'm so sorry, Brodie,' she said. It felt like she was looking at a ruin of a man. She had just blown up his entire life. 'I had to tell you.'

He nodded, too emotional to speak.

'You can stay if you want, spend some time with Harvey, take some time to process...'

Brodie waved away her concern. 'Thanks, but I need to get going.' He patted Harvey's head on the way out, almost stumbling in his haste to leave as she opened the door for him. She felt for him, she really did, but she'd nothing left to give him. He had made his choice.

Glancing at her watch she walked through to her bedroom to get changed, a flutter of anticipation in her stomach. Tonight, she had a date with a hot fireman, and she had a feeling Harvey was going to approve.

# A LETTER FROM THE AUTHOR

Dear reader,

Huge thanks for reading *Murder at Whiteadder House*. I hope you were hooked on Grace McKenna's latest adventure. If you want to join other readers in hearing all about my new releases and bonus content, you can sign up here:

www.stormpublishing.co/jackie-baldwin

If you enjoyed this book and could spare a few moments to leave a review that would be hugely appreciated. Even a short review can make all the difference in encouraging a reader to discover my books for the first time. Thank you so much!

I was inspired to write this book after reading articles about recent breakthroughs in the quest for longevity. I was shocked to come across real-life examples of covert experimentation on human subjects.

Thanks again for being part of this amazing journey with me and I hope you'll stay in touch – I have so many more stories and ideas to entertain you with!

Jackie Baldwin

# KEEP IN TOUCH WITH THE AUTHOR

facebook.com/JackieMBaldwin1

x.com/JackieMBaldwin1

instagram.com/Jackie.baldwin.1088

# ACKNOWLEDGMENTS

A big thank you to my fantastic editor, Kathryn, for her invaluable insights and feedback. Thanks also to the whole team at Storm including copy editor Liz Hurst and proofreader Amanda Rutter. A special thank you to Tim Burton for his beautiful cover design. Grateful thanks go to my Twisted Sister friends for their unflagging support and keeping me sane when the going gets tough. They have made my writing life so much more fun than I ever thought it could be. I would also like to thank those friends I have made within the blogging community for sharing the book love. A special shoutout must go to Kelly Lacey of Love Book Tours for her friendship and support over the years as well as organising fantastic blog tours for me. Finally, the biggest thank you of all to my lovely husband, Guy, for his constant and unwavering support over the years. I couldn't have done it without you!

Printed in Great Britain
by Amazon